HA'VEN'S SONG

CURIZAN WARRIOR BOOK 1

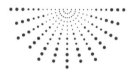

S.E. SMITH

MONTANA
PUBLISHING

ACKNOWLEDGMENTS

I would like to thank my husband Steve for believing in me and being proud enough of me to give me the courage to follow my dream. I would also like to give a special thank you to my sister and best friend, Linda, who not only encouraged me to write, but who also read the manuscript. Also to my other friends who believe in me: Julie, Jackie, Lisa, Sally, Elizabeth (Beth), Laurelle, and Narelle. The girls that keep me going!

And a special thanks to Paul Heitsch, David Brenin, Samantha Cook, Suzanne Elise Freeman, and PJ Ochlan—the awesome voices behind my audiobooks!

—S.E. Smith

Summary: Emma Watson is a withdrawn and damaged human female,
and once Ha'ven, Crown Prince of the Curizans, sees her, he can't
imagine loving anyone else.

ISBN: 9781494238339 (kdp paperback)
ISBN: 9781078731119 (BN Paperback)
ISBN: 978-1-942562-15-3 (eBook)

Romance (love, explicit sexual content) | Science Fiction (Aliens) |
Paranormal (Magic) | Contemporary | Royal | Fantasy | Urban |
Angst/PTSD

Published by Montana Publishing, LLC
& SE Smith of Florida Inc. www.sesmithfl.com

CONTENTS

Prologue	1
Chapter 1	3
Chapter 2	11
Chapter 3	17
Chapter 4	24
Chapter 5	33
Chapter 6	42
Chapter 7	51
Chapter 8	65
Chapter 9	74
Chapter 10	84
Chapter 11	91
Chapter 12	99
Chapter 13	107
Chapter 14	116
Chapter 15	122
Chapter 16	131
Chapter 17	139
Chapter 18	145
Chapter 19	156
Chapter 20	161
Chapter 21	169
Chapter 22	176
Chapter 23	182
Chapter 24	189
Chapter 25	195
Chapter 26	200
Chapter 27	205
Chapter 28	211
Chapter 29	216
Chapter 30	225
Additional Books	232
About the Author	235

SYNOPSIS

The Curizan have a secret, kept even from their closest allies, & Emma is more like them than she knows....

Ha'ven Ha'darra is Prince of the Curizans, a species known for their technology. Not even his best friends are aware of his magic, but his powers are getting out of hand, and soon they might find out first-hand what he can do.

Emma has withdrawn from the world and wants nothing more than to fade into a peaceful death. After she was rescued by aliens, she was healed of her physical wounds, but they could not touch the ones deep inside her. Ha'ven, however, annoyingly ignites her temper, bringing her fully into the moment with his impossible claims that her magic reached out to merge with his, that they belong together....

PROLOGUE

*O*ver a century ago a Great War raged between three of the fiercest species in a galaxy known as Heron Prime. The species were the dragon-shifting Valdier, the cat-shifting Sarafin, and the powerful Curizans, a species whose skills in technology were only surpassed by their ability to use and manipulate the energy surrounding them.

The war raged long and fierce for nearly a century as the skills of each species matched the other. It was only when two young princes and a very young king came together in a surprise alliance that it was discovered forces from within their own worlds were behind the war. These forces were determined to eliminate the ruling Houses so they could gain control and rule through deceit and terror.

The friendship that developed between Ha'ven Ha'darra, Prince of the Curizan, Vox d'Rojah, King of the Sarafin, and Creon Reykill, Prince of the Valdier became unbreakable as they worked together to bring peace to their people and capture those responsible for the death and destruction on each of their worlds.

The traitors, still determined to eliminate the royal families, had kidnapped Zoran Reykill, Leader of the Valdier in the hopes of restarting the war. Zoran, severely injured, escaped in his symbiot warship to an unknown planet in a distant star system. Landing on Earth, he is rescued by a young female. Claiming her as his mate, he returned to his world with her and several other females. On a return visit, other women from Earth were brought back to Valdier.

CHAPTER ONE

urizan Home World of Ceran-Pax:

Ha'ven breathed deeply as he ran through the twisting paths. His focus was on reaching his living quarters and the re-enforced lower chamber beneath it. He cursed when he felt another blast of heated energy surging up inside his body.

I should have returned to my living quarters hours ago, he thought darkly.

He stumbled and slowed as he approached the fork in the path. He carefully scanned the huge garden that separated his home from those of his parents and brothers. Dread engulfed him as he realized he would not make it home in time as the surge built until he was breathing heavily from the effort of holding back the dark power inside him. His eyes shifted as he came to a stop at the crossway and he found himself staring up into the clear night sky wishing for a miracle. His eyes burned as he felt himself losing control.

Why? he demanded in silent agony. *Why can't I find a way to harness the deadly power that was unleashed during my captivity? How long will I be forced to suffer before it drives me mad or I kill those I care about?*

The stars glittered down at him, as if mocking him for his lack of self-control. His body was humming with pent-up power. He had wanted to get further away from the palace, but had been in meetings all day and had waited too long. Now, he feared he would be unable to control the excessive energy building inside his body like a volcano that had lain dormant for far too long. Colors swirled around his fisted hands, moving up his arms. He gritted his teeth, fighting against the energy threatening to scorch him from the inside out.

Drawing in a ragged breath, he glanced around the gardens once more to make sure no one was near him. With a loud groan he sank to his knees and unclenched his fists, spreading his hands palms down toward the ground. A shudder shook his tall, broad form as he closed his eyes. He released the long tentacles of energy that swirled around him before it burst downward into the soft soil. The ground buckled and moaned under the onslaught. A cry ripped from his lips as a powerful surge exploded from him. He knew everything within half a kilometer would be destroyed if he didn't rein in the surge of power escaping his body. He breathed heavily as he pulled back, trying to regulate the flow, but it was useless. He was out of control... again. He could only hope he was far enough away from everyone as the power inside him broke free.

"No!" Ha'ven roared out, opening his glowing eyes and looking up to the stars. "No!" he groaned again, clenching his teeth as pain flooded his body as the raw power burst from him in waves resembling the effects of a massive stone being tossed into a still pool.

"Ha'ven!" His father yelled in a harsh voice. "Focus, son. Release it slowly. You can do it," Melek said in a quieter voice. "I'll help you if you can't."

Ha'ven hissed as he fought to control the ropes of swirling energy. He could feel the bands wrapping around his thick forearms. He drew in deep, steadying breaths, fighting to clear his mind of everything but the strands.

Closing his eyes, he focused the way his grandfather had taught him. He imagined the energy moving deep into the ground, nurturing the garden. Red and gold bands wove together, digging deeper in the darkening soil. He didn't see the new life bursting from the ground, the trees stretching higher, or the vines winding along the lush soil. Just when he thought he might have control once again, another wave struck harder and longer this time.

Ha'ven threw his head back and roared as dark energy bands shot out like a supernova, flattening the new growth and shattering trees like toothpicks. Just as quickly, the swirling colors of energy faded, leaving him weak and sick. He fell forward onto his hands and lowered his head almost all the way to the ground. Breathing deeply, he fought against the paralyzing weakness threatening him. Forcing his head up, he looked over to where his father's voice had called out.

He forced back the nausea and stared back the way he had come. He released a sigh of relief when he saw his father standing several meters behind him. He turned his face away so the man who had only recently come back into his life couldn't see the shame on it.

Forcing himself into a sitting position, he slowly sat back on his heels until he was holding himself upright with his hands on his thighs. He continued to breathe deeply until the trembling finally stopped.

"You shouldn't have followed me," Ha'ven bit out in a dark, husky voice. He turned his head again to glare at the tall male as he slowly lowered his arms. The brilliant shield Melek had thrown up dissolved as his hands fell silently to his side.

"I could have killed you," Ha'ven growled as he rose on unsteady legs.

"You should have told me," Melek said gruffly as he walked over to where Ha'ven was standing stiffly.

Ha'ven looked at his father and grimaced in distaste. "Tell you what? That I've lost control of my powers? That I'll soon be too dangerous to be left alive?" he asked in disgust.

Melek laid his hand on Ha'ven's shoulder. "I cannot help if you do not let me," he replied quietly.

Ha'ven stood frozen for a moment before he shrugged in resignation. He looked at the destruction around him. He drew in a deep breath and focused, pulling on the power deep inside his body. This time he was in control as he raised his hands. He sent the winding flows of energy that he had gathered from around and inside him and directed it toward the broken and mangled vegetation.

Melek watched silently as the swirling bands touched the damage and knitted the shattered pieces back together. Deep down, he felt sorrow that his oldest son could not do the same to his own soul. Bitter regret tore at him that he had not been there when Ha'ven needed him.

Once Ha'ven had finished the repairs, he turned on silent feet and continued on his way to his living quarters. He knew his father walked by his side, quietly analyzing what he had seen. A part of him wanted to rant and rave at the man beside him to leave him alone while another realized that was never going to happen.

If there was one thing he knew about his family, it was that they never turned their backs when one of them was in trouble. Hell, he was no different. He had sent his twin younger half-brothers, Adalard and Jazar, who everyone called Arrow because of his passion for archery, on missions that were supposed to ensure their safety. Instead, both had almost been killed by the assassins sent after them.

"Ha'ven," Melek started to say in a quiet voice.

"You cannot help," Ha'ven interrupted his father abruptly before stopping and turning to look at him. "There is nothing that can be done to save me," he continued in a quieter voice. "What Aria unleashed is consuming me."

Melek studied the grim expression on his son's face. His own darkened as he thought back to the damage his cousin's traitorous daughter had done. Aria had been born to the lineage of the Royal House of Ceran-Pax but she had been anything but satisfied with her pampered lifestyle. She had been greedy for power.

Aria had united with Ben'qumain, Ha'ven's step-brother, in the hopes of ousting the Ha'darra family from power. Ben'qumain had been jealous of his older step-brother's power as heir to the leadership of the Curizans. The two traitors had not been satisfied with bringing down just the Curizan ruling family though. They had joined in an alliance with Raffvin Reykill of the Valdier and rebels looking to overthrow the d'Rojah, the Sarafin ruling family, as well. Their plan was simple. They wanted to divide the three strongest species. They had been successful to a certain degree.

The Great War between the three species had been elaborately orchestrated by them. Thousands from each of the three had died unnecessarily. A plan that Melek felt guilty at not discovering sooner.

Melek put his hand on Ha'ven's shoulder to stop his son from turning away from him. He knew he would do whatever was necessary to save the family he had only recently been able to claim. He would not lose a single one of them again. Not his beloved mate, Narissa, nor his three sons. He had quickly claimed Adalard and Arrow upon his return.

"There might be a way," Melek insisted determinedly.

"How?" Ha'ven demanded, throwing his arm out and waving to the path behind them. "You saw what happened! I am slowly losing control. It grows more powerful each time. If I lose control at the wrong time, even your shield will not save you. Do you think I want to take a chance of killing you or mother or my brothers?"

"All I'm asking is that you do not give up," Melek said. "I will not lose you. I spent too many years watching you from afar. I will not lose my family again now that I have regained it."

Ha'ven opened his mouth to make a bitter retort, but swallowed it. He knew the sacrifice his biological father had had to make for his people.

Even in the darkness, Ha'ven could see the lines of anguish around the corner of his father's mouth.

As the second son of the ruling family, Melek had to step aside when the woman he loved was given to his older brother, Hermon, in an effort to strengthen the ruling family.

Hermon had not mated with the mother of his son, a woman from a lower social class. Ben'qumain was born just days after Narissa had given birth to Ha'ven who was conceived during the one brief night his mother and Melek had together before being torn apart.

Ben'qumain's mother had sent her newborn son to Hermon in an attempt to undermine the new alliance between the royal houses. Instead, Narissa had taken on the responsibility of raising the two newborns as if they were her own. Six years later, she had given birth to twin boys, Adalard and Jazar. Ben'qumain's resentment grew over time as it became obvious he had not inherited the powers that Ha'ven and his two younger brothers possessed.

During this time, Hermon had fallen in love with his new mate, unaware that her heart belonged to his younger brother or that Ha'ven was not his own son. Over time, Narissa had come to care deeply for Hermon although not with the deep passion that she had for Melek. Melek, out of respect for his brother's rule, had chosen assignments that had kept him away from the palace as much as possible. He had commanded the Curizan military, eventually guiding and working alongside Ha'ven during the Great War when he was old enough. He had cherished his time with his son even if he could never claim him as such.

It was not until recently that Ha'ven discovered that not only had Ben'qumain been responsible for Hermon's death, but that Melek was his true father. He had always respected Melek for his integrity, honor, and wit. Still, it was difficult to accept the male that he always thought of as his mentor was indeed also his father.

Fortunately, Melek had returned in time to prevent those working alongside his nephew from killing his mother and younger brothers.

Zoran Reykill, King of the Valdier, had eventually killed Ben'qumain when he made the mistake of attacking Zoran's human mate. Ha'ven's lips curved as he thought of the dragon-shifting species they had fought in the war and who had eventually become one of their strongest allies.

He and Creon Reykill, the youngest of the royal family, had become good friends after finding themselves trapped in the same mining tunnel during the war. Not long afterwards, Creon had met and fallen in love with his cousin, Aria, unaware of her devious plans for power.

Aria had used her connection to them both against them. She had used her knowledge of him to kidnap and imprison him. She had used Creon to find out information to help those trying to overthrow their governments. Eventually, Creon had learned of her betrayal and had saved his life.

Their alliance was sealed and Ha'ven knew he would do whatever he could to help Creon and his brothers defeat their uncle. Unfortunately, he still needed to deal with the Curizan traitors who had worked alongside Ben'qumain. They were now desperate to overthrow the ruling family because they knew the moment they were uncovered they would be sentenced to death for treason against their people.

"I… would appreciate any help you can give," Ha'ven admitted reluctantly.

Melek nodded solemnly before he looked up at the stars shining high above. "The ancient archives might hold information. I will work with those in charge of keeping them," he said, looking back at Ha'ven.

Ha'ven gave a brief nod. "Talk with Salvin. I trust him to keep the issue quiet," Ha'ven replied. "I need to review a few things before Adalard and I leave in the morning for Valdier. A trap has been set for Raffvin. It is my understanding that things have changed that makes it likely we will soon eliminate another major leader in the rebellion."

Melek drew in a deep breath and released it. "I will be glad when the rest have been brought to justice. I will work with Arrow to continue to uncover those here who are still working against the royal house."

"Thank you," Ha'ven said, turning to continue down the path.

"Ha'ven," Melek called out quietly. Ha'ven turned and looked back at the dark shadow of his father. "Be careful. Your mother made me promise to tell you that."

Ha'ven didn't bother trying to stop the small grin that curved his lips as he looked back at the man who was fighting to find his place in his adult son's life. He could see the concern, the pride, and the worry. This was one reason why he wanted to avoid all serious relationships. He had enough to worry about without adding a female into the mix.

"Now, where is the fun in that?" Ha'ven replied with a chuckle as he turned and disappeared into the darkness.

Melek released a sigh and shook his head. "That is exactly what your mother said you would say," he muttered before he turned back toward his own living quarters.

CHAPTER TWO

*H*a'ven maneuvered the transport ship through the thick clouds almost ten kilometers from the royal palace on Valdier. He had left Ceran-Pax several days before with Adalard as his only companion. Only a select few on the planet knew he and Adalard were arriving. He had made the decision after talking extensively with Creon Reykill. Both men had decided it would be prudent if as few people as possible knew of his and Adalard's presence.

Normally, he preferred traveling alone when he could, but Adalard had insisted on traveling with him. Ha'ven knew that his brother wanted to make sure for himself that Mandra had recovered from the wounds he had suffered while fighting Raffvin and his forces not long ago. His younger brother had taken a shine to the human woman Mandra Reykill had taken as his mate.

Personally, Ha'ven was beginning to think it best to avoid the species. When he had first heard about the females and had met Carmen, Creon's mate, he had been curious. After all, it wasn't often that he found himself hanging upside down from a female dragon's tail, or trapped under a pile of bodies with her sitting on top of him and taking a nice size slice of his hair as a prize.

It was just, the more he was around them, the more he saw the pull they had on the other species and it worried him. He liked his freedom, and while he wouldn't mind playing with one for a night or two, he had no desire to become entrapped by whatever spell they cast.

He honestly didn't know what it was about them, but every single one of the Reykill brothers had fallen for one of them. If what Creon told him the other night was true, it wasn't just the female of the species either.

Ha'ven had been shocked when Creon had informed him that his mother had been claimed by the father of the human female called Trisha. Ha'ven just hoped there weren't any more of the species running around. If there were, he planned on avoiding them at all possible cost.

"I want to see how Ariel and Mandra are doing," Adalard commented, breaking into his reverie as he switched on the landing gears. "You should have seen Bahadur trying to sweet talk Ariel away from Mandra."

"Bahadur?" Ha'ven repeated in surprise, looking at his brother in shock. "That cold bastard wanted Mandra's human mate for himself?"

Adalard chuckled and nodded. "Yeah, I think he is making plans to take a break when all this is over. He was fascinated by her and has been asking me to find out the location of her planet."

What Adalard didn't tell his older brother was that Ariel had mentioned a female back on her planet that she thought would be perfect for him as well. He wasn't interested in anything permanent, like a life mate, but he wasn't opposed to having a little fun. If this Samara that Ariel was talking about was half as interesting as Ariel, he wouldn't mind meeting her and exploring the differences between her species and his own for a short period of time.

"Well, tell Bahadur no. I know I mentioned it might be interesting to play with one or two, but I've changed my mind about wanting to meet any of them," Ha'ven said with a shudder. "The last thing we need is a bunch of this human species on our planet. You've seen how fast they have brought the Valdier royals to their knees – literally. Creon told me his mate beat him up and Mandra's knocked him out!"

Adalard's husky laughter filled the cockpit of the transport at the thought of the tiny females beating up males over twice their size. He joked with Ha'ven about some of the other stories he heard from members of the crew traveling with Mandra. He related tales from Ariel's collection of pets to his own observations of watching her beat up the traders in the bar on the Spaceport where they had picked him up.

Ha'ven listened with half an ear, wondering what had happened to the huge dragon shifters that could change them. From what Adalard was telling him and from the little that he had seen, there was definitely something about the species that played havoc with his friends and their symbiots.

Hell, even Vox had fallen head over heels for a human female the Antrox had! The damn cat-shifter was as deadly as any of them and known to like having his women hard and fast. The human female had his furry friend so mixed up the Sarafin King was practically chasing his own tail the last time he had talked to him!

"If that is not enough, now they have younglings to worry about," Adalard was saying as he finished the landing procedure as Ha'ven guided them to a clearing just large enough for the transport. "I know they are worried Raffvin or those working with him might try to attack them."

Ha'ven looked sharply at Adalard before he turned his attention back to the final approach. Hovering over the thick grass, he set the transport down in the center of the small meadow. He turned off the engines with a wave of his hands, pulling the swirling bands of energy back into his body. Another benefit of traveling in the transport was he could use his own energy to power it, thus reducing the chance of a repeat of the other night.

"Creon told me of his daughters," Ha'ven admitted. "I will do everything in my power to protect them and his mate."

Adalard just nodded. He knew his own powers were considerable, but they paled in comparison to his older brother. Adalard and his twin had always looked up to Ha'ven who had protected them against Ben'qumain when they were still young and vulnerable. He had encouraged them to work together to develop the power held inside them. Since his captivity on the asteroid prison known as Hell, Ha'ven's powers had grown until both he and Arrow worried about its effect on him.

"Ha'ven," Adalard said, turning to look at his older brother as he started to rise. "Are you alright? The other night I felt…" Adalard's voice faded as he studied the huge male across from him.

Ha'ven saw the concern on his younger brother's face. His eyes swept over the long scar marring Adalard's cheek. His brother refused to have it removed, stating it reminded him of the dangers around him.

"I'm fine," Ha'ven said with a short nod. "Let's see what plans have been set up. Raffvin is not the only danger. We still have traitors of our own to deal with."

Adalard nodded and stood up. He followed his brother down the corridor and out through the small hatch located under the belly of the spacecraft. Once Adalard was clear of the transport, Ha'ven pressed a button on the belt wrapped low around his hips. The transport shimmered for a moment before disappearing.

The Curizans used a combination of technology and 'magic' as some of the worlds called it. In reality, they were able to gather energy from the world around them and harness it within their bodies. Once there, they could manipulate it to do whatever they desired.

Each Curizan was born with a different ability and level of control. Some used it for healing, some became better pilots, some better warriors. Those that ruled in the Royal House of Curizan could contain and manipulate it in ways beyond the limited abilities of most of the citizens of Ceran-Pax.

The Ha'darra family had ruled for centuries. Their power was boundless as Ha'ven was discovering. Never had the full extent of what they could do been explored as there had been a fear that, if unleashed, it could destroy not only the one who wielded it but the world itself.

Ha'ven had always thought it was a myth passed down through the centuries to warn those that followed of the dangers of absolute power. After all, a dead man could not rule a dead planet. Now, he knew the warnings were real. If he was unable to find a way of controlling the power building inside him soon, there would be no other choice but to eliminate the threat to his world.

"Ha'ven, are you ready?" Adalard asked, touching his arm. "The transporter room is ready when you are."

"Give them the go," Ha'ven said as he jerked and muttered a low curse as he realized that Adalard was still looking at him with concern.

Seconds later, he and Adalard were in the central transport room inside the palace. If he had been on one of the larger Curizan warships, he would have just materialized down to the room, but there was no way they could leave the transport in space uninhabited. It contained new technology that he and Adalard had recently developed.

The small, yet sleek, transport was perfect for missions like this. It was designed so a small crew of two or three could travel for months in it quite comfortably if necessary or for stealth missions like this one. They had designed it to work specifically with the power they could manipulate. The weapons, navigation, and shields were enhanced as they fed their powers directly into it.

He mostly used the transport for short trips such as this, preferring to travel alone when possible. At first, he planned to travel by warship with Bahadur and Adalard, but after a lengthy discussion with Melek and his brothers, they had decided to send several of their trusted generals, including Bahadur, to deal with some of the rebel bases that Arrow had recently discovered.

Arrow would lead the effort while Adalard and he worked with the Valdier. Raffvin was one of the key instigators behind the rebellion and one of the most deadly. He needed to be stopped once and for all.

He breathed deeply as he felt the energy surrounding him as the controller locked onto his position. His eyes narrowed as he felt the energy of the transporter beam meld with the energy inside him. He did not feel the disorientation that many others complained about at first. He could see and feel his body breaking into the smallest form and reveled in the sense of freedom it gave him. He almost groaned as he felt his body rematerialize on the platform.

I really need to figure out how to do that on my own, he thought before his eyes met the dark golden ones of Creon Reykill.

CHAPTER THREE

"Zoran has called a meeting," Creon explained as they walked through the corridors of the Valdier palace. "*Dola's* mate will be there as well. He has a plan that he believes will work. Have you found out anything else about those on your world that were working with Ben'qumain?"

"Yes, it would seem even in death my former stepbrother is causing trouble," Ha'ven said heavily.

"I'm just glad he is dead," Adalard said, running his fingers along the long scar on his cheek. "I wish I had been there when Zoran burned him."

Ha'ven didn't respond. He had been there. In fact, he had been the one to draw Ben'qumain's power away from him so he could not use it to attack Zoran. While his stepbrother had been royalty, he had not been very powerful. That was one of the things he had been jealous of in Ha'ven. Unfortunately, Aria had been and had known how to imprison Ha'ven. What neither of them expected was the power that she would unwittingly unleash during his time on Hell.

The men strode down the long, gleaming hallways. Glossy white and black marble glistened on the floors and walls. Ha'ven shot his friend an amused look. He didn't want to say anything but his friend looked like he had been held on the asteroid and tortured as well. Lines of exhaustion showed around his eyes and mouth, not to mention his hair was bound crookedly behind him as if it had been done in haste.

"How is mated life treating you?" Ha'ven couldn't resist asking. "You look..." He finished his comment with a wave at Creon's hair instead.

"What?" Creon responded distractedly before he released a small grin. "Mated life is great," he said, ignoring Adalard's choked cough of disbelief. "It is being a father that is... challenging. Having two tiny females is nerve-wracking. They are so small. I fear I'll hurt them just picking them up. Carmen insists they are tougher than they look but I do not understand how that is possible. You should see Trelon," he added with a huge grin. "If you think I look bad, he looks a million times worse. I don't think he has slept more than a few hours at a time since his two were born."

Ha'ven's shook his head. "I am just glad it is you and not me, my friend," he said in distaste. "I can't believe you and Vox have fallen for this species. What is it about them that made both of you lose your control?"

Creon stopped in the hallway and studied his friend. He wasn't the only one looking tired. Something was wrong with Ha'ven. He knew the huge Curizan warrior well enough to know better than to ask though. If he was patient, he would learn what was bothering his friend. Despite the tiredness, he could also see curiosity shining in his intense stare as well.

"She fills the empty space inside me," Creon said quietly. "I was worried when I returned with her to her world."

"Why?" Adalard asked, moving to stand next to his brother. "What happened?"

Creon looked down the long corridor for several long moments before he turned back to face both men. His face was grim. He glanced around once more before he nodded toward a small alcove near a set of windows. He walked over to it and leaned back against the wall near the long windows that looked out over the central garden.

"Carmen needed closure," Creon began, looking fiercely at both men. "Her first mate was murdered and she was gravely wounded by a very dangerous male back on her world while she was protecting the youngling of another. She was pregnant when she was attacked and lost her babe as well. She wanted…" Creon paused, drawing in a deep breath as he turned to look out over the gardens. "She needed the closure before she could accept her new life. She wanted to find and eliminate the male who had taken so much from her. I knew she would not be able to move on unless she was able to do this."

Adalard cursed under his breath. "I cannot hold that against her, but how could you risk placing her in the same danger again?" he asked in disbelief. "She was carrying your younglings at the time, wasn't she?"

Creon turned and scowled at Adalard. "Yes, but you have met Ariel. Carmen is even more stubborn than her sister! What do you think would have happened if I had denied her? She and Ariel had already tried to escape once. Do you truly think I would take a chance with her life? It was the only way I could think to keep her with me. She… she came close to ending her life more than once. I was not about to take the chance of it happening again," Creon retorted tersely.

Ha'ven put his hand on Creon's arm. "We give no judgment of your decision, Creon. I, better than most, know you would never purposely endanger those you care about," he said quietly.

Creon's eyes jerked to Ha'ven's. He saw no recrimination in them even if it would have been justified. It was his fault that Ha'ven had been captured and tortured. It had been his stubborn refusal to believe Aria, the woman he thought he loved, would betray him.

His denial had almost cost Ha'ven his life. He had killed Aria, drawing every traitorous act she committed from her before he gave her the relief of death. After he and Vox had rescued Ha'ven from the prison he had been held in, he had wished he had taken even more time in killing the bitch.

Creon's eyes flickered to Adalard who nodded in agreement. "I meant no disrespect, Creon. It is just hard to believe females react so differently. Even our females are not fighters in the true sense. They can be lying, deceitful bitches, but they do not know how to fight as a warrior. I have seen Mandra's mate in action. I can just imagine what your mate must be like," he said with a twisted grin.

"I made sure she was protected at all times, not that it made much difference. She still took matters into her own hands. Shortly after we returned to her world a man she knew contacted her and told her where she could find the human she hunted. I, along with Carmen, Jaguin, and Gunner, went to confront him," Creon paused and his eyes turned a dark gold, revealing his anger. "The male had two females in the room with him. Both females had been brutally beaten and tortured. He did this in retribution for an injury that he blamed on Carmen. The human looked for any female that remotely resembled my mate. Once found, he would torture and kill them. According to one of the females we rescued, he had already killed two others shortly before we arrived."

Ha'ven hissed as he stepped back. He knew all too well what it felt like to be tortured. The feeling of being helpless. The feelings of hopelessness and finally the rage at being at the mercy and control of another. Then came the next wave of feelings.

The wish to escape from the pain, whether through death or by any other means. He could not imagine someone inflicting such pain against innocent women simply for the pleasure of causing it. It went against every principle inside him.

"What of the females?" Adalard asked curiously. "You returned with them?"

Creon nodded. "Yes, one of them is Jaguin's life mate," he said.

Ha'ven turned as the door across from them opened and Zoran stood in the doorway frowning at them. Mated life must be good for the huge leader of the Valdier because it wasn't exhaustion causing the frown on his face, it looked more like impatience as his eyes darted down the corridor.

"What are you doing there? I want to get this over with," Zoran growled out. "Abby and Zohar will be waiting dinner if we don't get this over with soon."

Ha'ven rolled his eyes. "As usual, I see you are your typically pleasant self," he drawled out as he stepped out of the alcove first.

"Shut up, Ha'ven," Zoran retorted. "Creon should have let me burn your ass. I don't know why he likes to hang with you and that fur ball so much."

"Maybe because we don't have a stick up our asses like you?" Ha'ven couldn't help the taunt about how uptight Zoran usually was about everything.

"One of these days, pretty boy, you won't have your fancy technology to hide behind," Zoran snapped, but the amused gleam in his eye took the bite out of his words.

Ha'ven chuckled. "Never. It is as much a part of me as your dragon and symbiot are of you." He didn't add it was more than technology that protected him.

"Greetings, Lady Ariel, Lady Reykill," Adalard spoke up as he came in the room behind his brother. "May I say you both look as enchanting as ever. I see Bahadur has not been able to entice you away from the huge ass dragon who has claimed you, Lady Ariel."

Mandra's dark growl rippled through the air as he pulled Ariel closer to his hard body. His eyes darted past Ha'ven and Adalard to Creon. He watched his little brother shake his head showing that Bahadur was not there. He released the breath he had drawn in.

"You are going to need a new general if that bastard doesn't stop sending her gifts. I'm going to cut him into little pieces and send him back to his home world in a very small box," Mandra growled in a deep voice.

Morian's and Ariel's laughter filled the room as the men began competing to discover the best way to kill Bahadur. Even Ha'ven couldn't resist adding a few suggestions. Things did not calm back down until a strange male quietly entered the room.

Ha'ven's eyes swept over Paul Grove as he entered. A ripple of unease brushed over Ha'ven as he realized that this male had in a matter of seconds taken note of everything in the room and he had no doubt that the male would be a deadly opponent if confronted. The male's gaze settled on Morian Reykill who flushed a delicate pink before she and Ariel quietly excused themselves.

"Paul," Zoran called out from where he had taken a seat at the head of the large rosewood table. "I would like to introduce you to some of the most experienced and deadly warriors in the known galaxies."

Ha'ven rolled his eyes at Zoran's introduction. "Don't forget the best looking," Ha'ven drawled out.

That comment started the group of men going again. Ha'ven sat back, a small grin curving his lips as he listened to the jokes, rude comments, and watched the even ruder gestures being exchanged. This was good. It built a comradeship between the warriors that would make them stronger.

You fought harder for those you trusted and respected, he thought as he watched Calo, one of Creon's fierce warriors, throw a small knife at his younger brother who caught it with ease. Things didn't calm down again until Creon erupted in impatience.

"Enough!" Creon impatiently growled. "Adalard, if you aren't careful you are going to end up with another scar to match the one on your face. Let's get back to business," he said in exasperation as he glared at the men sitting around the large table. "The babies didn't sleep well last night," he added sheepishly as he sat back in his seat.

"Mine never do," Trelon Reykill groaned out, running his hands through his tousled hair. "They escaped again last night. They are up to something new. I just know it."

"This is why I never want to find a mate. It turns a man...." Ha'ven muttered in a low voice.

".... Into a man," Paul said, standing up.

Ha'ven raised his eyebrow at Paul's interruption, but listened silently as the male continued to outline what had happened and the plans to finally trap and kill Raffvin Reykill. He leaned forward, listening intently. There was something about the male that was... strange. He looked at Adalard who returned his glance with a small nod. Ha'ven focused inward, pulling on the power inside him and muttered a small meditation chant under his breath to help him focus the power.

Everything in the room faded as power pulsed out from his body to the other male. A golden glow formed around the male, casting him in a mist of the shimmering color. Within seconds, Ha'ven was focused back on the room and staring at the male with a combination of mild shock and curiosity. This was a very powerful male who had been touched by the Goddess herself.

Ha'ven shook his head to clear the vision as another large male suddenly entered the room. A grin broke across his face as he recognized the short dark hair, equally dark scowl, and vivid spots showing under the black vest the male wore. Intense eyes narrowed on Paul Grove before the Sarafin King opened his mouth and put his foot in it as usual.

"Who are you?" Vox asked, sniffing loudly. "You look and smell human, but there is another smell on you."

Ha'ven chuckled as a chorus of smothered chortles met his statement. The huge cat-shifter had a habit of saying what was on his mind and it almost always ended in either a riot or trouble of some type. It took another ten minutes before the human was finally able to calm everyone down again.

Yes, if I have to go into battle I can think of no one else I would want by my side than the men in this room, Ha'ven thought as he flexed his fist to keep the power that he had drawn from building even further.

CHAPTER FOUR

"*D*o you want something to eat?" a soft, concerned voice asked.

Emma didn't respond. She wasn't even sure she could if she wanted to. It had been so long since she had used her voice. It didn't change the fact that she didn't want to answer. It took too much effort and would make her accept where she was and what had happened to her.

Instead, she sat curled up in the chair by the window, looking out over the clear sky, waiting for darkness to fall again. She liked the darkness. It didn't bring scary nightmares or horrible monsters. No, the light did that. In the dark, she was invisible, hidden from the sight of everyone and everything. In the dark, she was… safe. Or at least as safe as she would ever be.

Emma heard Sara sigh when she received no response. She really didn't know why Sara kept trying to bring her back to life. She didn't want to live, not anymore. There was nothing to live for. She had lost everything that had ever mattered to her.

"You have to eat, sweetheart," Sara said, kneeling in front of Emma and cupping one of her slender hands. "You are losing way too much weight. The food is delicious. We can go for a walk through the garden afterwards. There are so many interesting and unusual plants here I swear it will take me the rest of my life to discover them all. If we were back home…"

Sara's voice faded when she felt the faint tremble in the hand she was holding. A knock on the door had her releasing Emma's hand and she stood up to answer it. Emma immediately tucked her hands under the light cover that had been carefully tucked around her. She heard a quiet conversation before another figure came into the living quarters they had been given.

Valdier… Emma thought. *What a strange name. It goes well with the strange creatures that live here. So different from Earth. I wonder how my mother is doing,* she wondered distractedly. *I wonder if she misses me.*

"Emma, Abby is here to see you," Sara said softly. "She brought Zohar as well. Isn't he adorable?"

Emma didn't turn to look at those who came into the room. That took too much effort, as well. She knew the other woman was from Earth. She had been by every day to see how she was doing. Recently, she began bringing other women from Earth as well. The one called Cara was funny. Emma liked it when she came. Even though she didn't let the others know it, she thought the young woman's love for life was fascinating to watch.

"Hi Emma, how are you doing today?" Abby asked gently as she came over to sit on the floor near the window.

The infant she had in her lap immediately leaned forward and tried to squirm away from her. Emma watched as he finally succeeded and immediately made a beeline for her. Abby started to stop him, but appeared to decide to let him explore. Emma's eyes reluctantly lowered until she was staring into a pair of very curious golden eyes.

Gold eyes, Emma thought as she pulled further away into herself. *Aliens, another world. So far from home. So very far from home,* she thought sadly as she closed her eyes to block out everything.

Several months earlier:

"Momma, I'm going to South America," Emma said excitedly as she walked into the cheerfully decorated room where her mother spent her days. "I've been accepted by the Reaching Kids through Music troupe. All those years of you and Poppa working with me has paid off."

The woman sitting at the window turned and smiled as Emma entered. She was dressed in the pretty new pastel dress that Emma had purchased for her the week before. She stood up and held out her hands to take the flowers Emma was holding.

"Are those for me?" Alice Watson asked with a smile. "Thank you so much, dear. Do I know you?"

Emma sighed as she handed the flowers to her mother who immediately took them over to the vase on the small side table and began changing out the wilted ones with the fresh ones. Today was going to be another heartbreaker. The advanced stage of Alzheimer's made her daily visits more and more difficult to deal with. Her mother very seldom remembered who she was from one minute to the next, much less one day to the next.

Her parents had been older when she was born. Her father had been a singer while her mother had been a dance instructor who began her career as a ballerina before becoming a choreographer. Emma's world had revolved around her parents as much as theirs had revolved around her.

They had been her best friends as well as her mentors. There had always been music and laughter in their home. She had helped her mother in the dance studio and played the piano and other instruments while singing along with her father.

Her world had crashed around her when her happy, imaginative father died of a sudden heart attack when she was eighteen. Two years later, her mother had been diagnosed with Alzheimer's. The disease had progressed until Emma was no longer able to take care of her mother by herself anymore. Fortunately, her parents had been financially well off and Emma was able to find a private nursing home specializing in patients like her mom.

"It's me, Momma, Emma... your daughter. I'm going to Colombia, Brazil, Argentina, and Costa Rica. I'm going to teach kids how to dance and sing, just like you and Poppa taught me," Emma replied, picking up her mom's hairbrush and walking over to her. She gently led her over to the chair near the window. "I... I won't be gone long," she said as she began brushing her mother's long, silver hair. "I haven't done anything since you came here a few months ago and I thought it would be good for me to, you know... get out and maybe see the world a little bit."

"That's nice, dear," Alice said as she ran her withered fingers over the petals of a pink rose. "I like pink. It is my favorite color. What was your name again, dear?"

Emma bit her lower lip to keep the pain in her heart at bay. "Emma, Momma," she replied as she laid the brush down and divided her mother's hair into three parts so she could braid it.

"That's a pretty name," Alice said as she leaned back in the chair. "I knew a girl named Emma once. She was a dancer with the Rockettes."

Tears burned Emma's eyes. "I know. You named me after her," Emma said quietly. "You said she could dance on a cloud she was so light on her feet."

Alice's soft chuckle echoed in the quiet room. "She was amazing."

Emma listened as her mother talked about things she had heard a million times growing up. They went for a walk around the gardens and Emma took her to the recreation room where she played the piano for her mother and sang the songs she had grown up singing, silently hoping that the music would wake her mother up and help her remember who she was.

She stayed for over four hours, helping her mother with her bath and into her nightgown. She fed her dinner before helping her into bed for the night. She leaned over, brushing a soft strand of silver hair away from the lined face before giving the wrinkled cheek a light kiss. Straightening up, she smiled down at the innocent look in her mom's cloudy eyes before she walked toward the door.

"Honey," Alice's tired voice called out as Emma opened the door to her room.

"Yes, Momma?" Emma asked, holding tightly onto the door.

"I... I wish I had a daughter like you," Alice said quietly. "You are a good girl. One day you will sing a song and a wonderful man is going to hear and come snatch you up. You just wait. My darling husband did that. He heard me sing and said I opened his heart. I was his nightingale," she murmured before her voice faded as she fell into a sleep filled with wonderful dancers and a tall, lanky man who swept her off her feet.

Emma stood at the door to the room for several long minutes gazing at the relaxed face of her mother. A single tear coursed down her pale cheek as she remembered the love her parents shared. She could only hope she could overcome her shyness long enough to meet the man who would fill her life the way her father had filled her mother's life.

"I know, Momma," Emma said as she brushed the tear away. "He loved you so much you could dance across the clouds and never touch the ground. I love you, Momma. Sweet dreams."

She had left for Colombia three days later for a two month tour. The performing troupe had signed a contract for a twelve city tour to promote the arts. When they had reached Florencia, Colombia, a month into the tour Emma thought she had a chance of breaking through the overwhelming shyness she had suffered from her whole life. That was one reason she had loved her parents so much... with them, she didn't have to look for friends outside of her home.

Working with the children in the different cities helped her realize they weren't the only ones benefitting from the workshops that were sponsored by the Performing Arts Company that was hosting the Reaching Kids through Music program. It had been the day before they were to leave to travel to Brazil that she and Betsy, another girl from the troupe, were kidnapped from out front of the small hotel they had been staying at as they returned from dinner at a restaurant across the street. Two other members of the troupe had tried unsuccessfully to help them. Emma could still hear the gunshots and see the blood as the two men were gunned down.

Emma's mind closed in on itself as she fought to bury the rest of the memories of what happened. She had tried to protect Betsy but things became foggy after her head had been slammed into the stone wall of the small cell they had been tossed in. She could do nothing but watch helplessly as Betsy was brutally murdered in front of her. She could still hear the beautiful girl's anguished screams as she died.

Emma jerked, her eyes opening wide in terror when she felt a hand against her cheek. Her mouth opened to scream, but nothing came out. It was as if her vocal cords were frozen and couldn't move any more. Her unfocused eyes finally cleared and she found herself staring into Sara's warm brown eyes.

"We are going to a dinner tonight," she said quietly. "I think it would be good for you to go. You have hardly been out of our rooms at all."

Emma wanted to protest that she didn't want to be around anyone else. She was happy staying in the rooms. Besides, she did get out... frequently. She waited until after Sara was asleep before she slipped outside into the gardens.

She had learned how to avoid the dragon-men who guarded the area. She became one with the shadows. She moved safely under the cover of darkness with nothing but the stars to light her way. She loved slipping down to the edge of the garden where a low wall ran along the cliffs leading down to the ocean far below. The stars caused the water to sparkle like diamonds on a clear night and she could almost imagine dancing among them.

The flowers that Sara loved so much opened at night and glowed with hundreds of different colors. If she touched them, they would close up. They reminded her of herself, opening when they thought they were alone and safe and closing when others came close. She would sometimes sit among them and gently touch them just so she could watch them open again. A part of her hoped that she would one day be able to have the courage to open up again.

Most of all, she loved the solitude and silence of the darkness. She pulled it to her like a cloak, hugging it tightly around her. She could look out on the world and no one could look back.

"Sara," Abby started to say as she rose and scooped up Zohar, who had crawled off to hide under the low table. "Do you think...?"

Sara glanced at Abby. "It will be good for her. She needs to get out more," she responded quietly.

Abby looked at Emma's calm, blank features. She nodded in silent understanding. "I'll send the seamstress to you. She will make a special outfit for you both. We have several guests from other worlds. It... it might be safer if you both remained inside for the next several days. Zoran has asked me to tell you that you won't be allowed outside until a certain situation has been resolved."

Sara frowned in concern at Abby. "Are we in danger?" she asked tersely.

Abby sighed and looked at Emma, who remained unchanged. "No, not directly, but the men are very protective."

Abby's voice dropped as she fought with whether to tell the two women what was happening. With a sigh, she realized they deserved to know. Abby quickly explained the situation with Raffvin and what had happened to date. She went on to explain that a plan had been set into motion that would eliminate the threat to all of them once and for all.

"Jaguin and Gunner will be remaining close to protect you both," Abby continued. "I have to go get Zohar down for a nap," she said before she grimaced as he began fussing and pulling at her top. "And feed him."

Sara nodded and walked with her to the door. She brushed her fingers down Zohar's cheek as he whimpered. Her eyes softened for a moment before she turned and opened the door.

"I know where the dining room is," Sara said. "I don't think it would be a good idea for any of the men to come here. Emma becomes more withdrawn when anyone else comes near her."

Abby glanced over to where Emma was sitting and staring out the window. "I don't think that is possible," she murmured softly. "I'm worried about her. It is like she is fading away a little more each day. Should I send the healer to see her again?"

"No," Sara said heavily. "The last time he came, she locked herself in the bathroom. It took me two and a half days to get her to open the door. This hasn't been easy... for either one of us, but especially her. She was held longer and that man...," her voice broke as she remembered what she had been subjected to.

"What about Audrey?" Abby said, looking at Sara. "She is human. She is an OB-Gyn."

Sara looked over her shoulder at Emma and nodded. "That might be a good idea. Maybe she can come see her tomorrow. The only time I really see Emma react is when Cara comes to visit with the twins. She actually smiled the last time she came."

"How could anyone not smile when those two are in the room?" Abby asked with a roll of her eyes. "They are so much like Cara it's scary. They get into everything. I swear Trelon is going to lock Amber and Jade in a tower when they get older to keep all the 'dragons' away," she added just as Zohar let out a loud cry cutting any further conversation short.

Abby gave a muttered apology before she hurried out the door. Sara turned and looked at Emma and let out a deep sigh. She was at a loss as how to help the young woman. She hoped Audrey could do something before the girl with the soft voice that had kept her sane during their captivity disappeared forever.

CHAPTER FIVE

"Do you have the equipment ready?" Adalard asked as he met up with Ha'ven later that night.

"Of course," Ha'ven remarked with a raised eyebrow. "I finished setting up the shield late this afternoon. Now the only thing that needs to be done is to tie Trelon's mate up before she dismantles the damn thing. She drove me nuts with her questions and I swear if I catch her 'tweaking' it again, I'm going to be the one tying her up and delivering her with a bow on her head to Trelon. How he can keep up with her I have no idea. I was exhausted and needed a strong drink after just thirty minutes in her company," he finished dryly.

Adalard chuckled. "I was talking to Jarak, Kelan's head of security from his warship. Did you know that she broadcasted Trelon's PVC out over the *V'ager's* communications system?" Adalard asked, biting his lower lip to keep from laughing.

"She did what?" Ha'ven asked in disbelief. "Why would she do that? What did Trelon say? What happened? I mean, I can't believe she is still alive."

Adalard tried to keep a straight face, but it was impossible. He was fighting the laughter so hard tears were rolling down his cheeks. He breathed deeply and opened his mouth to tell Ha'ven what happened, but every time he did he burst into laughter again.

"What's so damn funny?" Trelon asked as he and Cara came up to where Ha'ven and Adalard were standing in the hallway outside the dining area.

"I was… I was… trying… to tell… Ha'ven about… your…" Adalard struggled to say before he gasped in a deep breath and burst out. "PVC!"

Trelon's face turned dark with a scowl at the reminder of what Cara had done to his Personal Virtual Companion. Not that he needed it any longer, but it still burned that everyone in the known galaxies knew his every fantasy. If that wasn't bad enough, he still got requests for copies.

Cara rolled her eyes and put her hands on her hips. "It wasn't *that* funny! Besides, I didn't know what it was. I thought it was about plumbing pipe. That is what we call it back on Earth."

"Plumbing pipe?" Ha'ven asked, confused. "How could you mistake it for piping? Didn't you see what was on it?"

Cara rolled her eyes and looked at Ha'ven like he was a first class idiot. "Duh! I didn't look at the video before I sent it because I thought it was an instruction on plumbing. Besides, I was more interested in seeing if the modifications to the communications system would increase the distance of the distribution of the signal. If you ask me, there really isn't that much difference between the piping from home and what was on the video."

"Do you even know what a PVC is?" Ha'ven asked in disbelief, looking at Cara like she had lost her mind.

Trelon looked at his friend like he would love to kill him right there while Adalard melted back against the wall holding his sides. Ha'ven looked at Trelon who was glaring at him and waving his hand back and forth across his throat behind Cara's back. Ha'ven shook his head and turned to look at Cara, whose lips were curved into a mischievous smile.

"Of course," she replied cheerfully. "The only differences between your PVC and the ones back home is you can only watch yours. Personally, I like the real thing. Of course, Trelon is built like you wouldn't believe. His cock is the size of …" A low curse broke Cara's detailed description off.

Ha'ven's mouth dropped open, Adalard crowed in delight and Trelon groaned as he wrapped his arms around his tiny mate and carried her into the dining room. Ha'ven's eyes followed his friend whose face had turned a decidedly darker shade of red at his mate's words. He decided that Trelon not only needed to tie his mate up, but he needed to gag her as well.

"Did she just describe Trelon's….?" Ha'ven asked, looking at Adalard who was wiping the corner of his eye on his shirt.

"Yes, she did," Adalard said with a grin. "I'm telling you, this species is very entertaining."

Ha'ven shook his head as Adalard went into the dining room. He drew in a deep breath and thanked the Goddess that he had no desire to be entertained by one of them. He had several females he enjoyed company with back on Ceran-Pax and that was all he needed. Besides, until he could find a way to contain the sudden waves of power that ebbed and flowed inside him, he couldn't even think of having a permanent mate. A slight shudder went through him at the thought.

I would rather go back to war with the Sarafin and the Valdier before settling for just one female, especially from a frustrating species like these humans, he thought with a grimace.

Unfortunately, it would appear the Goddess was not listening to his offering of thanks. He knew he was in trouble the moment he stepped into the dining room. A wave of power unlike anything he had ever felt before swelled inside of him, swirling and churning until invisible bands burst from him and shot across the room.

His first thought was he had to find a safe place to release it before he killed everyone in the palace. His second thought was there was no way he would get far enough away to be able to protect them. But, it was his third thought that almost brought him to his knees in front of everyone in the room… he had found his mate.

Emma sat quietly next to Sara looking down at the empty plate in front of her. She hadn't wanted to come. She wanted to stay in the safety of their rooms until darkness fell. Then, she would slip out and find her way to the edge of the garden.

Sara had refused to let her stay behind. Emma wished she could be as strong as Sara. Sara had been thrown into the cell next to hers the night after Betsy had been murdered. Emma had listened as she had cursed at the men who had brought her. She had no idea of what was about to happen to her but Emma did.

They had ignored Emma throughout the night and the next several days. She heard one of them joke that it was no fun killing when the victim was unaware of what was happening. Emma had crawled over to the metal door and tried to warn Sara. It had been hard to think as her head hurt so badly. Sara had finally quieted down enough to hear Emma's softly spoken words.

They had been left blissfully alone for the next four days before they had both been dragged out of their cells to the beautifully decorated office of Javier Cuello. The horrid man was back and this time, Emma knew she would not be given the reprieve of just a beating. Sara had cursed and fought until they strung her up on the poles. Even then, she refused to give in. By the fifth lash of the whip, her wretched screams echoed along with the men's laughter and taunts. By the fifteenth, she was barely conscious and still they continued.

When Emma struggled to throw herself in front of the man with the whip, another had struck her in the head knocking her to the floor. Cuello had ordered the man who hit her to force her to sit up and watch. Shortly after that, things had become very strange when the door suddenly burst open and long, golden tentacles stretched out through the room, imprisoning the men. She didn't remember much afterwards until she awoke in a strange room and learned she was no longer on Earth.

She refused to look at the strange creatures who had taken her. They had been kind so far but she didn't trust them any more than she trusted the men who had kidnapped her. She saw what they changed into. She saw them fighting with each other when she was on the warship. They had been savage in both forms.

The golden creatures had been kind but they had also changed into horrifying shapes with long, dagger-like teeth and claws. None of them came near her. It was as if they knew she was terrified of them.

She had finally just remained in the small cabin they had given her. She had sat for hours looking out at the black nothingness and wondering what would become of her. Eventually, she had stopped caring.

Sara came to visit her every day, but even that didn't brighten Emma's mood. She was worried about what would happen to her mother if no one went to visit her. Was this her punishment for leaving her mom alone to seek out a life of her own? She had been wrong to think it was better to live life to the fullest. Her life had been full before, only she had been too short-sighted to appreciate it.

Emma gasped as a sudden shock hit her slender body, jerking her out of her private torment. Her head jerked up and she looked around in confusion. Her body tingled with a strange awareness that she had never felt before. She felt like someone had just hit her with a Taser.

Her blue eyes searched the area, pausing at the doorway where a tall, muscular male stood staring back at her in equal astonishment. His violet eyes stared at her with an intensity that made her blush and she had to force her eyes to pull away from him. Her face flamed as she looked down at her clenched hands.

Why is he staring at me? she wondered in confusion. *I don't want him staring at me. What if he comes near me?*

Panic built at the thought of the huge male approaching her. She knew there was no way she could escape him. He looked like he could break her with one hand tied behind his back. She doubted if she even came up to his chest!

"Are you alright?" Sara asked, leaning toward her. "You look flushed."

Emma looked at Sara with huge, wary eyes before she turned away when the large male who was sitting on the other side of Sara leaned forward to look at her as well. The male had shown up as they exited their living quarters. Sara had gripped Emma's hand so hard when she saw him that there was no way Emma could have escaped back into their rooms.

"Does she have need of a healer?" Jaguin asked, looking at the delicate figure that appeared to shrink into her seat at his question.

Sara shook her head. "No, I don't think so. Can't you go sit somewhere else?" she asked testily.

Jaguin smiled at Sara. "No," he replied.

Emma listened as Sara snorted and said something rude to the male. Her eyes rose just far enough so she could look to see if the male by the door was still staring at her. She breathed a sigh of relief when she didn't see him. Her heart was just slowing down when the chair beside her pulled away from the table and someone sat down. She was too busy processing the strange feelings rushing through her to acknowledge the person.

In the back of her mind, she hoped it was Cara. She had watched as the perpetually cheerful woman with red and purple hair had been carried into the room by another enormous male. The tiny woman had been laughing. Emma loved to listen to Cara's infectious laugh.

"What is your name, female?" a dark voice whispered in her right ear. "I am called Ha'ven."

Emma froze as the voice washed through her, crashing against the wall of ice inside her. She wanted to gasp out in anger at the feelings that were threatening to awake in a torrential wave. She wanted to push away from the surge that threatened to tear down the barricades that she had erected to protect herself.

"You are too thin," Ha'ven continued harshly. "You need to eat."

Emma turned her head when long, slender fingers held a piece of meat in front of her mouth encouraging her to take a bite. Her lips tightened and annoyance burned through her. She would bite something if he didn't leave her alone.

I'll bite one of those fingers off! she thought savagely, shocking herself.

"You will eat, *misha petite*," the honey voice continued.

"Leave her alone," Sara hissed protectively under her breath.

Ha'ven's eyes glittered back in challenge at the dark anger reflected in the pale female sitting on the other side of the woman who had knocked the breath out of him. No one would keep him from his mate. The pull of her power against his would not allow him to turn away even though he wanted to. The force with which his power blended with hers was like two super strong Neodymium magnets attracted to each other.

"She is too thin," Ha'ven replied with a shrug as he picked up a piece of the delicious fruit from his plate and held it up to Emma's lips. "If she does not wish me to feed her, she can tell me herself," he added mockingly.

"Ha'ven," Jaguin said quietly, looking at Emma's still face as she stared straight ahead. "This one is not for you, my friend. She is not well."

Ha'ven's eyes narrowed as he took in the translucent complexion of Emma's face. He pulled at the energy pulsing feverishly inside him and directed it toward the female sitting beside him. He could see the colors of his essence swirling furiously around her as if seeking a way in.

Astonishingly, she was pushing it away. He had never known another species with an ability similar to the Curizan. One who could harness power and manipulate it the way they did. Nor did he know of any other that could push his power away except perhaps a member of the royal family.

A silent curse escaped him as he looked first at the woman sitting on the other side of his mate before shifting to look at the other human females in the room. He could see no other evidence of power, such as those of the Curizan pulsing from them. The only other one had been the human male. His eyes glanced briefly at Paul, who was watching him through narrow, thoughtful eyes.

His gaze locked with Adalard. His brother had turned and looked at him in warning. Adalard shook his head and touched the corner of his eye. Ha'ven realized his eyes must be glowing with the barely contained power pulsing through him. Breathing deeply, he forced it back down and muttered a small meditation chant to strengthen the shields he had erected to contain it.

"What is wrong with her?" Ha'ven asked, moving his hand to touch one of Emma's hands which were clenched in her lap.

"She was…" Jaguin started to say before he looked at the woman at his side.

"We were kidnapped, tortured, and almost killed," Sara said through clenched teeth. "We just want to be left alone. Is that too much to ask? Emma was held longer and…" Sara's voice faded before she muttered a low curse under her breath. "She hasn't spoken since she woke on the spaceship. I can barely get her to eat. Please…" She looked at Ha'ven with a combination of a plea and a demand. "Just… leave her alone."

Ha'ven looked at the pale hand clenched tightly in his own. A smile curved his lips. He could see what no other could, the colors of her power twisting with his own. The bands were beautiful as they danced with each other before twisting into an unbreakable bond.

He felt the uncontrollable power in his own body being absorbed into hers. He wasn't sure, but he may have discovered the miracle he was seeking. For the first time since before his capture, he felt… balanced.

Leaning closer to Emma, he let her sweet scent fill his nostrils as he breathed deeply. "You are mine, *misha petite*. There will be no leaving you alone. The power within your body has already recognized mine. I do not know what magic your species wield, but you are mine and I will not let you go," he bit out huskily.

Fury washed through Emma. She pulled her hand out of the male named Ha'ven's grip with a sharp jerk and rose out of her seat with the grace earned from years of dancing. She schooled her features to remain blank as she turned to leave. Sara started to rise, but Emma wanted to be alone. Resting her hand briefly on the other woman's shoulder, she shook her head before hurriedly walking out of the room.

CHAPTER SIX

*H*a'ven's eyes followed the slender female as she rushed from the room. He turned and looked at Adalard who was watching him with raised eyebrows and a confused look on his face. He didn't have time to explain to his brother what was going on. Hell, he wasn't sure what was happening. He just knew he needed to find the woman before she disappeared.

Shrugging his shoulders, he rose from the table and turned to follow the woman. Whether either of them liked the fact, she was his mate and some instinct deep inside him knew he needed her. He paused when he found Creon standing between him and the doorway.

"You haven't eaten," Creon pointed out, shifting slightly to the left when Ha'ven moved to step around him. "If you wish some company, my friend, I'm sure I can find more than one female in the palace that would be happy to be with you tonight."

Ha'ven glowered at his soon to be former friend if he didn't move out of his way. He had no desire to visit with any other female. The only one he was interested in was getting further away as he stood wasting time.

"I want only one female," Ha'ven said in a deadly calm voice. "And you are keeping me from her."

Creon shook his head. "The human females are off limits, Ha'ven. Especially the one that just left. They are under our protection."

"She no longer needs your protection," Ha'ven said gravely "I will assume it."

Creon frowned as he looked at the huge male staring intently back at him. Was this the same one that only earlier said he had no desire to settle down? Now he wanted to assume responsibility for a human female that was obviously not well. Creon shook his head again.

"Not with this one," Creon said quietly. "She is not well. I am not even sure she will survive, my friend. You saw her. She grows weaker each day. Abby and Cara have been going to see her daily and she still does not respond to them."

"She responded to me," Ha'ven growled, waving his hand to the door behind Creon. "You saw for yourself."

Creon raised his eyebrow at the dark tone in his friend's voice. "She runs from you just as she runs from the rest of us."

"She is my mate," Ha'ven bit out darkly.

"She's..." Creon's voice broke in shock as he stared in disbelief. "Are you sure?"

Ha'ven drew in a deep breath before responding. "Yes."

He didn't elaborate. How could he when Creon didn't know of the power he held inside his body? His friend thought all their power came from the gadgets they enjoyed. He did not know that the gadgets they created were merely tools for focusing the power held within their own bodies. He could no more explain how his power inter-twined with the human female than Creon could explain how he, his symbiot, and his dragon all knew when they found their mate. It was a force of nature they did not question, just accepted when it came as being a part of who they were in the universe.

Ha'ven shifted to the right and breathed a sigh of relief when Creon stepped aside to let him pass. He knew he had shocked his friend. Hell, he was still in shock. He never expected to find his mate in a species unknown to him.

Nor did I expect my mate to not be willing when I found her, he thought suddenly as he walked out of the dining area.

No, this was definitely a new experience. He frowned as he hurried through the corridors following the quickly fading swirling colors of the female's energy. His own surged as if trying to absorb it.

The female had walked away from him. In fact, she had not only walked away from him, but she refused to even look at him.

When was the last time a female did that to me? he wondered silently as he reached a section where the corridor divided.

The traces of color were gone. He turned, glaring at the intersection where the hallways divided. He had three different directions in which she could have gone.

"Which way did you go?" he muttered softly. "Show me," he whispered and waved his hands outward.

Colorful bands of energy burst from his fingers moving a short way down one corridor before moving back to try the next. On the third corridor, glittering sparkles of energy flared as his own touched the residual energy left behind as the female passed down the corridor. Ha'ven's lips curved in triumph as he moved down the corridor to the left.

He sent small bands searching periodically trying to find which room she may have entered. He paused when a large set of doors on the right suddenly burst into color.

"You are mine, *misha petite,*" Ha'ven growled. "You cannot escape me."

Emma raced through the empty corridors. She wanted to get back to the safety of her and Sara's living quarters. She would find the dark cloak she used to hide her pale coloring and escape into the gardens. She would hide so deep that no one would ever find her.

She pushed open the door leading into her living quarters and rushed through the elaborately decorated living room down the hallway to her bedroom. The floor-length black cloak lay on the end of her bed where she had dropped it early that morning. Sweeping it up in a hand that trembled violently, she pulled it around her like a suit of armor and headed for the balcony doors.

Pushing the double doors leading out onto the balcony open, she drew in a deep breath of the scented night air. A feeling of calm swept through her. This is what she wanted.

I don't want to feel again, she thought fiercely to herself. *Feeling hurts too much. I don't want to remember. I just want to fade away like the stars do before dawn.*

But, they do not fade away, a husky voice whispered in her mind. *They are still there, unseen but there.*

Emma gasped and looked around the balcony. She turned in a circle, backing up until her hip bumped against the balustrade running along it. Her eyes widened in fear and she raised her hands to her temple.

Am I finally losing my mind? she wondered in terror. *Am I going to go mad before I die in this strange world?*

You are not losing your mind, misha petite, the voice responded softly before hardening. *Neither will you die.*

Who are you? Emma whispered silently as she let her hands drop to her side.

No answer came. Emma bit her lip to keep the cry of frustration from escaping. Twirling around, she ran to the steps leading down into the garden. She ran down the long winding paths heading for the edge of the garden where it overlooked the ocean far below.

She was breathing hard by the time she reached the low wall. She half fell, half leaned on the smooth stone. Her whole body trembled, exhausted as overwhelming fear choked her.

What was happening to her? Was she turning into something else like the other women? She knew strange things had happened to the other human women. She had been out in the garden late one night a few weeks ago when two dragons had flown over her. She had hidden under the thick branches of a tree and watched as they landed on the balcony high above her living quarters. Trelon Reykill had shifted and turned in time to catch Cara as she changed back into a human as she touched the top of the balcony. Cara's giggles had echoed through the cool night air but that was not what had given Emma goose bumps. It was the fact that a human could change into something else.

Never! Emma thought fiercely, looking down at the glittering water. *I can never fit in and there is no way to get back home. There is nothing here for me.*

Tears blurred her vision as she sank shakily down onto the low wall. She stared out over the ocean, becoming almost hypnotized by the rolling waves as she let her mind drift. Her body moved without her realizing it, turning around until her legs were over the side of the short wall. In her mind, she could almost see herself dancing and twirling across the gentle swells like she used to do with her mom and dad in the dance studio. How she longed to be with her parents again, surrounded by their love and safe in her own home.

She closed her eyes, lifting her arms up and out as she imagined being back in the dance studio with her mom and dad. The cloak fell from her shoulders. She shivered as the cool night air brushed along her bare arms. Sliding forward so she could stand up, she reached for the imaginary hand of her father as he smiled down at her. She wanted to dance again. She wanted to sing. She wanted to…

"What the hell do you think you are doing?" a dark angry voice demanded harshly.

Thick arms wrapped around her waist, pulling her backwards and out of her memories. Emma's eyes flew open in alarm and she gasped as she realized she was hanging over open space. She would have fallen to her death if the male had not grabbed her.

A low, animalistic cry built deep inside her as she realized that the image in her mind was just that… a memory from her life before.

Ha'ven's heart thundered in his chest and he was actually shaking. He didn't know if it was from adrenaline, anger, or fear. It didn't matter which one it was, he didn't like it and it was the fault of the female in his arms.

"What were you thinking?" he demanded.

He pulled her back over the low wall and set her down. Once her feet were on the ground, he roughly turned her around and shook her. When she looked up at him with wide confused eyes, he let out a low, tortured groan before capturing her parted lips with his own and pulling her against his hard body, fear and relief warring inside him.

Ha'ven moaned as the taste of her washed over him. The moment his lips touched hers, he knew he was in trouble. The power Aria had unleashed surged through him and flowed around them. From the corner of his eye, he could see the bands of power swirling around both of them, encasing them in colorful whirling ribbons of energy.

He moaned louder as he felt the shift inside himself. It felt like a huge weight was being lifted from his shoulders. The feeling of relief was impossible to describe. He had never felt anything so….

His body jerked and he gasped as pain suddenly overcame the pleasure he had been experiencing. He rocked backwards, grabbing his crotch as the first wave of excruciating pain eased into a second, longer one. He breathed deeply through his nose as he fought to stay on his feet while the tiny figure he had been holding seconds before fled into the darkness.

"I hate to say this, but that looked painful," Adalard commented as he stepped out of the shadows.

Ha'ven pulled in a hissing breath as he glared at the retreating figure of the woman who had been in his arms just moments before. He finally turned his heated glare on his younger brother as he slowly straightened up. He closed his eyes as another wave of pain, thankfully lesser than the first two, washed through him.

"What are you doing here?" Ha'ven bit out harshly, slowly opening his eyes again.

"I was worried about you," Adalard admitted before he grinned. "It looks like I had a right to be. She kneed you pretty good."

Ha'ven grimaced as he turned and sat on the low wall. He breathed deeply as he sent a small amount of healing energy to his bruised crotch. He had definitely not been expecting the female to do that. Normally when he kissed a female they were more interested in doing something much more pleasurable with his balls. Relocating them up to his throat had never been one of those things.

"That was... painful," Ha'ven finally admitted. "And very unexpected."

Adalard chuckled as he sat down next to his brother. "So, what was all that about?"

Ha'ven threw Adalard a disgusted look. "It is called kissing. I thought you would know that by now," he remarked dryly.

"I know what you were doing," Adalard responded with another chuckle. "I'm talking about the fact that you both were glowing bright enough to be seen from the Spaceport orbiting the planet."

Ha'ven drew in another breath and realized he didn't feel the crushing pressure inside that had been his constant companion since Aria's betrayal. A small satisfied smile curved his lips. His mate was turning out to be an enigma he was determined to solve.

"This is what happens when you discover your true mate," Ha'ven finally responded to his brother's observation. "I had heard stories. We all have. I thought it was a myth that when a true mate is found their powers merge, becoming one. Father," he grimaced as he stumbled over the unfamiliar use of Melek's position. "Father said the same thing happened when he was with mother."

"But, that female is not from our world," Adalard pointed out. "From everything I have seen and heard, they do not have the ability to manipulate energy the way we can."

Ha'ven looked up into the night sky and sighed. "My mate can. I do not know if she does not want anyone to know that she can or if she is unaware of it, but the fact remains, she can." He looked over at Adalard. "I need her, Adalard. I can no longer control the power that builds inside me. She is the only thing between me and total destruction," he reluctantly admitted.

Adalard hissed loudly as he stared in disbelief at the male who had been his biggest role model. He had never known Ha'ven to lose control. He had known he had changed a lot after his capture, but he had never dreamed the situation was so dire.

"What are you going to do?" Adalard asked sharply.

Ha'ven grinned, suddenly feeling more like his old self. "I'm going to claim my mate," he said.

Adalard's eyebrow rose as he looked skeptically at his brother. "She didn't look like she was interested in being claimed from where I was standing. What if she refuses?"

Ha'ven shrugged and rose to his feet. "Then I'll kidnap her and hold her until she agrees. It shouldn't take more than a day," he said, flexing his shoulders. "Have you ever known a female who could resist me?"

Adalard stood and shook his head. "No," he admitted. "But, I've never known one to try to rearrange your balls before either."

"She'll be eating out of the palm of my hand before the sun sets," Ha'ven responded confidently. "She was just surprised tonight."

Adalard stood watching as Ha'ven started back toward the palace. He thought about the look on the female's face as she kneed his brother and shook his head. If the look of fierce determination was anything to go by, he had a feeling it was going to take a little bit longer than a day to get the female to cooperate.

"I don't think it is going to be as easy as you think, brother," Adalard said doubtfully as he started after him. "I think you have met a female who is as stubborn as you are hard-headed."

CHAPTER SEVEN

*E*mma stood on the balcony to her room later that night. She had rushed back to the safety of her bedroom after she escaped from the dark male who had grabbed her in the garden.

He did save my life, a small, obstinate part of her admitted. *If he had not grabbed me, I would be fish food right now.*

Yes, but he didn't have to kiss me! she argued silently with herself.

Frustrated, she realized that she would never be able to sleep. Her body was humming with unexpected energy. She felt like she had stuck her finger in an electrical outlet only to discover it was live. Every nerve-ending in her body was tingling, especially where he had touched her.

She had waited over an hour, staring intently out into the darkened garden for any sign of movement before she finally grabbed the little courage she had left and stepped out onto the balcony.

At once, the cool dark silence cocooned her in its magic. She closed her eyes and soaked in the sounds of the night. She loved the darkness.

Walking over to the railing, she leaned on it and looked up at the stars. She wondered where Earth was in relation to where she was at now. A sense of longing engulfed her as she thought of the small, blue marble that had been the only home she'd ever known until now. She lowered her eyes, letting them sweep over the dark gardens with their strangely lit plants. A movement under one of the trees to the left drew her attention.

Emma gasped as a dark figure stepped out of the shadows of the tree into the moonlight. She stumbled backwards in fear as Abby's words about a threat echoed through her mind. Turning, she bolted for the door leading back into her bedroom and safety.

"Wait… please," a familiar deep voice called out.

Emma paused with her hand on the door as she recognized the voice of the man who had kissed her earlier in the garden. She fought between the desire to run and hide and the need to find out what he wanted. Drawing in a shaky breath, she reluctantly turned until she was facing him. She stared at him in silence, wary of what he might do next. As a safety, she kept her hand on the door just in case she needed to bolt inside.

"I never properly introduced myself," he said, stepping onto the first step. "I am Ha'ven Ha'darra, Crown Prince of the Curizan."

Emma tilted her head and studied him silently, waiting to see what else he had to say. She really didn't care what his name was. She was more interested in why he had kissed her.

A light blush rose as she remembered the heat of the kiss and the feel of his arms around her. She swore she could feel electricity moving through her body when he touched her. That was what had scared her so much. She had never felt so alive before.

She bit her lower lip to keep from smiling when he shifted uncomfortably from one foot to the next when she didn't respond to his introduction. She honestly didn't know what he wanted or why he was even talking to her. It wasn't as if she had done anything to encourage his attention. In fact, she would have thought after she kneed him, he would have done everything in his power to avoid her. A low curse filled the air as he waved his hand at her.

"Most women are impressed when I tell them who I am," he grunted out in annoyance.

Emma couldn't keep the twitch of amusement from curving the corner of her mouth or lighting up her eyes at his statement. It was obvious he was not used to women ignoring him. Studying him in the soft light of the moon, she could understand why. He was huge!

Emma guessed him to be well over six and a half feet tall. He had broad, muscular shoulders. She had felt the hard muscles under her palms when he kissed her. She also knew there was no way she could wrap both of her hands around his forearms. Long, dark hair hung down his back almost to his waist.

He wore a long-sleeve black silk shirt tucked into black pants that hugged his thighs. She blushed as her eyes brushed over the front of his pants. She wondered briefly if the rest of him was built as big as well. She was mortified by her thoughts. She had never thought of a man's...

Emma blushed a brighter red and was thankful that it was dark so he couldn't see her rosy face. She remained silent instead, curious as to what he would say next. She had to lower her head to hide her amusement when he growled in frustration at her lack of appreciation for his position.

"You are called Emma?" he asked with a frustrated glare.

She lowered her chin in acknowledgement. The smile that had been threatening to escape disappeared when he climbed the next two steps. Her eyes darkened with mistrust when she realized he stood on the balcony not more than a few feet from her. Her hand tightened on the door and she started to open it when he asked his next question.

"Why do you not speak?" Ha'ven asked, desperate to keep her from leaving.

Emma briefly closed her eyes before she looked past him into the dark garden. *I can't.*

"Why?"

She didn't know how to respond to his softly spoken question. If she answered him, then she would be forced to remember. If she remembered then the nightmares and feelings of what she had gone through and what she had lost would overwhelm her.

Shaking her head, she opened the door. It had been foolish for her to stay outside. She should have just remained inside where it was safe. Where she could hide. How could a man as strong as the one standing in front of her understand what it was like to feel weak and helpless? He would never understand what it was like to feel hopeless and lost.

"Don't leave," Ha'ven called out softly. He hated the feeling of emptiness that filled him at the thought of her pulling away from him. "Please, I...." He paused, desperate to think of some way of convincing her to stay longer. He waited until she turned to look at him again before he continued. "I promise not to touch you unless you say I can," he rashly vowed.

Emma studied him for several long minutes before she reluctantly let go of the door. She relaxed when he stepped back down onto the steps. She watched as he sank down to sit on the top step. It was as if he knew she didn't trust him to keep his word. She finally walked over to one of the chairs and sat down. They both recognized and understood the uneasy compromise that they had silently agreed upon.

They sat like that for hours. She listened attentively as he spoke of his world. She loved the images he shared as he described the great waterfalls and thick forests where he played as a child with his two younger brothers. She couldn't stop from giggling when he explained how his youngest brother, Jazar, earned the nickname Arrow.

"Even as a child, he loved the tales that Salvin, our teacher, would tell of the old ways. He could barely walk when he found one of father's bows. He would drag it out of the chest where it was stored. Of course, it was much too big and heavy for him to use but he didn't care.

Melek, my father, gave him his first bow when he turned six. Mother finally gave up trying to take it from him. Jazar ate, slept, and would have bathed with it if it wouldn't have ruined it. Adalard started calling him Arrow and it just stuck until that is the only thing we call him anymore," Ha'ven said, leaning back against the wall, staring at her as he spoke.

He loved watching how her eyes sparkled in the moonlight and the way the colors of her aura changed as he spoke. When he first saw her standing on the balcony, the colors around her had been dark and ominous. He didn't know what she had been thinking about but he wanted to chase the shadows away. Her mind had been protected by the icy walls of protection that she used to hide behind when he tried to reach her in the dining room.

He had not returned to the dinner after their meeting earlier. He had parted ways with Adalard after one of the female servants had caught his brother's eye. Another tried to catch his but there was only one female he was interested in now. Instead, he had wandered through the gardens again hoping to figure out what was happening to him. It didn't take long before his power had flared, pulling him through the shadows until he found himself staring up at the cause of his confusion.

There were so many questions he wanted to ask her but he didn't. He could see that she didn't trust him. He could see the stiffness in her body as she fought against her instinct to flee. He also saw the hesitant curiosity in her eyes when she glanced at him when she thought he wasn't looking.

Everything about this female confused him. He wanted her with a desperation that he had never tasted before, but he also knew that if he was not careful, he could lose her. So, he continued to tell her about his world. He also asked her simple, harmless questions like what her favorite color was… violet like his eyes. He bit back a grin when the thought swept through her mind when she let down her guard. She loved to sing and dance. He saw the images of her with an older man as they twirled around in a circle.

He realized questions about her past were off limits at the moment. She withdrew from him the moment he asked her if she could go to any place in the star system where would that be. He hid his grimace of frustration behind a calm mask as the icy walls in her mind rose, blocking him from seeing into her thoughts. Even so, he could feel the pain and grief before she hid it from him. Understanding that she was not ready to share that part of her life with him yet, he continued with his tales of adventure.

Emma curled her legs under her on the seat and leaned back. She enjoyed listening to Ha'ven's deep, rich voice, though she would never admit it. At first, she had been uneasy when he would ask her a question and she realized he could 'see' what she was picturing. It was only when she realized that she could also 'block' him from seeing into her mind that she relaxed a little.

After the first couple of hours, she was surprised to realize that she didn't even think of it anymore. Sometimes she answered him with a flickering thought, other times she would hold the wall she had built around her and just look out over the garden at the softly colored glow of the plants. She found she enjoyed the comfortable silence between them just as much as when he spoke. They reluctantly parted ways as the sky began to brighten on the horizon.

"I will not be able to see you tonight," Ha'ven said as he stood up and stretched. "You must promise me you will stay inside until you are told it is safe again, *misha petite*. Promise me that you will listen. These are dangerous times and it is important that you understand that."

Abby already told us, Emma replied, wrapping her arms around her body. *She said two warriors would remain with us until it is safe.*

Ha'ven bit back a low growl of jealousy at the thought of another male being near Emma. He wanted nothing more than to bundle her up and hide her away until all the danger was past. Instead, he gave a tense nod.

"I will return as soon as I can," he promised, aching to kiss her again but mindful of his promise.

Not for me, Emma whispered back. *This has been... nice, but I just want to be left alone.*

Ha'ven stared at Emma, a dark frown marring his face. "I will see you, *misha petite.* I promise to keep my vow to not touch you... for now, but I will see you again," he swore in a steely voice filled with promise.

He watched as Emma shook her head in denial before she slipped into her bedroom. His hands clenched at his sides as he fought the over-whelming urge to follow her. His eyes darkened as he thought of the battle ahead. Not just the one with Raffvin but the one to earn his mate's trust.

The next day, she and Sara were told they had to stay inside their living quarters for a couple of days. Emma remained in her bedroom. She wasn't comfortable being around the two warriors who were assigned to protect them.

She heard Sara talking with Audrey, the human doctor who had been by to see her before. Audrey tried drawing her out into the living room. She finally gave up, realizing that as long as the men were there, Emma would not come out of her room.

"Emma doesn't like it when others are around," Sara explained softly to Audrey, looking over at where Jaguin and Gunner were talking quietly. "Those are the two that brought us aboard the warship. They were there when we…" Sara's voice broke as memories crowded her.

"It will take time," Audrey said soothingly. "I worry that Emma isn't showing any improvement, though."

Sara nodded and turned her head to hide the tears in her eyes. "It's hard," Sara whispered. "I never used to be afraid. Now…," she glanced toward the men when she realized they had stopped talking and were watching them. "Now, I don't like being around other… people. I can understand where Emma is coming from." Sara bowed her head, ashamed to admit to Audrey, she was scared of being around people, especially men.

Audrey touched Sara's arm. "Sara, you and Emma have been through a very traumatic experience. I wouldn't be surprised if you both weren't suffering from some form of PTSD. There is nothing to be ashamed of," Audrey assured her.

"What is PTSD?" Jaguin growled. "You said you were fine! I thought my symbiot healed your wounds," he bit out, glaring at the huge golden shape lying at Sara's feet.

"Do you mind?" Sara snapped out. "I was having a private conversation and you were not invited to participate!"

Jaguin ignored Sara's retort and turned to glare at Audrey. "Do you know how to heal this PTSD?" he demanded.

Audrey folded her arms across her chest and looked pointedly at Jaguin. "This is a private conversation between myself and Sara but I will explain what PTSD is. It stands for Post-Traumatic Stress Disorder. It often occurs after an individual has suffered a terrifying ordeal, often from physical harm or the threat of physical harm. What Emma and Sara went through would definitely classify as such an ordeal."

"Audrey," Sara whispered in a strained voice. "I don't want to talk about it. Especially with him here."

"I was there, Sara," Jaguin said tightly. "I saw what was done to you."

Sara's eyes darkened in distress and she let out a low, wounded cry before turning and rushing from the room. Jaguin took a step to follow her but Audrey put her hand on his chest and scowled up at him.

"Enough!" she said in an authoritative voice. "I'll go to her. You two… just stay here and make sure no one takes the silverware," she ordered before turning to follow Sara.

Gunner walked over to where Jaguin stood near the couch. He laid his hand on his friend's shoulder and squeezed it in support. His own eyes followed the figure walking stiffly down the hallway, a golden symbiot by her side.

"Give her time," Gunner said quietly. "You were there. You know what was done to her."

"But not everything," Jaguin said, a muscle throbbing in his jaw as he gritted his teeth in frustration. "I don't know everything that was done to her."

Gunner looked at his friend's tortured expression. "You may never know," he responded. "Just accept and support her. That is all you can do."

Jaguin nodded stiffly. "I will be there for her, even if she refuses to accept me."

Gunner grinned and smacked Jaguin hard on the shoulder. "Since when have you ever accepted defeat?" he asked. "You have a challenge, my friend, to get her to accept you. Now, you must think of the best way to break down her barriers."

Jaguin's eyes narrowed for a moment before a slow smile curved his lips. "You are right, Gunner. I think it is time I took this challenge to more familiar ground. Somewhere I know and somewhere that she won't be able to resist going."

Gunner's eyebrow rose. "How do you plan to do that?"

"She loves unusual plants," Jaguin said, looking at Gunner with a devious smile. "I know a place where there are all kinds of unusual ones."

Gunner stared into Jaguin's cunning eyes and saw the determination in them. His friend had a plan. He grinned and laughed.

"You are too cunning for your own good sometimes," Gunner said. "Now, what do you think my mate meant when she told us to make sure no one took the silverware?"

Emma glanced over as Sara entered her bedroom two days later. She sat at the small table looking out over the garden. She was replaying the unusual meeting with the huge warrior once again. It was like a broken record in her head. She couldn't stop thinking about him and it was beginning to drive her even crazier than she thought she already was!

Sara walked quietly across the room and sat across from her. They sat in silence for several minutes before Sara sighed loudly. Emma knew something was wrong when she felt the tremble in Sara's fingers as she touched her hand.

"I'm going away for a little while, Emma," Sara said reluctantly. "I've been invited to go up into the mountains where there are some very unusual plants. I… I miss my research," she admitted softly. "I need to find a place for myself on this world and this is the one thing I know I'm good at."

Emma looked at Sara's tear-filled eyes. She could see the guilt waging a war with the need to start living again. She knew that Sara had put her own wants and desires on hold in a misguided effort to help her. She felt the weight of her own guilt surface as she realized that Sara was waiting for her approval to move on.

Emma forced herself to respond. She gently touched Sara's cheek with the tips of her fingers. Her lips curved into a ghost of a smile in understanding and acceptance. She didn't blame Sara at all for wanting to move on. Sara squeezed her hand in return.

"You have to fight back, Emma. This is a good place to live even if it is different. The people here are…" Sara paused as if searching for the right words. "The people here are strange and different as well but they would never hurt us. Not like Cuello did. You have to fight back. I can't stand watching you fade away any longer. I… I need to heal and I can't do that unless I get back to doing what I love," she finished in an emotion-choked voice.

Emma stroked her thumb over the dampness on Sara's cheek and nodded. She understood what Sara was saying. Sara was strong. She had fought against the men who had kidnapped them. She had lived a life back on Earth. Something had broken deep inside Emma during her captivity. She wasn't sure if she could ever be fixed.

I just don't fit in, she thought sadly. *Neither here nor on Earth.*

I think you fit perfectly with me, Ha'ven's husky voice broke through her dark thoughts.

What are you doing back in my head? she asked testily. *I thought you were busy,*

Never too busy for you. Will you have dinner with me tonight?

No, she thought back, looking out the windows. *I… I think it best if you left me alone.*

Never, came the dark promise before he had faded away again.

Emma sighed as she picked at the hem of her skirt. She sat at the small table near the windows overlooking the gardens, impatiently waiting for the sun to set. Her mind was focused on a certain tall, dark-haired alien. She touched her lips as she remembered his kiss yet again. She swore she could still feel his lips touching hers!

She impatiently rose from her seat and looked around the empty room. Everything seemed so much quieter since Sara had left almost a week ago to travel to the mountains to study the plant life there.

At first, Emma had wandered around the empty space trying to convince herself that it was what she wanted. She thought if she was alone she would be able to find the icy solitude that she had surrounded herself with before. So far, it wasn't working, thanks to one very irritating male who refused to leave her alone.

She still didn't understand how or why he could talk to her the way he did. She had briefly fought against it before she just accepted that there was no way to totally shut him out. She had tried to understand how this could have happened, but she kept coming up with a blank. She finally decided it was just part of the crazy world she now lived in and should just accept that she would never understand it.

She glared out the windows into the brightly lit garden in frustration. She was looking forward to nightfall when she could escape out into it without fear of running into anyone. Well… anyone but the male who refused to leave her alone for the past ten days.

I look forward to our time as well, a husky voice broke into her thoughts.

I didn't say I was looking forward to seeing you! Don't you have somewhere else you need to be? Emma snapped back in exasperation. *Why don't you just leave me alone?*

Because, like you, I cannot forget the sweet taste of your lips, he teased.

Emma pictured rolling her eyes so he would know she didn't believe him. *Don't forget you promised you wouldn't touch me again without my permission,* she reminded him once again.

A promise I regret making, he growled back in frustration. *Why do you fight me?*

You… wouldn't understand, Emma whispered back. *Any more than I understand how you can talk to me this way.*

Misha petite, he started to say before he broke off with a low growl of annoyance. *I must go. You will come to me tonight?*

Emma folded her arms around her waist and rolled her eyes again. *I don't 'come' to you. You are the one who finds me, remember?*

A low chuckle echoed briefly through her mind. *I will find you again tonight in your favorite spot by the wall, my stubborn little mate. Think of me until then.*

Not likely, Emma snorted before she threw up the wall in her mind to block him from knowing how his words affected her.

I will be thinking of you and dreaming of holding you in my arms, came his soft reply before he faded away.

Emma shook her head. One thing she was learning was when it came to pickup lines, Ha'ven Ha'darra never seemed to have a shortage of them. He had been slipping in and out of her mind since the night of the dinner. He also had an unerring way of always knowing where she was.

She was still surprised by his reluctant promise not to touch her without her permission. He had given it to her the same night as the dinner and, so far, he had kept his word. A soft smile curled her lips as she remembered how he had called out to her. She still didn't know why she had stopped. Maybe it had been the desperation in his voice. She had also heard the confusion and hesitation in it. It was as if he was as puzzled by her as she was of him.

The night Sara left was the beginning of their almost nightly meetings once Emma was allowed to venture out again. He had found her later that night and each night afterwards near the low wall looking out over the ocean. Each night, he brought a basket filled with food and a soft blanket that he would fold for her to sit on.

Tonight was no different. She sat on the folded blanket, listening in silence as he shared more of his home world and his family. She was thankful that he did not ask about hers. She wasn't ready to share and she got the feeling that he understood she needed more time. He spoke of light-hearted moments as well as some of the darker ones during the Great War. Emma was shaken when she saw a brief glimpse of him hanging by his arms in a dark cavern, blood running in thick streaks down his body before a different image replaced it.

War is never good, she said silently. *I am glad that Creon did not kill you.*

"I am thankful as well," Ha'ven responded with a chuckle as he placed several slices of fruit on her already full plate.

I can't eat all of this, she silently told him in exasperation. *You don't need to fill my plate like I'm a child. You keep putting too much on it.*

Ha'ven reached out to run his fingers along her cheek. He paused when she jerked back and turned her head away from his touch. He dropped his hand to his lap and clenched his fist in frustration.

"When will you give me permission to touch you?" he growled out in a low voice.

Emma turned to look up at him with dark, troubled eyes. *Never,* she whispered back.

Ha'ven's eyes darkened with frustration and suppressed desire. Every night for the past eight nights he had fought against the growing hunger deep inside him. The need to claim her was growing to unbearable levels. Each night, he craved the feel of her soft skin against his and the sweet taste of her lips again.

"That is not the answer I want, Emma," he growled out, standing to look out over the ocean. "I cannot keep my promise forever. I have to return to Ceran-Pax for a few days to take care of several issues," he said before turning to look at her. "When I return, you will be mine. I give you these few days to accept that. My promise will be over."

Then it is best if you do not return, Emma responded, standing up and looking at him with a determined tilt to her chin. *I don't want to see you again. If you do return, I want you to leave me alone.*

I could no more leave you alone as I could stop breathing, Ha'ven growled out silently. *I have claimed you, Emma. You have a week to accept that or not. But I promise, when I return you will be leaving with me.*

Creon has promised me his protection. You can't claim me against my will, she responded passionately before she turned and bolted for the safety of her rooms.

"I already have, *misha petite,*" Ha'ven growled out possessively as he watched her flee into the darkness. *I already have,* he repeated silently, making sure she heard the resolve in his promise.

CHAPTER EIGHT

A knock on the door pulled her head around. She frowned as it drew her from her thoughts of her last meeting with Ha'ven almost a week ago. He said he would return to Valdier in another two days, but Emma was sure that he had forgotten all about her and his silly claim by now. After all, what could a man like him possibly want with someone as messed up as her?

I should never have let him inside. I should know better. It only hurts when I start to care about someone else. They will only leave me, she thought as she turned to look back out the window. *He will have realized by now that my turning him down was for the best.*

Whoever was at the door would go away when she didn't answer it. It wasn't like she was expecting anyone, anyway. All the women had already been by to see her. They had made a habit of visiting with her for a few hours each day since Sara left.

Trisha was the last one to come see her for the day. She had stopped by a short time ago with her son, Bálint. Emma had smiled at the serious expression on the infant's face as he stared back at her. He looked like he trying to figure out who she was.

He was so different from Cara's two little ones who were into every-thing. She couldn't resist smiling when the little golden symbiot on his arm changed into a pacifier when he started fussing as he grew tired. There was just something magical about it.

Trisha told Emma about escaping into the woods outside the palace, not long after she came to Valdier. Emma had listened in fascination as Trisha talked about how she had hidden from Kelan and the trackers pursuing her for days before she 'tagged' them. Emma smiled as she thought about how frustrated Kelan must have been when he couldn't capture Trisha.

She sighed in relief when whoever was at the door didn't knock again. Her thoughts drifted once again to Ha'ven. She had done the right thing when she told him to leave her alone. He had probably found someone else anyway. Someone who was beautiful and strong.

She had overheard some of the women who came in to clean her quar-ters talking about him. Two of them even had the nerve to brag about how great a lover he was in front of her! Silent rage built when one of the women complained that he hadn't asked for her when he was here last week. The other joked that it was because he had been with her. Jealousy and hurt burned inside Emma even when the woman finally admitted that it was Adalard that she had been with instead.

Emma turned when a movement out of the corner of her eye drew her attention back to the door. She started in fear when the form of a man suddenly began forming just inside of it. Her mouth opened to scream before she snapped it shut as the form solidified. Fury blazed in her eyes instead as they met the mocking, yet determined, violet eyes of the male she had just been thinking about.

Ha'ven stood outside the door to the living quarters of his mate and waited to see if she would answer the door. He shifted impatiently as nothing but silence greeted him. He had left the following day after she ran from him, but not before he had tried several times to talk to her.

Frustration ate at him when she refused to see him. Hell, she even refused to answer his silent requests! The last time he tried to see her Abby had answered the door and said it was up to Emma if she wanted Ha'ven to enter. A locked bedroom door had been his answer.

Out of desperation, he had slipped into her mind when she finally fell into an exhausted sleep right before he and Adalard departed. Agony and sorrow burned deep into his soul as her vivid dreams filled his mind. The pain, fear, and overwhelming grief had been suffocating. Held in the grasp of her memories, he had done what he could to soothe her, but even then, she refused to let him ease her pain.

He had cursed violently as they lifted off to return to Ceran-Pax. He hadn't wanted to leave without Emma, but he had promised her a week to come to terms with his intentions. Creon had told Kelan and Zoran about his claim on her. They understood his feelings, but their mates had not.

Abby, Carmen, and Trisha were concerned about Emma's continued silence and fragile mental and physical health. Zoran had reluctantly given his permission for him to court Emma but he stressed she had to be willing. He had agreed to the terms before he realized just how stubborn and uncooperative Emma could be.

If Bahadur hadn't returned with two rebels from the hidden base Arrow had discovered, he would never have had to leave. He thought for sure he was on the verge of wearing her down that last night before she ran from him. Now, he decided both rebels could have taken a page out of his mate's book when it came to being obstinate.

The rebels had been stubborn, but Ha'ven had learned a thing or two about torture during his time on Hell. Both men had eventually revealed additional names. He had ordered Arrow, Adalard, and Bahadur to work on finding them while he returned to Valdier for Emma.

Just a few days away from her showed him that the emptiness inside him grew to irrepressible levels. He was done with waiting. He was done with making promises that separated him from his mate. He needed to get her away from Valdier where she could hide in her living quarters and behind the royal family. He needed to take her back to Ceran-Pax where she would be under his control.

"No more hiding, *misha petite*," Ha'ven said, taking a step toward where Emma was standing glaring at him. "You have hidden from me for the last time."

"Get out!" Emma whispered in a rusty, shaky voice, surprised that she could remember how to talk. "Get out!" she repeated a little stronger this time.

"So you can speak when you want," Ha'ven said mockingly. "I thought we would live our lives in blissful silence."

Emma's eyes blazed with uncontrollable fury as she thought about what the two women said about him and his 'skills'. She looked wildly around her. Snatching up an empty cup on the table, she turned and raised her arm.

"I wouldn't if I were you," Ha'ven bit out, his eyes narrowing on the cup in her hand.

Emma pulled back and threw it as hard as she could at him. Unfortunately, she was not a very good shot. The cup shattered a foot from where he was standing. Growling out in rage, she darted toward the hallway leading to her bedroom. She skidded to a stop when Ha'ven's huge frame stepped in front of her. Twisting, she darted around the couch.

"You are going to be difficult, aren't you?" Ha'ven said, releasing a sigh. "You do realize most women would give anything to be in your position."

"Go... find one of them, then," Emma forced out slowly. "I... I'm not interested. I know where... you can find... a couple who are," she retorted angrily.

Ha'ven threw his head back and laughed. Never had he had to chase a female before and to be told one was not interested in him was... strange. He grunted when a pillow from the couch hit him in the face.

His eyes widened when he saw she had a figurine to throw next. He looked warily at her as she pulled back and let loose, barely ducking out of the way. Her aim was definitely improving. He dodged when she picked up a large bowl and threw it next.

Cursing, he went one way trying to catch her only for her to go the other. She was determined to keep the couch between them and find anything loose that she could throw at him. When she raced to the dining area, he jumped over the back of the couch and chased after her.

"Ouch! That hurt!" he growled when she tipped a chair in front of him and it landed on his foot. "Will you stay still?" Emma ignored him and continued pulling the chairs over as she rounded the table.

"Never!" she said breathlessly when she saw him heading in the opposite direction. "Not until... you... disappear back to where you came from... like you did... before."

Ha'ven growled in frustration as she tipped another chair in front of him before turning and quickly jumping the ones that were lying on the floor. His foot caught in one and he almost went face first into the floor.

"That's it," he snapped as he pushed up.

With a wave of his hand, chairs began flying out of his way. Emma's eyes widened as they began moving on their own. She let out a loud scream and turned. She ran as fast as she could to her bedroom.

Slamming the door and twisting the locks, she backed up as she heard his booted feet against the polished tile. She glanced frantically around looking for a weapon she could use against him. A decorative sword was set against the far wall.

She rushed to it. Rising up, she groaned in frustration when she realized she was too short to reach it. Turning, she raced for the chair near the vanity.

Pulling the heavy chair across the floor, she pushed it up against the wall and quickly climbed up onto it. She was shaking from head to toe as she yanked on the heavy piece of metal. It came free at the same time as the doors leading into her room burst open, hitting the wall with a resounding bang.

Emma grunted as the sword came free, almost toppling her off the chair. She turned on the narrow seat and tried to hold the large weapon in front of her, but it was too heavy for her to lift. She glared at the huge male standing in the doorway with his hands on his hips and a dark scowl on his face.

"You are the most aggravating, stubborn, and hard-headed female I have ever met," Ha'ven bit out. "Why are you fighting me? I told you I was claiming you when I returned."

Emma let the heavy sword rest on the edge of the chair. She looked at the male who actually looked like he was confused that she was not jumping into his arms. He honestly didn't understand why she was running from him. If she wasn't so angry and confused herself, she might have found the situation funny.

"I want you… to leave me… alone," she forced out quietly. "I don't know why… you won't. You could ha… have any woman you want. Why are you… picking on me?"

Ha'ven looked at the petite figure standing on the chair holding a large war sword between her slender hands and biting her lower lip. Her eyes were huge and she looked as confused as he felt. He slowly took a step toward her, biting back a chuckle when she tried to raise the sword that had to weigh more than she did. With a wave of his hand, the sword disappeared as he stepped in front of her.

"What…? How…?" Her shocked words echoed in the room.

"There is much you will need to learn, my Emma" Ha'ven answered quietly. "The first is there is only one woman for me and you are her. I thought I had shown you that during our nights together."

A loud banging from the outer rooms drew his attention. Shouts sounded as evidence of their struggle drew the attention of more guards. In the background he heard Creon and Kelan's voices. It was time to take his mate and leave before they thought to stop him.

Ha'ven wrapped his hands around her tiny waist and pulled her off the chair, ignoring her squeal of protest. He turned just as Creon and Kelan stepped into the room, their swords drawn, and their symbiots in the shape of huge Werecats.

"Ha'ven!" Creon said in disbelief before his eyes narrowed. "Release her."

"I think not," Ha'ven replied darkly.

"Let me… go," Emma breathed out as the thick arms pulled her closer. "Help… me," she pleaded, looking at Creon. "You promised… you'd protect me."

Creon's eyes darkened at the plea. "Ha'ven," he said, taking a step closer. "She has asked for my help. I have promised. I cannot deny her request."

Ha'ven's eyes narrowed as his friend raised his sword. "Six months," he said suddenly. "Give me six months. If she wishes to return still, I will return her to you."

"No," Kelan began to say before Creon put his left hand out to stop him from moving any further.

"You will not force her to accept you," Creon argued. "She has to accept you of her own free will."

"Creon," Kelan began again.

Creon looked at his brother. "She is his mate," he said quietly. "She has spoken. She responds to him."

"No!" Emma wailed, pushing against the arms imprisoning her. "You... promised you would protect... me. You can't do this. I don't want to... go."

Creon turned back to look at Emma who was glaring at him through tear-filled eyes. He didn't see fear in her eyes. He saw anger. He knew if she remained here that she would never heal or learn to accept her new life. In a way, it was much as it had been with him and Carmen. They had been forced to live again.

"Six months starting today. Take her," Creon bit out harshly and turned away.

"Creon," Kelan began one last time. "Our mates are going to skin us alive, not to mention Paul when he and *Dola* return."

Creon glanced toward Ha'ven and Emma. He stopped in shock to see they were already gone. He looked around, puzzled. He had not seen a transport beam initialize in the room.

Ha'ven must have another new toy, he thought in disgust.

"Would you have walked away from Trisha?" Creon asked, turning back to look at Kelan.

Kelan shook his head in resignation. "No," he acknowledged heavily. "No more than you could walk away from Carmen. I just hope he knows what he is getting into."

Creon looked up at the wall where the ancient war sword hung. If he had to guess, he would think the female who had been half dead had been doing her best to get it down in order to use it on his friend. He couldn't hold back the chuckle that escaped as he imagined Ha'ven's face if she had been successful.

"Personally, I don't think he has a clue. I just wish I could be there to see how he handles it," Creon replied.

A moment later, Kelan's chuckles joined Creon's as they both remembered their own trials and tribulations while trying to court their mates. If the human female had decided she was ready to join the living again, Creon figured his friend was going to need all the help and time he could get. With a sigh, he motioned for one of the guards to notify the servants in charge of Emma's living area that it needed to be righted and that their mistress was temporarily away.

Yes, Creon thought as he saw his mate and Trisha heading toward them with grim expressions on their faces. *Ha'ven has no idea the fury he may have just unleashed.*

CHAPTER NINE

"*I* hate… you!" Emma growled out, hitting Ha'ven in the back with her fist as hard as she could as he carried her on-board a small spaceship. "I hate you. I hate you. I hate you!"

Ha'ven grimaced as he walked down the narrow passageway to the bridge where he set her down forcefully in the co-pilot seat of the small transport. He caught her hands as she swung at him. Unfortunately, he wasn't quite fast enough to miss her foot, which connected with his stomach. If he hadn't bent over to grab her arms, he would have been in a lot more pain.

"Will you stay still?" he growled out as he slipped a strap over her shoulder. "I don't want to break you. You are too small and thin."

Emma glared up at him as he pulled the strap tighter. "Well, if you don't like what you see, you can always zap me back to where you got me. I didn't ask to come with you, you… you… overgrown ox."

Ha'ven pulled back and glared down at Emma's furious face. If he wasn't so damn horny he would have been furious himself. Instead, the sight of her flushed face, flashing eyes, and pouting lips were begging him to do things he didn't have time to do… yet. The moment he could program the return trip into the sleek transport, he was taking her back to his cabin.

"You are so beautiful," he muttered, shocking them both. That had NOT been what he had planned to say. "We will be underway soon," he added gruffly, sitting back in his seat.

"I don't want to be underway," Emma whispered, looking at him as he sat across from her. "I just want…"

Ha'ven glanced at Emma as her voice faded and she looked down at her clenched fists. He saw them tremble and a moment later, a small drop of moisture glistened on one hand. He cursed silently and turned back toward her.

Cupping her trembling chin in his large palm, he was amazed at the difference between them. His darker skin was a dramatic contrast to her fair complexion. He gently tilted her chin up, forcing her to look into his eyes.

"I will not hurt you, little one," he promised in a husky voice. "I could never hurt you."

"What do want with me?" Emma asked, mesmerized by the glowing swirls of color in his dark violet eyes. "Why did you take me away?"

Ha'ven studied the confused eyes staring back at him. He ran his hand tenderly up her jaw to carefully push the loose pale strands of hair that had fallen forward back behind her ear. He was fascinated by every detail of her. He could see her aura. It shimmered with colors that he had only seen in the clear skies after a fierce thunderstorm. She was… breathtaking. An air of innocence clung to her as she looked at him, waiting for his answer.

"You are mine," he responded simply, letting his hand fall away and turning back to the controls.

Emma opened her mouth to demand he clarify what he meant by 'mine' but snapped her mouth closed instead when colorful bands formed around his hands and merged with the grips he used to pilot the ship. A moment later, the soft hum of the engines engaged and the spaceship began rising up off the field of waist deep purple grass.

"How did you do that?" she asked instead, staring as the bands changed color. "What is that?"

Ha'ven shot her an amused look as he notified the control tower that he was leaving Valdier orbit. He could see the curiosity fighting with her desire to continue arguing with him. He breathed a sigh of relief when curiosity won.

"It is the way of the Curizan," he said cautiously. "We do not share what we can do openly with other species. Your species is the same. You do not share your ability to harness the energy around you either."

"Humans can't do that," Emma said, pushing another loose strand of hair back from her face. "Well, except in books, but the characters aren't usually human."

"Of course you can," Ha'ven responded, checking the transport as they entered orbit. "Your energy melded with mine the first night before I even saw you. I had barely entered the dining area when I felt your power reach out and link with mine."

Emma stared open-mouthed at him. "I did not! I mean, something hit me. It felt like what I imagine a Taser would feel like, but I never did anything to you. Ever since I met you, crazy stuff has been happening. I hear you in my head and you make me see colors and feel things that I don't understand," she mumbled under her breath.

Ha'ven glanced at Emma with a frown forming a crease between his eyes. "Of course you did something. I could see it. The colors of your essence reached out and called to mine."

Emma didn't know how to respond to his statement. None of what he was saying made any sense to her. She turned as a small transport flew ahead of them and looked through the front view-screen in wonder.

They were passing a very busy Spaceport. All types of spaceships in a wide variety of shapes and sizes were docked at it. She watched as several paused in the distance, as if waiting for permission to arrive while others moved slowly away as they departed.

"Why?" she wondered, not realizing she had asked the question out loud.

"Why what?" Ha'ven asked as he sped past the Spaceport heading toward deep space. Once they moved through the first Jump-gate, he would program the transport.

Emma turned and looked at Ha'ven. "Why did this happen to me?" she asked huskily. "I just wanted to see a little tiny piece of the world before returning... home to run the dance studio and take care of my mom. Why did this happen to me?"

Ha'ven heard the hurt, confusion, and pain in her voice. Her pain pulled at him. He had never before let the feelings of another touch him the way hers did. He did not think even his younger brothers could touch him the way she did with her simple question.

"Only the Goddess knows why she does the things she does," he told her. "Perhaps she believed you needed to see more of the world than you thought. Or..." he broke off.

"Or...?" Emma asked, waiting for him to finish his sentence.

"Or perhaps she knew that I needed you," he finished.

Emma watched as the huge male who had basically kidnapped her carefully balanced a tray of food in one hand while he picked up a cup with his other. They had traveled for almost four hours before they made it to the first 'Jump-gate' as he called it. She had closed her eyes and prayed she wouldn't throw up when they had first gone through it. It had taken her several minutes of breathing deeply before she realized that warm calloused hands were caressing her face.

"It gets easier with time," Ha'ven told her quietly before he carefully unstrapped her from the chair. "Come, I will fix us something to eat."

Emma paused before she slowly took the hand he offered. An electric shock swept through her every time he touched her. That was one of the reasons she had been so insistant that he not touch her again after he kissed her. She wasn't sure if it was static electricity or the 'power' he said he had inside him. Nothing in her past had prepared her for what was happening and she was at a loss as to what to do.

"How did you make the sword disappear?" she asked as she reached for the tray and set it down on the small table. "I mean, one minute I was pointing it at you and the next it was gone."

Ha'ven nudged her over a little, enjoying the soft pink that washed up into her cheeks as she moved over enough so he could sit next to her. He set the drink down between them. Creon's words that she might not survive had haunted him every night since he first saw her. That was one reason why he had brought a meal each night. He wanted to make sure she ate. He would do whatever was necessary to make sure she did.

"Everything is made up of energy," he explained, waving his hand over the tray and making it disappear while leaving the plates of food. "I simply focus on what I want to do with the energy and change it to suit my wants and needs."

Emma ran her fingers over the table where the tray had been seconds ago. She looked up at him with a look of wonder and fear. This was a part of him that she hadn't seen during their late night chats. She glanced back down at the table before she carefully tucked her hands back into her lap.

"Can you make me disappear?" she asked quietly. "For good, like you did the tray and the sword."

Ha'ven watched as Emma bit her lip and refused to look at him. He touched her cheek with his finger, running it down along her silky skin until he touched the tip to her lips. Her lips parted and he felt the soft, warm air as she released the breath she was holding.

He tilted her face toward him. "The tray and the sword merely moved to a different location. Their energy is still there, just as I moved us when we left the palace. I would never let you disappear, Emma. I told you, I need you."

Leaning forward, he carefully replaced his finger with his lips. Something told him he needed to take this slowly. Over the past several hours, he discovered something that he had never considered before – that success was not always guaranteed. And, for the first time in his life, he was afraid of failing.

Ha'ven closed his eyes as intense desire and something he didn't understand moved through his body, making it taut. A low moan escaped him as her lips parted under the pressure of his. He slipped his tongue into her mouth, wanting to taste the sweet fruit of her essence that he had been taunted with since the first time he kissed her.

His hand moved around to cup the back of her neck, pulling her closer. His head tilted ever so slightly, allowing him to deepen the kiss. He tried to pull her around so he could press her delicate form against his aching body, but the table prevented him from gathering her closer.

With a muttered curse, he pulled back and rested his forehead against hers. Both of them were breathing heavily. After several long seconds, he sat back and pulled his hand around to pick up the cup. He paused in shock when he saw it tremble.

"What are you doing to me?" he muttered under his breath.

"What... what?" Emma asked softly, raising a hand to her swollen lips.

Ha'ven shifted his eyes away and glared at his plate. "Eat," he said gruffly. "You are too thin."

Emma glared at his dark face. "I've gained weight since I met you. Besides, I haven't been very hungry since..." her voice faded and she looked away as tears filled her eyes as memories suddenly flooded her. "I would like to go to my cabin," she finished dully as her stomach churned with the stress she always felt when she remembered what happened and where she was.

"No," Ha'ven said sharply before calming. "Please, eat with me," he said in a softer voice. "Tell me about your world. I have told you about mine. What is it like? Do you have family there?"

The moment the last words were out of his mouth, he felt like kicking his own ass. He thought to distract her from her memories and here he was asking for her to open up and tell him about it. He knew how much it hurt her to think about it. He had to be the stupidest male in all the known star systems – after Vox. Even he wasn't as stupid as that crazy cat shifter.

Emma's giggle surprised him and he looked at her with a raised eyebrow in question. She grinned at him, showing off small, pearly white straight teeth. Her eyes sparkled with amusement.

"You were thinking pretty loudly," she confided with a blush. "I didn't mean to eavesdrop, but I wanted to know what I had done to make you mad," she confessed.

"I was not mad at you. You make me feel things I am not familiar with and it confuses me," Ha'ven admitted with a grin of his own. "I don't like things that confuse me."

"Mm, does that mean you don't like me?" Emma teased, tilting her head to look pointedly at him.

Ha'ven groaned and broke off a piece of bread on his plate and stuffed it into his mouth. He chewed it slowly, glaring at her as if to say he was not about to dig the hole he had started any deeper. Emma giggled again before picking up a piece of fruit off her own plate.

"There is only my mom and me," she began, pausing to take a bite of the sweet fruit and swallow it before she continued. "My father passed away a couple of years ago from a heart attack." She looked at him before continuing. "My parents were older when I was born. Mom was in her late forties and dad in his late fifties. They had given up ever having any kids. I was a huge surprise to them. Mom thought she had a stomach bug and went to the doctor to see if it was bacterial or viral. You can imagine her and dad's surprise when she found out she was pregnant!" Emma smiled and took another bite of food before she continued. "They were ecstatic. My dad had the most beautiful voice and my mom was a professional dancer. I grew up singing and dancing with them. They were the best parents in the whole wide world."

Ha'ven watched as a wide range of emotions crossed Emma's expressive face as she talked. He picked up a piece of vegetable with his fork and held it in front of her mouth. His lips curved when her mouth opened like a small bird. He bit back a groan when she reached out and tucked her tongue under it to pull it off.

"You speak as if your mother is no longer living," he observed. "Yet, you said it was just the two of you."

Emma nodded and her eyes clouded with regret. "My mom has advanced Alzheimer's. She doesn't remember who I am. It became so difficult to care for her on my own that I finally had to place her in a special home so she could get additional care," she said quietly. "I didn't want to, but she left one night while I was sleeping. I had locked the doors but she undid them. The police found her walking almost two miles from the house in the early morning hours in her night-gown. It was only when I called that they knew who she was. I couldn't stand to think of something happening to her while I slept, but I was so tired. I tried to keep her with me."

He took her hand as she waved it in aggravation. Raising it to his lips, he pressed a kiss to the tips in an effort to comfort her. He could tell she was very distressed at having to give up caring for her mother.

"How long did you care for her? You could not be expected to care for her alone," he assured her.

"Two years," Emma admitted. "Two very long, very lonely years." She looked down at her plate, surprised to see almost all the food on it was gone. "Momma never had many friends. She always thought of Poppa as her best friend. She was just beginning to suffer from dementia when he died. After that, she went downhill fast and the few friends they had stopped coming by. In a way, I don't think she wanted to remember a life without Poppa." She sighed and looked up at Ha'ven.

"I went to see her every day. I spent time with her, helped her with bathing, fed her, and put her to bed every night. Who is doing that now? Who is taking the time to be there for her with me gone? I just wanted a little time to feel alive." Emma's voice choked with tears. "I wasn't going to be gone long. I just wanted to know what it was like to be young and free to discover the world."

Ha'ven reached out and touched the strand of hair that fell across her cheek. "What happened?"

Even as he asked the question, a part deep inside warned him he wouldn't like the answer. He had seen bits and pieces in her dreams. Even in those, she closed him off when things became too dark. He could feel her terror before she woke and shut him out.

Emma looked away. "I don't like to remember," she said before she scooted out from behind the table and stood up. "I'll take care of the dishes since you prepared the meal. Shouldn't you be checking the engines or where we are going or something?"

Ha'ven knew he would get nothing else out of her. She had closed him out again. He could feel the icy touch of the wall she threw up when she didn't want him seeing into her mind. He was getting better at finding a way to be a shadow in her mind, just as she had found a way to slip into his without him being aware of it. Still, she was very stubborn and very good at withdrawing tightly into herself. He could feel the rough edge of pain and fear, but nothing to tell him what caused it.

With a sigh, he stood up and gathered the dishes. "I will show you how to work the cleansing unit, then show you where you may rest. I have a few things I need to do."

He didn't add that his plans for bedding and claiming her had only slightly changed. He knew now that he needed to proceed with a caution and slowness that was totally alien to him. He had always charged in and to hell with the consequences. That was not an option this time. His first and foremost concern was for Emma. He wanted... needed to know her. He wanted to chase the fear and pain away, not cause more. He looked on as she loaded the cleansing unit and released a silent sigh.

This is going to be one of the toughest battles I have ever fought, he thought as his eyes swept over her rounded bottom and down over her long legs that peeked out from under the skirt she wore. *Sometimes being honorable really sucked.*

CHAPTER TEN

"How goes your journey?" Adalard asked, sitting back behind the console on his warship. "Were you finally successful in getting your little mate to talk to you?"

Ha'ven ran his hands through his hair and grimaced. "Yes… and no, but more yes than no," he replied.

Adalard rolled his eyes and snickered. "Did she knee you again?"

Ha'ven dropped his arms and snorted. "No, she did not. She pulled a Valdier War Sword on me," he said with a grin.

Adalard choked out a laugh before he turned and spoke to someone to the left of him. A moment later, Arrow's face appeared on the screen. His dark violet eyes were lit with amusement.

"I just wanted to see if you were still in one piece," he grinned. "Adalard told me what happened. Did she really pull a sword on you?"

Ha'ven grunted when he saw his youngest brother grinning like a Sarafin cat who had just discovered a treasure of *nippa*, one of their favorite treats. His brothers were having far too much entertainment from his love life. The last thing he wanted was for them to say anything to Emma that might make her mad or scare her.

"Yes, she did," he growled out. "I want you two to be on your best behavior when we get back to Ceran-Pax."

"You talked her into coming back already? Damn, I thought for sure it would take at least a couple more days," Adalard exclaimed.

"Yes, well, I didn't exactly talk her into coming," Ha'ven muttered under his breath.

"What did you say?" Arrow asked.

Ha'ven glared at his little brother, if you could call being over six and a half feet tall and almost three hundred pounds of muscle little. He knew Arrow had heard him. Nothing had ever escaped his notice. That was one reason why he had been so good at staying one step ahead of the assassins Ben'qumain had sent after him.

"I said I didn't exactly talk her into coming," Ha'ven replied a little louder.

Adalard crowed and slapped his twin on the back. "I knew it! What did you do? Have you claimed her yet?"

Ha'ven released a sigh and sat back. "I kidnapped her and no, I have not claimed her as yet. Things are a little… complicated."

"Define complicated," Arrow said, sitting down in the chair next to Adalard. "How complicated? We are not going to war with the Valdier again are we? I have to tell you, I was only battling them for a year, but they are a deadly lot to piss off."

"No, we are not going to war with the Valdier. I have given my word to return Emma in six months if she wishes," Ha'ven replied slowly. "She is different."

"What do you mean by different?" Arrow insisted. "Adalard said her species can harness and use energy like ours."

Ha'ven shook his head. "She insists they cannot. She was shocked when she saw me using it, and frightened. I do not understand what is going on yet. I can see the power surrounding her and it calls to my own. She calms me," he admitted reluctantly.

"How can that be?" Adalard asked, sitting forward and looking at Ha'ven with a dark frown. "Do you think she is trying to hide it from you by denying it? Surely she knows we can see the power in her aura."

"What does it look like?" Arrow asked. "Is it like ours?"

Ha'ven thought for a moment before he shook his head. One advantage he had was he could recognize another's aura. The color and strength of it defined what they could do and how powerful they were. Melek's aura was a powerful red, wrapped with gold and yellows. His mother's was filled with soft greens, pinks, and purples. He knew his own was black with swirls of red, gold, and dark greens. Each reflected his strength. Before his captivity and torture on Hell, the black had only been thin bands, but since it had grown until it was difficult to see the other colors.

"Ha'ven, does it look like ours?" Arrow asked again impatiently.

Ha'ven looked at both of his brothers on the vidcom and shook his head again. "No, it is strange but it is softer. It appears to glow from the inside out of her and it changes with her moods instead of being a constant color like ours."

Arrow groaned and rubbed his hands over his face in frustration. Out of the three brothers, his fascination with science and technology knew no bounds. Anything strange or different demanded his attention. When he was younger, Ha'ven was constantly finding creatures, plants, and experiments hidden away.

"I want to meet her," Arrow said, looking pointedly at Ha'ven. "When will you arrive on Ceran-Pax?"

"We should be there in a day or two," Ha'ven replied. "I don't want you scaring her. I need time alone with her to get her to accept what has happened to her and to accept me," he added, shooting both of his brothers a warning look that dared them to make a smart-ass comment.

"We should be back by the end of next week," Adalard said with a small grin before his expression turned serious. "We tracked one of the names given to us to the Sanapare Spaceport, but by the time we got there, Kejon was gone. He is the assassin that tried to kill me."

Ha'ven's mouth tightened. He knew Kejon. He was a lethal, cold assassin whose unethical methods had gotten him in trouble during the Great War. He refused to listen to his superior officers and had killed anyone, Valdier, Sarafin, Curizan or any other species that had gotten in his way. He had been sent to Hell after he tried to kill one of his commanding officers. He had escaped shortly afterwards and disappeared. Ha'ven had a feeling his stepbrother had a hand in the escape.

"Where is Bahadur?" Ha'ven asked.

"He has gone to the Marastin Dow star system," Arrow replied with a grin. "He never was one to take the easy way. One of the men on the list was supposedly trying to seek assistance from them."

Adalard snorted. "Yeah, good luck with that. They would just as soon gut him and steal his credits than earn them."

"Those purple bastards are like a swarm of *Rougeworms*. I swear if you kill one, there are ten more coming at you," Arrow growled out.

"Do what you can to find Kejon. I don't like the fact that bastard is still alive and free," Ha'ven said before a sharp pain struck him.

He breathed deeply as it faded before another more intense took its place. He focused on where the pain was originating. It took a moment before he realized it was not his pain but Emma's. She must be dreaming again.

"I have to go," he bit out grimly.

"Be safe, brother," Adalard said with a sharp nod.

Ha'ven didn't bother replying. He was already out of his seat and heading down the corridor as fast as he could go. Another sharp pain hit him at the same time as a soft whimper echoed in the narrow corridor from the open door leading to the small cabin he had shown her to earlier.

Emma bit back a cry. He liked it when she cried out. He laughed when she did. She refused to give him the satisfaction. Her body jerked as she felt the slash of the whip again. The pain was excruciating.

She pulled further into herself trying to escape it. If she could just lose consciousness, maybe he would quit. He didn't like it when she fainted. He wanted her awake. She felt herself being pushed aside as they reached for Betsy. She lay on the cold stone floor trying to catch her breath as her back burned.

Betsy's high-pitched scream broke through the haze surrounding her as she turned her head. The man had handcuffed the other girl to the bars of their cell and was running the tip of his knife along her shoulder across to her breast. Blood followed the trail.

Emma forced herself up onto her hands and knees. She bit her lip until she tasted blood, but she refused to just lay there while they tortured Betsy more. She ignored the man with the cane.

He was the one who ordered the man with the knife to hurt them. He was the one who laughed as they cried, begged, or screamed. He was the monster.

If she could get the knife away from the man, she could kill them both. She didn't think of how impossible an act that would be. She didn't care if he used it on her. She was ready for the pain to end. She and Betsy had been held for almost three weeks.

Three weeks of constant pain until they thought they would go mad. Only the man would not let them. If it looked like one of them would die, he would tell the man to leave them alone until they healed a little.

He had a young local girl come and doctor their wounds, uncaring that the young girl was crying along with them.

He had become livid when Betsy had told him she would do anything he wanted. Anything... He had asked her if she would do disgusting things to him, with him, to the other man. Betsy had sworn she would. She would do it all, anything he wanted if he would just not kill her.

Emma thought Cuello might actually agree to Betsy's suggestions. At least until he had shown her what was left of his leg. Betsy had gasped and turned away in horror. That was when Emma's beating had ended and Betsy's torture had begun.

Emma felt her body lurch toward the man with the knife as he cut deeper into her friend. She managed to grab his arm, but Cuello swung his cane out, striking her on her shredded back. She had cried out and released the man's arm.

The huge man swung around, grabbing her by the throat and slammed her head against the stone wall so hard she immediately lost consciousness. When she finally came to, it was to find Betsy barely clinging to life as the man continued to cut her. Blood soaked the floor around the tiny blonde's limp body.

Emma released a terrified scream when a hand grasped her shoulder. She didn't think, she just reacted. Her hand came up, palm flat, and stuck the vulnerable nose while her leg came up and stuck out with every ounce of her strength. The sound of bone breaking and the harsh curse as the body went flying backwards woke her out of the paralyzed daze she was in.

Rolling, she was on her feet and running. She jumped when a hand reached to grab her ankle and flew through the door, hitting the wall on the other side of the corridor hard before she turned. Her eyes were wild with terror and her only thought was to find a place to hide where no one could find her. Somewhere dark. She had to find a safe place.

A choked cry escaped her as she ran blindly down the narrow corridor. She turned when she reached the end and frantically searched for an opening. Spying a hatch, she pulled it open and began half climbing, half sliding down the narrow rings that made up a ladder.

She jumped the last few feet and ran along a narrow catwalk between long tubes and wiring. She turned at the end and saw a small, shadowed area under a large tube. She scrambled down off the catwalk and rolled under the tubing until she was in the corner. Once there, she curled up as small as she could and closed her eyes.

I'll disappear. I'll disappear where no one will ever find me, she thought desperately.

She pictured in her mind that she was invisible and no one could see her hiding. A soft glow surrounded her as she imagined herself hidden in the shadows. As the glow intensified, her body began to shimmer and dissolve until there was no sign that she was there. Soon, not even the glow was visible. Emma had succeeded in disappearing.

CHAPTER ELEVEN

*H*a'ven cursed as he grabbed his bloody nose. He rolled over and stumbled to his feet. Sending an impatient burst of energy to his nose and bruised ribs, he strode out of the cabin looking both ways.

He had been so focused on what Emma was experiencing he didn't think about the fact that she was locked in her memories. It was the first time he had really seen a small part of what she had suffered. Uncontrollable rage flared toward the humans who had done this to his mate.

His own power swelled as it sought an outlet for the damage done. His eyes glowed with the suppressed feelings of helplessness and a thirst for justice that he would never be able to give. He knew from the brief conversations that he had with Creon that the man who did this to his mate was dead, but there was no satisfaction in the knowledge.

"Emma!" Ha'ven called out, waiting to see if she responded. "Show me where my mate went," he demanded when nothing but the soft hum of the ship responded.

Ha'ven directed the swirling energy out from him. It danced for a moment before twisting and curling in flowing waves along the corridor. It paused for a moment at the end before dipping and flowing down through the hatch. He hurried toward the opening leading down to the engine room.

He didn't bother with the rings. He simply dropped down through opening, landing with a light clang as his booted feet hit the metal catwalk. He sent out another wave of energy. Thin red and gold strands burst out, but it was the black that worried him when it danced, growing larger, as it moved down along the catwalk to the far end. Ha'ven moved cautiously down the narrow metal walkway.

"Emma, *misha petite*," he called out softly. "It is just me, little one. Remember, I promised not to hurt you. I could never hurt you, little mate. Come out and let me help you."

Ha'ven cursed silently when nothing but silence greeted him. He opened his mind as he followed the flow of his energy. He paused at the end, frowning as the red and gold bands shimmered back and forth before dissolving. It was as if it were confused. He could sense Emma was near but he could not see her.

Little one, you are safe. Come to me, he called out silently.

Frustrated when he received no response, he lifted his hand and concentrated. "Show me where my mate is," he commanded again.

Red and gold bands formed and spread out, only to dissolve as soon as it left the area around the catwalk. Ha'ven frowned as he swept his gaze around the maze of tubes and wires. He could see nothing, but he knew she was near. He could feel the faint, icy wall when he reached out to her. There was nowhere else for her to hide and he knew she came down here.

Desperation swept through him as he felt a sense of foreboding that she was fading further away from him. A knowledge born of survival and instinct told him if he did not find her soon he may never find her at all. Pulling on the dark energy that threatened to overwhelm him, he opened his palm to a swirling black mist.

"Show me my mate," he commanded in a low voice.

The black mist shot out from his palm and flowed under the tubing to the corner. The moment it touched the shadowed area, silver sparks flared as if a million tiny diamonds had captured the light of the sun. A fragile shape formed in the shimmering mist. Pale blue eyes slowly opened and lifted to gaze at him with such deep sorrow that his heart broke for the tortured soul looking back at him.

Ha'ven moved slowly. He knew instinctively that if he were to move too quickly he could very well lose her forever. She had moved herself to a plane of existence between two worlds, neither here nor there.

"Emma, *misha petite*," he said soothingly as he knelt on the metal catwalk before carefully climbing off it so he could get as close to her as possible. "You are safe, sweetness. Nothing will harm you here. I will always protect you."

Emma shook her head furiously back and forth. Her pale hair danced with sparkles as the energy that composed her physical form danced between the realms. Her lips parted as if she wanted to speak, but nothing came out. The look in her eyes still held the terror of her dream.

"Come to me," Ha'ven whispered, holding out his hand. "Touch me and let me protect you."

"You… you can't," she finally whispered back. "He'll kill you just like he did my friends. He'll hurt you because of me. Please… I don't want to hurt anymore."

"He cannot touch you ever again," Ha'ven assured her. "He is dead. There is no way for him to ever harm you, little one."

Tears filled the pale blue eyes and coursed in silvery trails down her cheek. He could tell she didn't believe him, trapped as she was in her memories. He felt the dark power building in him begging for release. It was like a living thing inside him, begging for a chance to avenge the wrong done to its mate. It wanted to destroy the males who hurt her.

Ha'ven cursed under his breath when he saw the hand he was holding out tremble and black tentacles swirl from the tips of his fingers toward Emma. The thin strands greedily reached out for her. He clenched his fist and started to pull it away from her.

How can I help her when I cannot even help myself? he wondered in despair.

His eyes widened when he felt the tentative touch against his fisted hand. The swirling black bands arced from him to her, wrapping around her slender wrist and pulling her closer. Concerned about her reaction to the dark power that threatened to destroy him, his eyes swept over her face. Instead of the fear that had been present only moments before, wonder and hope fought to replace the fear and horror of her memories.

Her hand solidified as she slowly pulled his fingers back so she could run her fingers up over his palm. Her eyes remained focused on the black bands that shimmered and glittered as she touched him. Her brow was creased, as if she was trying hard to decipher a hidden message within the dark strands.

"What is this?" she asked softly. "It feels… warm."

Ha'ven wrapped his fingers tightly around hers. She was not out of danger yet. Only her hand and a small part of her arm had returned. He tugged on her hand a little to see her reaction. She allowed him to pull her closer to him. As she moved out of the shadows, a little more of her solidified. He ran his free hand up her other arm as she placed it on the tubing separating them. The moment he knew he had a good hold on her, he quickly pulled her out of the shadows. Breathing out a sigh of relief, he reached over the large tubing and lifted her over it and into his arms.

A shiver ran though his body as he wrapped his arms tightly around her. He buried his face in her hair and breathed deeply until he felt a measure of calm settle over him. Once again, the moment his power wrapped with hers, it settled. He did not understand what was going on. When they returned to Ceran-Pax, he would meet with Melek and Salvin to see if they had found anything in the ancient archives.

Sliding his arm more securely under her legs, he turned and walked back to the small lift that was on the opposite wall from the hatch. He issued a short command and the door slid open. Stepping inside, he turned as the door closed them in the narrow space.

"I'm sorry," Emma said quietly. She wrapped one hand around his while her head rested against his chest. "I hurt you. I didn't mean to. I was scared and reacted without thinking."

Ha'ven chuckled as the door opened to the upper level. "You have a very good punch when you want to for someone so small. I will have to remember that in the future. You do a good job with your feet as well. That is the second time you have kicked me," he said as he stepped into the small sleeping area.

Emma blushed and turned her face into his chest. "I've never hit anyone in my life," she admitted.

He walked over and sat down on the edge of the bed she had been sleeping in only a short time ago. He refused to let her go. He was shaken by her ability to slip into the shadow realm. If what she said earlier was true, then she was unaware of the power she wielded inside her delicate frame. It was imperative that he teach her how to control it before something bad happened.

"Then I am honored that I was your first victim, though I prefer to not be on the receiving end again. The first time you almost emasculated me and this time you broke my nose. I can happily attest to the fact you are proficient in self-defense," he teased.

Emma raised her head in alarm. "I broke your nose?" she gasped, looking at the long, narrow appendage. "It doesn't look broken," she said, looking confused as she reached up to gently touch it.

Ha'ven lifted his head enough to brush a kiss against her fingers. An unfamiliar emotion swelled inside him and suddenly all he could think about was how close he came to losing her. Fear choked him. Both emotions were foreign to him and left him bewildered.

"I healed the damage," he said gruffly. "You must promise me to never do what you did again. It was very dangerous."

"I told you I didn't mean to hit you," Emma started to say in a small voice.

"I'm not talking about that. I'm talking about disappearing into the shadow realm," he said. "If you had become trapped there, you could have been lost."

Emma shook her head. "I don't know what you are talking about. I can't just disappear into a shadow even if I wanted. I was just looking for a safe place to hide," she said with a hint of exasperation before she laid her head tiredly down against his chest. "I don't know why I'm so tired."

Ha'ven threaded his hand through her hair and pulled her head back far enough for him to look into her eyes. He was shocked to realize she really didn't understand what she had done. She didn't have a clue that she had been able to dissolve the molecules of her body until only her natural energy remained. This was much more serious than he realized.

"Oh, little one, you are dangerous in more ways than I ever expected," he groaned out, sealing his lips over hers.

Emma froze as Ha'ven's hot lips sealed over hers. The same warmth that flooded her when he touched her earlier in the engine room filled her. There was something about him that made her feel safe, needed… loved.

She had been so lost until he touched her and the strange black bands had wound around her. The moment she felt the dark strands wrap around her wrist, it was as if someone had shot pure energy into her. She felt invincible. The bands had drawn her forward from the dark shadows that she had imagined hid her from everyone. It was as if they were pulling her closer to the huge male who made impossible promises to her.

She moaned softly, opening her mouth and drinking him in like a desert rose that was waiting until the first rains before blossoming. Her arms slid up, her fingers touching him lightly as she searched for the warmth of his skin. A deep sigh escaped her as she found what she was looking for. Her fingers caressed the skin on the sides of his neck before burying in his thick black hair.

She didn't protest when he shifted around to lay her gently back against the soft covers of the bed. A loud whimper escaped her when she felt his hot palm cover her left breast. Unable to resist the sensation of pleasure, she pressed up against it, begging for more. Her fingers tightened in his hair as he kneaded her breast before slipping his hand down and under her loose shirt to touch her skin.

Emma pulled her mouth away from his and pressed upwards with a loud hiss. She stared up into his eyes as he gazed down at her with an intensity that almost hurt to look at. His hand paused briefly before he moved it slowly up along her ribcage.

"Tell me to stop and I will," he bit out harshly. "Tell me, Emma, and I will, but if you do not I will claim you as mine."

Emma stared up into his eyes, heat pooling low inside her at his words. She nervously licked her lips before biting her lower one. His hand paused again, this time just under her left breast.

"For how long?" she asked huskily. "For how long will you claim me?"

Ha'ven's eyes darkened at her husky question. "Forever, my Emma. I will claim you forever," he vowed in a soft voice filled with determination and possession. "Forever," he whispered again, leaning until he was a breath away from touching her lips again.

"If you promise not to leave me again, then the answer is...," she paused as she leaned up enough to rest her lips against his. "... yes."

Ha'ven's loud groan filled the small cabin as he captured her lips in a desperate kiss at the same time as his hand captured her unbound breast.

CHAPTER TWELVE

*H*a'ven swore he would have gone mad if she had denied him. He would have left her if she had, but it would have come at a great cost. His body throbbed painfully with the need to claim her. The essence that gave him his power burned to complete the joining that would bind them together forever.

He had not been just saying the words to make her feel better. Once he claimed her fully, she would carry the very essence of him inside her as he would her. Their powers would combine to make them extremely powerful. That power would be seen as a threat by those that wanted to destroy him and his family. Emma would become a target, her life in constant danger if he and his brothers did not eliminate the threat.

"Emma, *misha petite*," Ha'ven groaned. "I need you."

Emma drew in a shaky breath as he pulled back far enough so he was kneeling over her. Her eyes widened as he waved his hand over his body and his clothes dissolved. She gasped loudly when he did the same to her and she found herself lying under him, nude. Her arms fell to cover her breasts as a bright, fiery blush rose over her cheeks.

"Ha'ven?" she asked, looking up at him with wide, startled eyes.

He grinned crookedly down at her. "I never really appreciated our ability until now. I think I will enjoy removing your clothes… often," he growled in a playful tone. "Very, very often," he added as he reached down and gently cupped her hands in his and lifted them to his chest. "Touch me," he asked huskily. "Please."

Emma fought her shyness. She hadn't been undressed in front of anyone except her mother her whole life. She had never even undressed for a doctor since she hit puberty. She had been mortified when her mom had taken her when she was seventeen to the doctor and the nurse told her she would have to undress. Instead, she had bolted from the room and her mom had taken her home. Shortly afterward, her father had died and her mother's dementia had grown worse.

Her fingers trembled as she touched the firm skin of his stomach. Her lips parted in wonder as she focused on exploring him. The sensations rushing through her were foreign, but the ageless fire of desire burst to life inside her. She forgot her own nudity as she ran her fingers over the exquisite form kneeling over her.

"You are so beautiful," she whispered as she slid her fingers along his heated flesh. "So hard but soft as well. You feel warm, almost hot. Is it natural for you to be this warm?" she asked, flicking a glance up at him before returning her eyes to where her fingers were.

"Gods, Emma," Ha'ven muttered as he closed his eyes and breathed out heavily. "Your innocence is like a drug to my system. You have no idea what your touch is doing to me, do you?" He opened his eyes and gazed down at her flushed face.

Her hair was fanned out around her head, framing the delicate features of her face. Her body glowed with her aura, changing colors as she touched him. His breath caught as effervescent colors danced around her and across her skin. Pinks, soft purples, yellows, and oranges swirled across silky, pale skin. His fingers slid across her collarbone and the colors reached up and clung to him. His own spun around, mixing with it. He started to pull back when the black strands surged outward.

"I love the way the black swirls when I touch you," Emma murmured softly. "It makes me feel safe… warm inside. When I touch you, different colors stand out against it before fading and blending into it. Yet, if I touch you, they come back. It is like the black is protecting them, only letting them out when it is safe or when they want to come out to play against it," she explained in a faint voice.

Ha'ven froze as her words sunk in. She was not afraid of the darkness inside him. He looked down where she was running her hands along his stomach and up his chest. Just as she described, her essence danced in a beautiful pattern across his own before disappearing briefly, then coming out again. His breath caught and he was held mesmerized by both her hands and the joining between them.

His hands moved to touch hers. She turned her palms and threaded her fingers through his, looking up at him with her soul bare for him to see. A soft, tentative smile curved her lips as she gently pulled him down.

"I like it when you kiss me," she whispered huskily. "When you touch me, I don't feel afraid anymore. I don't understand this or why you make me feel safe, but I like it."

"You…" he started to say before his voice faded.

Ha'ven couldn't finish his sentence. The emotions that he had felt earlier rushed back through him again, this time with an intensity that took his breath away. He didn't understand the emotions that she unleashed deep inside him. He didn't know what they meant. The only thing he knew was that he would never, ever let the delicate female he held in his arms be taken from him. May the Goddess have mercy on anyone who tried, because he wouldn't. He would unleash every ounce of the power that Aria had awakened inside him and damn the consequences.

Ha'ven deepened the kiss even as he slowly lowered his body over her smaller frame. He groaned when her legs instinctively parted to let him rest between them. There was so much he wanted to do to her, but he honestly didn't know if he had the self-discipline this first time. The fear of losing her still brushed along the edge of his consciousness, making the need to claim her almost unbearable.

He pulled back just far enough to run small kisses from her swollen lips down along her jaw to the sensitive spot below her right ear. He nipped at her neck, enjoying the gasp that echoed from her reaction. He wanted to discover every inch of her body. He didn't think a life-time would ever be enough and Curizans were known to live a very long time.

"You make me feel things I do not understand," he whispered as he pressed a kiss against her collarbone. "The power inside you calls to my own."

"You make me feel... things too," Emma replied breathlessly as his firm lips teased the tip of her right breast. "Please, I want... you too.... This feels so good, so...."

"Right," Ha'ven muttered under his breath before he covered the taut peak with his hot mouth.

The feel of Emma's hands tangled in his long hair, holding him to the tip he greedily sucked on, fired his blood even hotter. Nothing in all of his other lovers ever prepared him for this rush of possessiveness. He wanted every part of her; mind, body and soul. Her fingers tugged on his hair. When his eyes lifted to her face, they locked with her wide ones. She stared at him with a hungry desire that poured over him in hot flames.

He released her small breast with a loud pop and slowly turned his attention to the other one. He loved the way her eyes followed him and her body tilted, trying to hurry him to the prize. His tongue slowly came out and her breathing became small pants as her own tongue imitated his. He didn't think his cock could get any harder or his sack any fuller but the sight of her licking her lips as he teased the taut peak made him think of that beautiful tongue doing the same to his hard shaft.

They groaned in unison, her from his finally sucking hard on her nipple; him from the imagery of her sucking on him. He could feel the moisture of pre-cum escape his cock as it brushed along the inside of her thigh. He closed his eyes when she moved her leg, rubbing his swollen, aching tip against her silky skin.

Releasing her nipple with a muttered oath, he rose up over her. "Goddess be praised, Emma. I will have you now and pleasure you to madness later," he swore as he moved back up her body and gripped her thighs in his large hands.

"Ha'ven!" Emma cried out as he aligned his hard shaft with her slick vaginal channel.

"You will forever be mine, my mate," Ha'ven growled in a low voice as he pushed forward, impaling her on his throbbing length. "Forever, *misha petite*. I promise you forever."

Emma cried out loudly as he pushed forward through the barrier and sealed her to him. He released her right thigh and pressed his hand to her lower stomach, sending a wave of healing energy to ease the pain of taking her. He wanted no memories of pain, only pleasure. He knew the moment her discomfort dissolved as her right leg curled up and around the cheek of his left buttock, pulling him deeper.

"Oh!" Emma said breathlessly, looking up at Ha'ven in shock. "You… I… Oh!" She finished on a moan as he began moving, slowly.

His groan of pleasure drew a soft blush to her cheeks. "Oh, indeed, my mate. You are so beautiful," he said in a low voice. "I claim you as my partner. In this life and any other the goddess gives us after, you will belong to me, Ha'ven Ha'darra, as I belong to you, my Emma."

Emma ran her hands up his arms as he leaned forward. She locked her lips to his as he pulled her closer. For the first time in her life, she understood what her mom had meant when she told Emma that her father loved her so much she could walk on a cloud and never touch the ground. Emma felt like she was floating.

∾

Ha'ven lost himself in Emma's sweetness. The hum of power inside his body flowed around them, in them, and between them. Their essence blurred, mixing until there was no separating them now. He made sure of that. He wanted no doubt in anyone's mind who she belonged to.

His body burned and tingled as he fought to bring her pleasure before he found his own satisfaction. The fact that he was her first and only lover was not lost on him. He felt the weight of responsibility of ensuring she knew nothing but pleasure at his touch. Nothing but satisfaction at their joining. She had literally become his world.

He kissed her deeply, ravishing her mouth as the emotions burst through the dam he had tried to secure them behind until he could understand what they meant. His arms tightened around her, pressing her against his body as he rocked deeper and deeper into her. How someone could have such power as to make him lose all rational thought with just a touch shook him.

Her hands were doing things to his body that he had never even imagined. He'd had numerous lovers since he came of age, but never had the mere touch of their hands inflamed him the way hers did. Her essence wrapped around him, pulling the darkness unleashed during his torture away.

"You make me feel free," he whispered brokenly in her ear.

He buried his face in the curve of her shoulder, unsure of what to expect. He had never admitted to anyone the weight he had carried deep inside since his captivity. He never even acknowledged his own feelings of vulnerability to himself. Yet the words had slipped from his mouth without thought as he basked in the warmth of her embrace.

What he did not expect was to feel her slender arms wrap around him to hold him just as tightly as he held her or the touch of her lips near his ear. She squeezed his hard frame to her, seemingly uncaring that he could crush her if he let his entire weight rest upon her smaller form. He stilled as her softly whispered words flowed through him, bringing a warmth to his soul that he thought would never be warm again.

"Nothing will ever cage you if I can help it," she murmured. "I want to watch you fly to the clouds and dance on the rainbows."

A shudder shook his huge form. He rolled, shifting so she was on top. Her gasp echoed as she placed both palms on his broad chest. The move drove him deeper into her. Her eyes widened before drooping as he cupped both of her breasts in his hands.

"Come for me, my Emma," he choked out, looking up at her with burning eyes filled with emotion. "I want to see you come for the first time. I want… I want to see you fly to the clouds and dance upon them as you come for me."

The passion of his words flooded her as he pushed up in a slow rhythm at the same time as he pinched her swollen nipples. Her head fell back, the long length of her hair flowing around her as she splintered into a million pieces. Only his hands spanning her waist kept her upright.

"Ha'ven," she whimpered as her head fell forward and she stared at him, a soft tremble on her lips.

"So beautiful," he whispered hoarsely.

His hands tightened on her as the last of his control dissolved at the beauty of her flushed cheeks and wide, expressive eyes. Never in his life had he seen anything more beautiful. It was worth the unbearable pressure building inside him to hold back long enough to watch her as she came apart in his arms. Gripping her hips, he began moving frantically, pushing deeper and deeper as his own orgasm rushed forward.

He groaned loudly when she fell forward, kneading his chest with her fingers as he swelled inside her. Her low mewing grew as she came again, tightening around him until he was panting as he pushed upward. The feel of her vaginal channel squeezing him, wrapping him in her silky, slick heat pushed him over the edge.

"Goddess!" he roared out, arching under her.

Spots danced before his eyes as he poured himself into her. The room began glowing brighter and brighter as their essences burst outward, upward, and around them. He knew Emma didn't see the colors of his aura as they swirled and twisted upward, dancing with hers in an erotic joining that left him pulsing with the power. Her eyes were closed, her lashes crescents of the moon on her flushed cheeks. The black mixed with the colors of the rainbow that Emma whispered of to him and he could swear he could see them dancing together.

"You are right, *misha petite*," he murmured as he pulled her limp body down to drape over his. His arms wrapped as tightly around her as he could without crushing her. "I am flying free," he whispered in wonder as he smoothed his hand possessively down her back.

CHAPTER THIRTEEN

*H*a'ven jerked awake as the transport rocked. His arms tightened protectively around the body curled at his side. A warning alarm sounded before the lights flickered and the transport rocked again.

"Warning. Unidentified ship has initiated fire. Shields maintaining at ninety-eight percent. Defensive actions have been activated," the transport warning system announced.

"Ha'ven," Emma's sleepy voice whispered huskily. "What's happening?"

Ha'ven's mouth tightened as he sat up. With a wave of his hand, he was fully dressed. Standing, he looked down into Emma's sleepy and confused eyes. He held out his hand to her even as another blast hit the outer shields.

"Come, little one," he murmured calmly. "We are under attack. I want you near me."

Emma's eyes widened with fear and she scrambled up, grasping his hand. Even as she stood, he waved his hand and she found herself clothed in a pair of black leather pants, black silky shirt, vest, and boots similar to what he was wearing. She stumbled as the transport rocked heavily back and forth.

"Warning. Three additional ships have entered the vicinity. Immediate defensive action is recommended."

Ha'ven cursed and gripped Emma's hand tightly as he pulled her from the cabin and down the corridor to the bridge. He had delayed their flight path to the second Jump-gate as he wanted additional time with Emma. Now, that time may have become a grave mistake.

"Scan ships. Give me armament capability and defense specifications," Ha'ven ordered as he stepped onto the bridge.

Emma scrambled into the same seat she had occupied only the day before. So much had happened in a short time that her head was spinning. Was it only yesterday that the man sitting across from her had kidnapped her? She shook her head when he started to strap her in.

"I can do it," she assured him. "What are you going to do?"

"Kill them," Ha'ven bit out harshly.

Emma stared at the cold, hard face and shivered. Gone were the heated gaze and the tenderness of the night before. Now a killing machine…

No, a warrior of old, she thought, looking on as he moved gracefully at the controls.

The black bands were back along with darker, blood red and gold ones. They swirled, blending into the console in front of him. Another blast rocked the transport and a warning light flashed before he muttered a short command and it stopped.

"Open communications," Ha'ven ordered. "This is the *Sentinel*, identify yourself."

An image appeared within seconds. Kejon's scarred face filled the view-screen. The Curizan assassin had a smirk on his face as he stared coldly back at Ha'ven.

"Well, well. It would appear we have found ourselves a royal without his bodyguards," Kejon observed. His eyes flickered over to where Emma was strapped in, watching with wide, frightened eyes. "And one of his whores," he added, turning to look back at Ha'ven with a raised eyebrow. "Caught with your pants down again. Isn't that how you ended up on Hell the last time, as well?"

Ha'ven's mouth flattened as he stared back, refusing to respond to the taunt. "I am going to enjoy killing you, Kejon."

Kejon laughed. "It will be a sweet reward to see your brothers' faces when they find you dead. They are off on a wild hunt looking for me. They are too far to come to your rescue, Ha'darra."

"Who says I need rescuing?" Ha'ven replied calmly, looking at the data flowing in.

"You are outnumbered, Ha'darra. I have three warships to your small transport," Kejon sneered.

"I believe you have miscounted, assassin. You only have two," Ha'ven said with a sarcastic curve to his lips.

Kejon cursed and yelled out an order at the same time as the warship he was on rocked as the Marastin Dow warship to his left exploded. He turned deadly eyes back to Ha'ven. Without another word, he cut communications and opened fire on the *Sentinel*.

Emma bit her knuckle as she watched the torpedoes or whatever they were called coming toward them. There were at least a dozen. She didn't make a sound. She didn't want to break Ha'ven's concentration. His hands were glowing brighter than they had yesterday and the small transport was moving rapidly toward the torpedoes instead of away from them.

A small squeak finally escaped her as the transport tilted as two of the torpedoes swept by. He was driving, or piloting, the transport just like the taxi drivers down in South America. She didn't know it was possible to turn and twist a spaceship the size of a football field as quickly as one of the little taxis, but he was doing it. One scraped under them, exploding as it hit the outer shield. The transport shook violently and warnings sounded.

At the same time, Ha'ven was firing at the other two larger warships. One rocked and flared for a moment, but it continued to fire at them.

"Ha'ven?" Emma whispered as they came closer and closer to the two warships. "Ha'ven?"

"It will be alright, little mate," Ha'ven said calmly. "We are going to slip between them."

"Between them?" Emma whispered, looking at the narrow gap. "Will we fit?"

Ha'ven flashed her a smile. "Barely. But if Kejon fires, he will take out the other warship."

"He wouldn't do that, would he? I mean, he would be killing his own men," she asked, squinting her eyes as they got ever closer.

"Of course he will," Ha'ven replied. "I am counting on it. Then, there will only be one warship to destroy."

Ha'ven glanced briefly at Emma. A low chuckle escaped as he saw her pull her knees up into the chair and cover her eyes. His little mate, the one who would pull an ancient Valdier War Sword on a Curizan Prince, sat curled up, peeking through her fingers.

"I promised you I would not let anyone hurt you, *misha petite*," he said grimly. "I will keep my promise to you."

"I know," she responded quietly. "I… trust you."

Ha'ven gave a sharp nod as he gripped the controls. He let his power flow from him into the ship. He would not be able to maintain the flow for long, but it would be long enough.

Emma had been right. There would not have been enough room between the warships for the *Sentinel* to squeeze through without his manipulation of energy. The black energy inside him flowed through the metal of the transport, shifting and changing the structure. It became longer, narrower, and sleeker.

The change gave them the added inches they needed to sweep between the warships. As he suspected, Kejon ordered the side laser cannons to open fire. By the time they were activated, the *Sentinel* was behind them.

Ha'ven slowly released the power he was sending out. The transport shifted back into its former shape. He heard Emma's delighted laugh of relief. Increasing speed, he focused on getting to the second Jump-gate before Kejon's warship had a chance to reposition and pursue them.

He didn't dare release the controls. Weakness pushed at him. He had expended a large amount of energy and it would take him several days to recover. If Kejon caught up with them, he would be defenseless except for the weapons and shields aboard the *Sentinel*. Without his added power, it would not take long for the warship to deplete them and destroy the smaller spaceship.

"You did it!" Emma clapped and laughed. Her eyes glowed with excitement. "You really did it."

Ha'ven smiled at the flushed face of his mate. *My mate*, he thought possessively. *She is mine.*

"You have much to learn about a Curizan Prince when he is in battle," Ha'ven teased lightly. "We will be going through the second Jump-gate soon. Once through, we will be in Curizan space. Kejon would be stupid to follow. We have patrols scattered throughout."

"What if he does?" Emma asked worriedly. "Can you call someone to come help?"

Ha'ven grinned and nodded. "*Sentinel* to *Rayon I*."

Within seconds, Adalard's face appeared on the view-screen. "This is the *Rayon I*. How goes it, brother?"

"I have found your missing traitor," Ha'ven said tightly as a warning sounded from the defense system. "He and a Marastin Dow warship are hot on our tail."

A loud curse from behind Adalard showed Arrow was listening in as well. "Can you get away?" Arrow asked, looking over Adalard's shoulder.

Ha'ven glanced at Emma who was listening quietly to the exchange. He released a deep breath before he shook his head. From the speed of the approaching warship they would just be entering the Jump-gate when it intercepted them. Once through, there was no guarantee one of their patrol ships would be close enough to arrive before Kejon destroyed the *Sentinel*. There was only one thing he could do.

"When I hit the Jump-gate I'm going to send us through to Yardell," Ha'ven said grimly. "It is the only way to ensure we aren't blown apart."

"Are you sure?" Adalard asked with a heavy frown. "I've alerted General Tiruss that you need assistance. He can be there in four hours."

"We would not last half that time," Ha'ven responded as he calculated the time to intercept. "Come for us."

"We'll be there," Arrow said, yelling out an order. "It will take us at least three days, but we will be there."

"May the Goddess be with you, brother," Adalard said before signing off.

"What's going on?" Emma asked, frightened. "What is Yardell?"

"It is a Spaceport on the far side of our star system," Ha'ven replied.

He glanced at Emma briefly before turning back as the second Jump-gate came into view. The large towers stood like silent sentinels in space. As the transport passed through, it would complete a connection between the energy grids, opening a large wormhole that would take them to the Curizan star system.

He would tap into that energy and take them further, to the opposite side. It was a dangerous move. One only done in theory, never in reality. Arrow had first come up with the idea. They had joked about it for years, but there had never been a reason to try such a risky move until now. If he didn't, Kejon would catch up with them as they came out the other side and destroy them before help could arrive.

Ha'ven slowly began releasing the power within him that Aria had awakened. He felt the blackness swirl and churn, almost as if it was a living entity buried deep inside him. For once, he did not fight it as it rose inside him. Instead, he embraced it, letting it wash through and over him.

We will not let that bastard harm our mate, Ha'ven told the dark mist. *We will protect her at all cost.*

Yessss… came the answer as the black mist spun out and through the controls.

Ha'ven gritted his teeth as the *Sentinel* entered the Jump-gate. The moment the energy connected through the transport, he pulled it inward and linked it with his own power. His body jerked as the massive amount of energy centered through his body. He vaguely heard Emma's cry of terror. He felt like his body was being torn in a million different directions.

He shook as the dark power inside him greedily grasped the extra energy. He fought to remain conscious. Everything began to blur as the wormhole formed. He focused the energy and extended it outward, curving it.

Things slowed down as the image of the Yardell Spaceport formed in his mind. He looked around curiously. He could see Emma's eyes glued to his form, a look of fear and worry on her lovely face.

He turned and saw his own physical form gripping the control sticks. The muscles in his arms bulged as he held them. His eyes glowed a fierce violet swirled with black. The red and gold bands twisted into spirals threading through the black mist that had spread to coat the surface of the transport.

"Ha'ven," Emma cried out as if from a distance. "You have to stop! This is hurting you. I can feel it. Please, let go!"

He turned his head to look at where she was staring and saw the trickle of blood as it seeped from his left nostril. He raised his hand to touch it and realized that he was a mere ghost looking at his corporeal self.

He could feel the moment when his body gave in to the pain of holding so much energy within it. He was pulled back into his body so forcefully, he lost his focus. The sudden release of so much power at once splintered through him and he fell forward, barely conscious over the console.

"Emma," he whispered weakly. "You... have to help... me. Have... to... dock with... Spaceport."

Emma looked through the clear view-screen. She couldn't see a Spaceport, only a small blue and green moon circling a much larger planet of red. She bit her lip and quickly unstrapped the belts holding her into the seat.

"Ha'ven, I don't see a Spaceport. I only see a huge red planet with a smaller moon circling it," Emma replied huskily as she knelt next to his chair.

She gently cupped his lowered head. Dark red blood scorched a path from his nose. He was deathly pale and his eyes were glazed with pain. She murmured softly, chiding him while she wiped the blood away.

"You shouldn't have done this," she rebuked him. "Whatever you did was hurting you. I could feel it. You should have let go sooner."

Ha'ven tried to focus his eyes on Emma's sweet face. "I promised you..." he stated hoarsely. "Protect you."

"You don't even know me," Emma said, tenderly smoothing her hand over his cheek. "Not really."

"Know... you," he forced out. "You are... everything."

Emma's eyes filled with tears as she looked at the huge warrior who made her want to believe in forever. It terrified her to see him so weak. She started to lean forward to press a kiss to his forehead when an alarm rang out loudly, startling her.

"Warning! Warning! Power levels have decreased to dangerous levels. Multiple system failures are being recorded. Environmental, engine, and defense systems are at less than twenty percent. Emergency landing procedures have been initiated."

"Ha'ven, what's happening?" Emma asked in alarm, standing up as the lights flickered and the bridge lights went out.

"Strap into your chair," Ha'ven bit out weakly. "We have to land. If we don't, we won't make it. There is... too much... damage. If the environmental system shuts down, we would only... last an hour... at most."

Emma scrambled over to her chair and began strapping herself back into it. She watched as the small moon began to grow larger and larger. She braced her arms on the chair, her fingers gripping the ends until her knuckles were white.

"Entry in five, four, three, two, one... Emergency descent activated. Prepare for hard impact," the computer said.

Emma looked at Ha'ven. He was slumped forward, held up only by the straps of his chair. His battle to stay conscious lost. She turned back and watched as a small lake came rapidly into view. She braced for impact as the transport hit the tops of the tall trees before everything went black as she was thrown forward as the sleek vessel hit the water.

CHAPTER FOURTEEN

*E*mma shivered as icy, cold water rushed around her ankles. She jerked awake, looking around, disoriented for a moment until she remembered what happened. Gazing out the front viewport, she could see they were partially submerged in the lake. The transport listed at an odd angle with half the nose sticking up above the water line.

"Ha'ven?" Emma called out, worried.

When she didn't receive a response, she quickly fumbled with the release on the straps. Impatiently pushing them aside, she grabbed the console for support and pulled herself out of the chair. The water was rushing in from the corridor behind them. She could feel the transport shifting as the weight of the water rushing into the back of the ship pulled it into deeper water. She had to get them out of it before it completely filled.

She gripped the chair and console for support and pulled herself over to Ha'ven's chair. He was leaning to the side. Blood continued to seep from his nose. Emma was afraid he had some type of internal injury.

"Ha'ven," she said, gently brushing his hair back from his face. "Ha'ven, please wake up. I need your help. I can't get you out by myself."

She shivered as the water crept up to her knees. She looked worriedly around when he didn't answer or show any signs of hearing her. Even the cold water was doing nothing to help wake him. She pressed her trembling fingers to the side of his neck and breathed a sigh of relief when she felt a strong pulse beating in it.

"We have to get out of here before the ship sinks," she whispered.

She quickly undid the straps holding him into the chair. If she had to, she would drag him out. She wouldn't leave him to drown. Touching his cheek one more time, she pulled away from the chair, sliding down to the wall leading to the corridor.

"There has to be some type of emergency equipment for if the cabin lost pressure. They have them in airplanes back on Earth, for crying out loud. You would think aliens would have them in a spaceship," she muttered as she began pulling open anything that looked like it could be storage.

She pulled on several panels, opening them before growling in frustration when all she found were tools. They might come in handy later, but not right now. She was almost crying in frustration as the water reached her waist.

She fell when the transport shifted again. Icy water closed over her head as she rolled. She pressed her hands on the floor of the transport and burst upward with a gasp as the chill of the water sucked at the breath that she was holding. She pushed her tangled, wet hair out of her eyes and glanced frantically back to where Ha'ven was seated.

Her eyes lit on a panel to his left. It had a strange marking on it. She pushed against the wall, struggling against the slant of the ship and the water that was beginning to numb her body. She pulled herself up using the back of Ha'ven's seat and reached for the panel. Pushing inward, the door popped open to reveal several masks.

"Thank God," she breathed.

She pulled one down and saw what looked like a full-frontal oxygen mask. She pulled it over her head. The moment she took a breath, lights appeared on the outside of the mask and a thin membrane sealed around her head. Fresh oxygen poured into it.

Pulling another one down, she braced herself and gently pulled it over Ha'ven's head. She closed her eyes briefly and murmured a prayer of thanks when she saw the lights turn on. She checked to make sure it was sealed correctly before she pushed the release on the chair so that it would swivel.

She grabbed Ha'ven's arm and draped it over her shoulder before she slid her arm around his waist. She let their combined weight pull them forward and they toppled under the water.

Now, to find a way out of here before we become trapped, she thought as the water closed around them.

In a way, the water was a blessing as she would have been unable to carry Ha'ven's much larger, heavier weight. Emma kicked her legs and reached with her free hand to grasp the edge of the door and pushed through it. She had no idea where to go and could only hope wherever the water was coming in, the opening was large enough for them to squeeze through before they were dragged deeper.

She swept her head back and forth, looking down the long corridor. She was familiar with only a small part of the spaceship. She pulled Ha'ven's body closer to hers, worried about how the cold could be affecting him. She remembered watching a television show that said if someone is injured that it was important to keep them warm in case they went into shock.

Fear blossomed when the transport groaned and started to twist. She rolled, wrapping her arms and legs around Ha'ven's limp body. Her back and shoulder hit the floor before bouncing off the wall. A torrent of bubbles exploded around them as an air pocket was suddenly filled with water. The rush disoriented her for several precious moments. She realized they were facing the short, narrow passage he had carried her down when he first brought her on board the transport.

She released her legs from around Ha'ven's waist and braced her feet on the wall, pushing upwards toward the hatch. She released one arm from around Ha'ven to grab the latch on it. She frowned in frustration as she studied it. The words written under it meant nothing to her. They were just meaningless symbols. She flutter-kicked her legs back and forth to keep them in place as she reached for the bar situated to one side of the door. She could feel her body slowly draining of strength and cursed the months she had wasted because of the depression that gripped her. She had thought she was ready to die, but the last couple of days proved to her, she wasn't ready to give in after all.

"How do you open this stupid thing?" she grunted.

She was going to need both hands. She refused to let Ha'ven go, though. She was terrified if she did and she got the hatch open that she would lose him in the rush of water and darkness. Gripping the latch with one hand, she wrapped her legs around his waist again and locked her ankles together. Once she was sure she had a good hold on him, she reached up and grabbed the latch with both hands.

"You will open," she gritted out.

She struggled to pull the latch down, but it wouldn't budge. She was beginning to pant as fear that they were trapped rose up inside her. She closed her eyes and focused on calming down.

"Please," she whispered. "Please, I don't want to die. I just found a reason to live. I have to save us. Please, please help me."

She didn't know who she was asking for help from, just that she needed to hear her own voice to help calm her. She slowly opened her eyes and was stunned to see her hands shining with a soft pink glow. As she pushed on the latch, a strand of black rose up and circled her hands. Warmth flooded her and she knew that subconsciously Ha'ven was keeping his promise to protect her.

The latch slid down and the hatch burst open. The rush of water pushed her back before a surge lifted them up and through the hatch. Emma quickly wrapped her arms back around Ha'ven and kicked upward.

She breathed a sigh when they broke the surface of the water. She saw they were only about ten meters from the shoreline. Rolling Ha'ven onto his back, she wrapped an arm around his neck and began kicking. She was breathless and trembling with fatigue by the time she could touch the bottom. Stumbling forward, she pulled Ha'ven as far as she could out of the water before collapsing down beside him.

She reached up and gently pulled on the mask, hoping against hope that the environment was conducive for them. She held her breath as long as she could before she inhaled deeply. Sweet, fragrant air filled her burning lungs.

"Thank you," she mumbled, lowering her head in relief. "Thank you for looking out for us."

She turned and quickly pulled the mask off of Ha'ven. She touched his face, looking for any other signs of trauma. Except for still being very pale, he looked like he was in a deep sleep. She could only hope that was a good sign as she knew next to nothing about first aid except for how to take care of minor cuts and burns.

She forced herself to stand and looked around. It looked like they had crashed along a huge lake. The nose of the transport was barely visible. The water was crystal clear and she could easily see the outline of the transport.

The beach was covered in soft, colorful pebbles. As far as she could see, huge forests surrounded the area. Her eyes swept upward. She saw the huge red planet like a full moon shining during the day while the sky was a soft mixture of red, pinks, yellows, and purples.

"Ha'ven," she whispered as she watched a flock of large birdlike creatures fly over the lake in the distance. "This is so beautiful. I wish you would wake up so you could see this. I've never seen anything like it before."

She slowly sank down next to him in the shallow water. It was still cold, but not as bad as it had been. She didn't know if she was just numb from what had happened or if she had grown used to the temperature.

She scooted closer so she could cradle his head on her lap. Brushing his hair back, she looked down at his peaceful face. He was a very complex man, she decided. She had seen so many different images of him. The tenderness he showed the older woman in his dreams. The love he showed his brothers. The tenderness and protectiveness he had shown to her last night. Yet, she had also seen images of him being tortured and the cold determination when the other warships attacked them.

"Who are you?" she whispered as she tenderly outlined his face. "What do you want from me? You make me crazy. I don't understand any of this. When you touch me, I feel strange… wonderful and safe and warm. But, I don't understand why you would choose me."

Emma looked over her shoulder when she heard a noise coming from the forest behind them. Her arms tightened protectively around the man who had sworn to keep her safe. Her heart raced as several large furry beasts slowly lumbered out of the thick foliage. They looked like huge Mammoths from Earth's distant past, only they had one large horn in the center of their forehead and no long trunk.

Her mouth opened in surprise as they halted, forming a small cluster. It was not just the beasts that caused her heart to nervously flutter; it was what was on their backs. She carefully lowered Ha'ven's head down to the ground before scrambling to stand in front of him.

She shivered as a light wind danced across her wet skin. She stood gazing at what were obviously the local inhabitants of this strange but beautiful world. Her heart skipped when several of the creatures slid off the huge beasts and started walking toward her, sharp spears in their hands.

CHAPTER FIFTEEN

"Find them!" Kejon snarled out, looking in fury at the captain of the Marastin Dow warship he had paid handsomely for. "I don't want excuses. I want that Curizan Prince's head on a platter."

The captain of the *Traitor's Run* looked coldly back at Kejon. He would gladly have slit the Curizan's throat if he could have, but the man was too powerful. The former captain of the *Traitor's Run* found that out when he was suddenly on the outside of the warship... without protective gear... instead of on the inside.

"He must have done something to the Jump-gate. You saw the amount of energy the scanners were picking up. We should have come out just inside the Curizan star system. According to our sensors, we are halfway to the Yardell Spaceport," Captain Tylis replied stiffly. "That is impossible, but the sensors are not wrong. No ships are being picked up by the long range scanners."

Kejon glared at the captain before ordering one of the Ensigns at the navigation console to move. He sat down in front of the console and studied the information pouring in. His fist tightened in frustration as the information confirmed what Tylis had just told him.

He pulled up a map of the star system. He knew it like the back of his hand. It had been his job to know every possible habitable moon and planet for two reasons. The first, to know where rebels might hide once Ben'qumain had overthrown the current ruling family. The second was for a more personal reason. He wanted an escape route should Ben'qumain fail.

His gaze narrowed on a huge red planet slightly set off the normal trade route. It was a huge desert planet known for its metal ore mining and export. It had two small moons. Both were habitable, which made it unusual. One was a primarily water covered world while the other was a lush planet with an indigenous population that was not known for welcoming visitors to its world. He knew because he had barely made it off the moon alive.

Those were the only three places that they could have sought to hide on besides the Spaceport. He still had one contact on Yardell. He would have Bushnell see if the transport docked. He would order the *Traitor's Run* to send down scouts to the planet and the moons.

"Prepare three transports. I want one to search each of these locations thoroughly," Kejon said, pointing to the red planet and two moons. "I will hold you personally responsible if they should fail."

Captain Tylis' eyes narrowed at the barely veiled threat. "Done," he snapped, turning away and issuing the order to prepare the armored transports.

He could only hope that Kejon did find the Curizan Prince he was looking for. Anyone powerful enough to bend space and time was someone he had no desire to confront. If the bastard who had taken over his warship wanted to confront such a powerful male, let him die.

I have my own battles to deal with, Tylis thought as the cryptic message he had received earlier flashed through his mind.

~

Rayon I

"I don't like this," Adalard growled. "It has been two days and we still haven't received word from Ha'ven. He should have answered us by now."

Arrow looked up from the tablet he held. He had been running the calculations over and over. In theory, the combined energy should have taken his brother close to the Yardell Spaceport. It could also have blown him to smithereens.

"What did General Tiruss say? Have you heard from Bahadur?" Arrow asked gruffly as he looked over his calculations again.

Adalard dropped into the seat across from his twin. He rubbed a tired hand over his face before looking expectantly at Arrow. He was the science whiz of the family. Adalard was just good at killing... and making love to beautiful women.

"Yes," he replied heavily. "Tiruss said nothing came through the Jump-gate in Sector Twelve. Bahadur got word from his contact on Yardell that Kejon has one of his informants looking for Ha'ven. One of the freighters reported that an unidentified transport entered Sector Thirty before disappearing off his sensor. He suspected it might have crashed on the red mining planet or one of its moons. He never received a distress signal so he assumed it was an abandoned transport and continued on his way."

Arrow nodded thoughtfully. "If Ha'ven had to release the energy he was harnessing due to pulling too much through it that would explain why he was short of his destination."

Adalard raised an eyebrow at Arrow. "Can you explain that in plain Curizan for me?" he asked dryly.

Arrow grinned. "You should have paid more attention during your studies instead of chasing all those girls," he teased. "From what Bahadur said, it looks like Kejon is on the outer edge of Sector Thirty. If he entered the Jump-gate just as Ha'ven was focusing the energy he was pulling from it, Kejon could have piggybacked on it. The strain would have been too much for anyone, including Ha'ven. He would have had to release it or die, as that much energy would feel like it was pulling him apart. It still would have propelled him ahead of Kejon because he entered first. When he released it, the gravitational pull of the red planet would have sucked him closer to the planet while Kejon's warship wasn't due to being released further back."

"So you are telling me we are now four days out from Ha'ven, who might or might not be injured from either the pull of this enormous amount of energy or crashing, while Kejon is just a day?" Adalard growled out in a low, deadly voice.

Arrow's smile faded as he nodded. "Yes," he confirmed. "We need to push the *Rayon I*. I've made some modifications. We can probably shave a day to a day and a half off the trip."

Ha'ven grimaced as he felt the touch on his forehead again. It felt like someone was stabbing him with the end of their finger right in the center of it. It wouldn't have been so bad except his head still felt like it was about to explode.

By the third time, he'd had enough of it. He moved with lightning quick reflexes, grabbing the offending appendage as it poked him again. His eyes snapped open. A loud moan filled the air as a bright shaft of light struck his eyes and speared straight through to his brain. He was about to close his eyes again to block out the added pain when a furry white nose touched his.

"Do you mind?" he growled out in a low voice as he stared eye to eye at the creature above him.

A low chuckle was his answer as the creature sat back. Ha'ven almost changed his mind and asked the creature to put his ugly nose back in front of him. He would have been happy with anything that blocked the horrid light filtering in through the window.

Pressing his hands to his head, he released a small amount of healing energy. Intense pain splintered through him and he rolled as his stomach rebelled. The creature was ready for him. A small pail was quickly pushed under him as he emptied his stomach. After several long minutes, he rolled back onto the bed and covered his eyes with his left arm.

"Where am I?" he asked hoarsely before he remembered Emma. "Where's my mate?" he demanded, struggling to sit up.

"*Chumba mi tai nee,*" the creature said, coming back over to Ha'ven. This time a cup was pressed into his hand. "*Chumba mi tai nee,*" the creature repeated and motioned for Ha'ven to drink.

Ha'ven sniffed the liquid suspiciously before taking a sip. He started to spit out the horrid liquid but the creature raised his stick at him and repeated the sentence again… this time more sternly.

Ha'ven glared at the creature before he tilted the contents down his throat. He grimaced at the foul taste before lowering the cup and wiping the back of his hand across his mouth. He stopped in surprise when he realized his head didn't hurt anymore.

"Where is Emma? My mate," Ha'ven said slowly.

"Your mate is well. The women have taken her to the river to bathe," the gruff voice replied.

Ha'ven stared at the elderly creature sitting back in a low chair. He knew who he was. He had met him on two previous occasions. Once during the Great War and the other time after his father… Hermon was murdered. The elderly male had come to pay his respects.

The Monikers controlled the mining operations on the huge red planet below their small moon. Fiercely protective, they lived in surprising simplicity while having an advanced trading system. Because of the remoteness of their world, only the freighters arriving to pick up the mined ore came this far out.

"Saba Monda, I thank you for your help," Ha'ven said politely. "I did not have a chance to talk with you much at my… father's passing celebration."

A husky chuckle filled the air of the small hut. Saba Monda was the Chief Elder of the Moniker, a large, fur-covered creature that stood almost six feet tall. The younger males typically had black, brown, or reddish fur while the elder males were silver or white. The females were the same. They wore bright, colorful tunics most of the time, except when hunting. Then, they preferred to remove their covers allowing them more freedom to move through the huge forests that covered the moon.

Many of the young males spent time in the mines on the red planet. It was believed to build character and strength in the males. Those who were strong were successful in finding many mates among the females that ruled over the dozens of villages scattered over the moon.

"You have a long journey ahead of you, young Prince of the Curizan," Saba Monda said. "Your mate is very fierce and protective of you. My wives like her. You must be good to her or they will get upset."

"I don't remember much of what happened after we entered Curizan space," Ha'ven admitted. "I need to contact my brothers and let them know where we are."

"Come, I will show you your transport, not that it will do you much good, young Prince," Saba Monda replied, standing and brushing a hand over his chest.

Ha'ven nodded and stood. He paused, frowning when the room spun for a moment. He couldn't remember ever feeling so weak, not even during his captivity when Aria and her fellow traitors took turns torturing him. Then, anger had given him the strength he needed to survive.

"Emma," Ha'ven started to say as he took a tentative step forward.

Saba Monda glanced over his shoulder. "My wives have taken your little mate under their care. It has been many cycles since they have had a female to care for. Give them this pleasure as payment," he insisted with a mischievous grin. "When they are happy, I am happy."

Ha'ven looked doubtful for a moment but realized he would get nothing else from the old man. It took several minutes before he felt like he could walk and talk at the same time. His primary focus was not to fall flat on his face. He ducked his head as he exited the small hut before he stopped and grabbed the doorway until the world righted itself once again.

His eyes scanned the activities humming around him. Young children of all different ages ran around playing. Young women moved around, laughing, talking, and working at different jobs while the older women sat watching, chatting, or caring for the young.

"Did you receive the shipment of new mining equipment?" Ha'ven asked politely as his eyes continued to search for Emma as he moved through the small village.

Saba Monda nodded as he patted a young boy who ran up to him. "Yes. It has improved productivity. Harron said they are now able to get to veins of ore they were previously unable to drill for. The lasers are much safer and use less energy than the water based drilling that was being used. I believe one of your brothers helped design the method."

"Arrow has been working with the engineers on it for one of the asteroid mining camps. He appreciates your willingness to try the prototype," Ha'ven replied as they walked down a narrow path.

"It will be interesting to see what the Antrox will do when they discover it," Saba Monda replied with a touch of humor. "We have an unspoken competition with them. They have tried several times to send in mercenaries to capture our males. No other species, including the Antrox, compare to being able to move or work in a mine the way a Moniker can. We did steal a few of their Pactors. They work in the mines better than the Tuskus," he added, nodding to several dark shapes they were passing.

Ha'ven glanced at the large, hairy creatures that moved as if in slow motion among the thick foliage. One of the beasts reached up and rubbed the large horn on the center of its forehead along the bark of one of the trees. A thick swarm of insects rushed out of the deep cut. Several younger Tuskus rushed over and began lapping at the swarm with their long tongues as the adult moved to another tree.

"I did not know you had been attacked. No word had been sent. I can order additional security for this region if you wish," Ha'ven replied.

Saba Monda chuckled as they stepped out of the forest onto a wide expanse of graveled beach. The large crystal clear lake spread out before them. Only the nose of the transport showed above the water. Saba Monda looked over at Ha'ven and shook his head.

"I think you will need a new transport," he said with a grin.

Ha'ven stared grimly at the remains of his sleek transport. He wondered how in the hell Emma had gotten him out of it. Walking closer to the edge of the water, he stared down at the shadowed remains of it. It was possible he could repair it if he had the right tools. He would have to get it out of the water first.

"Do you think the Tuskus could pull it out of the water?" Ha'ven asked. "I need to see just how much damage has been done."

Saba Monda tilted his head and looked over the dark shape. He was silent for several long minutes as he calculated the size and weight. He finally gave a slow nod.

"Yes," he responded. "It will not be easy, but we should be able to pull it onto the beach. I will send for more help." He looked up at the sky, which was beginning to darken. "We will start first thing in the morning."

"Do you have a communication console I can use? I need to contact my brothers," Ha'ven asked, turning to look back at Saba Monda.

"Of course," the older male replied, turning back toward the path they had left just minutes before.

Ha'ven paused, looking back at the sunken transport. "How did she get me out?" he wondered out loud.

"Have her share her story tonight at dinner," Saba Monda suggested. "My wives were very impressed at her determination. I asked them if they would have done the same for me," he chuckled. "Only Olla said no. I made her mad when I did not compliment her dessert. I am still trying to get her to forgive me," he added with a twinkle in his eyes.

"I need to see my mate," Ha'ven said suddenly.

He had an urgent need to touch her, hear her voice, and see for himself that she was alright. He had tried to reach out to her, but every time he tried to touch the power deep inside him, excruciating pain radiated through his head. His stomach turned with nausea as he thought about how defenseless he was at the moment to protect Emma. He could only hope Kejon was unaware of their location.

CHAPTER SIXTEEN

*E*mma giggled as she splashed in the water with the other women and children. She had been mortified when they had first brought her down to the river. Large pools of warm water bubbled up from several hot springs overflowing into the shallow rock formations. Small groups of women of different ages played with young children who squealed and chased each other.

She now understood that Saba Monda had four wives, Sebra, Telmay, Olla, and Pollamay. Sebra was the lead wife as she was the oldest followed by Telmay, Olla, and the youngest, Pollamay, who still had the soft sable colored hair covering her body which was rounded with her first child. The four women had finally forced her away from Ha'ven's side where she had stayed for the last two days.

She had been terrified when the strange creatures had first approached her. She had frantically searched the beach for some type of weapon. She had finally grabbed a large piece of driftwood and stood holding it like a baseball bat as they approached.

She had been shocked when the silver-haired female that she later learned was Sebra chuckled when she growled at them to stay back. Sebra had waved the others to stand back as she and Saba Monda stepped closer to where Emma was standing protectively over Ha'ven's crumpled form. Sebra had tilted her head before speaking in a soft husky voice.

"We will not harm the young Prince," she had said calmly. "You are a fierce warrior, even for being so small."

"You... you know him?" Emma had asked hesitantly.

"Of course," Saba Monda had responded. "He is the Prince of the Curizan, Ha'ven Ha'darra."

"My husband has met the young prince before," Sebra commented. "He is injured."

Emma had been shocked when Sebra had turned and barked out several short commands. Within moments, a small group of women emerged from the forests. Several carried a large stretcher between them. Sebra touched Emma as the women came closer, pulling her gently to the side so an older woman could exam Ha'ven's injuries.

After several long minutes, the older woman stood up and waved to a group of younger females. Emma watched as two of the females opened the stretcher and laid it on the ground next to Ha'ven. Six females with black and brown hair gathered around Ha'ven's still form. They bent as one and gently lifted him onto it. Once he was centered, they lifted him and began moving back toward the forests.

"Where... what?" Emma started to protest.

Saba Monda stepped up to her left side while Sebra moved to her right. Sebra reached up and touched Emma's blonde hair with a reassuring smile. Emma glanced back and forth before she let the stick in her hand fall to the ground as weariness suddenly washed through her.

"He will heal," the older woman said as she came to stand in front of Emma. "This one needs rest as well," she said as she touched a small knot on Emma's forehead that she didn't know she had.

"Are you sure?" Emma asked, worriedly looking where the women had disappeared with Ha'ven. "Are you sure he will be alright?"

"Yes," the old woman snorted softly at Emma's doubt of her diagnosis before she turned.

The trip back to the village had passed in a blur. Emma had swayed for a moment when she tried to move forward. Sebra had gripped her around her waist and quickly climbed up the large beasts they had been riding. Emma had clung to the fur in terror as it turned to follow the others down the wide path. A brief thought flashed through her mind as the forest closed in around them. She wondered what other strange things could possibly happen.

"Catch me!" a small voice cried out.

Emma barely had time to lift her arms to catch the small bundle of brown hair that flew through the air. She laughed as the thin arms wrapped around her neck. She had been embarrassed when she found out they had brought her to the river to bathe.

She had refused to take her clothes off at first, but Pollamay had chuckled and began dancing around her, pulling at her clothing. Soon the others joined in and a very red-faced Emma had been left standing in the sunlight with nothing but her hair and hands to cover her. The women had quickly removed their coverings and stepped into the small basins of warm water where they splashed and teased each other.

Emma had reluctantly joined them and soon forgot her own nudity as the children came over to see if she would play with them.

"What happened to all your hair?" Beta asked, touching Emma's face. "Did it hurt when you lost it?

Emma nipped at the little girl's fingers. "I don't have hair like you do. I have a light coating on my arms and on my legs if I want. Human females mostly just have hair on their heads," she explained as she cradled Beta in her arms.

"You have some lower," Beta responded, looking at Emma, puzzled.

Emma blushed as Olla chuckled. "Beta, go play with your sisters and leave the poor female alone. You have made her face red again."

"I'm sorry if I made your face red," Beta said, looking at Emma with big dark eyes before she rubbed her nose affectionately against her cheek. "I think you are beautiful even with only a little hair on you," she whispered before she climbed off of Emma's lap to go find her older sisters.

Emma's eyes filled with tears and her hand rose to touch where Beta had rubbed against her. A warmth spread through her, melting the last of the ice around her heart that she had surrounded it with since she was kidnapped and her world changed. She looked at Olla, who sat across from her with a small smile on her greying face.

"Beta is right," Olla said. "You have unusual coloring. Even without hair I think our males would find you attractive. If you wish, I can…"

"No, you cannot," Ha'ven interrupted, standing near the edge of the clear pool. "She has already been claimed."

"Ha'ven," Emma looked up in surprise. "You woke up."

"Yes."

Emma didn't hear Olla as she silently climbed out of the pool. Her eyes were glued to the man who had become the center of her world. Her eyes roamed greedily over him.

Sebra and Saba Monda had both insisted that he was simply sleeping a healing sleep. She only came down to the river after the women insisted and Saba Monda promised he would stay with Ha'ven until she returned.

"I..." She blushed as she became aware of her lack of clothing. She glanced around and realized they were suddenly all alone. "Where did the others disappear to?"

Ha'ven reached up and tugged his shirt over his head. "I think Sebra let them know we needed time alone. We will join them later," he added as his hands went to the front of his pants.

"Why don't you do that hand-wavy thing?" Emma asked breathlessly.

Ha'ven's eyes darkened when she licked her lips. His body tightened as he felt it respond to her unconscious invitation. He toed off his boots before pushing his pants down and off.

"It appears I will have to do things a bit slower for a little while," he responded with a smile as he watched her eyes widen at his arousal. "There are some advantages to this way as well."

Emma opened her mouth to respond but nothing came out as he stepped lightly onto the smooth rock rimming the basin before stepping down into the warm swirling water. She rose up to meet him, her hands sliding up his chest and her mouth searching for his as he sank down.

She wrapped her arms and legs around him, kissing him frantically as all her fear and worry washed away at his touch. Her fingers tangled in his hair.

"Don't ever..." she whispered fiercely. "... do that... again."

Ha'ven moaned as his arms tightened around her, pulling her against his chest. He kissed her like a dying man given a second chance at life. His hands roamed over her slender form. The more he touched her, the more he needed to touch her. He buried his face in her shoulder, panting as overwhelming relief flooded him.

"I cannot live without you, my Emma," he whispered. "Just the thought of you being in danger almost destroyed me. All I could think about was getting you to safety."

Emma threaded her fingers into his hair and held him against her as she heard the desperation behind his words. He had promised to keep her safe. He had, but almost at the cost of his own life.

"You promised to keep me safe and you did," she whispered, pressing her lips against the side of his head before she pulled back far enough so she could look him in the eye. "But whatever you did, hurt you. I could feel it. You must promise never to do that again."

"Emma...," Ha'ven began before his voice faded as she pressed her lips to his to silence his protest.

Ha'ven had waited impatiently as Saba Monda took his time walking back along the path to the village. The need to see Emma grew deep inside him until it became an unbearable ache. He had breathed a sigh of relief when the village came into sight. Turning, he opened his mouth to demand the location of the river only to find Saba Monda's eyes twinkling as he pointed to a path to the right.

Ha'ven had dipped his head in appreciation before he strode over to the path. The moment he felt sure no one from the village could see him, he broke into a run. He had to stop several times and let small groups of women and children pass him as they came back from their baths. The women chuckled and shooed the children to the side when they moved to surround him. He nodded as he scooted around them.

When he broke through to the river, his eyes were immediately drawn to Emma's light colored hair. It shone with changing strands of gold, white, and yellow in the faint light of the late afternoon sunlight. Her aura glowed with the faint yellows, pinks, and purples he had grown to look for. Even from this distance, he could see the traces of black, gold, and reds from his own essence intertwined with them.

Several of the women had smiled at him in understanding, but he had ignored everyone but Emma. She held a small child in her arms. Her eyes were filled with a soft warmth as she listened to whatever the child said. Whatever the small girl said, it had drawn a rose-colored glow to his mate's pale cheeks. He watched as tears filled her eyes as the child brushed her nose along her cheek before scrambling out of the pool to join several older girls.

He could not hold back the jealous possessiveness that flooded him when he overheard Olla offering to find her a mate. A hot fury rushed through him at the thought of another male touching his mate. He realized from the mischievous twinkle in Olla's eyes that she had known he was there and listening.

What pulled the breath from his body was when Emma had looked up at him. The warmth from before was nothing compared to the blaze in them as she stared up into his eyes. He felt like he was melting under the spell she was casting.

He drew in a deep breath now as he ran his hands down to grip Emma's hips. He shifted enough to align her with his throbbing cock. With one swift move, he rose up, impaling her as he pulled her down over his thick shaft. Her loud cry fired his blood even hotter. He held her hips tightly as he rose up again and again. The need to claim her, to imprint his mark on her forever held him tightly in its grip.

"Goddess, Emma," he groaned as he felt his balls drawing up tight. "I do not understand these feelings, but I can never lose you."

Emma moaned as the tips of her nipples brushed along his broad chest. Each time he pushed up, they rubbed against him until she was ready to scream from how sensitive they were. Her fingers clamped down on his shoulder. Her nails left tiny crescents as the feelings inside her swelled.

"Ha'ven," she cried out as her body suddenly shattered around his. "I love you," she whispered hoarsely as her head dropped forward so she could look into his eyes.

"Emma," he groaned loudly as his body tensed before exploding into her.

He stared into her eyes as he filled her, holding her gaze with his own blazing one. He felt the power of his essence try to reach for her. Even as the pain flared briefly inside him as it reached for her, her own essence wrapped around his, calming him.

He realized in that moment that he did understand what was happening to him. He was... had fallen in love with his little mate. Shock held him mesmerized as he was pulled into the tender warmth of her blue eyes. He felt the darkness inside his soul open to the healing warmth of her love. His hand rose and he tenderly touched his fingers to her cheek. He traced the curve of her face until he touched her lips. He leaned forward, pausing a breath away.

"I... I love you, my Emma," he said in a shaken voice. "I love you."

"I know," she whispered tenderly as she closed the distance.

Ha'ven closed his eyes as her warm lips touched his. He wrapped his arms tightly around her, deepening it. He was in love! This little human had done something no other woman had ever done... she had captured his heart. Suddenly, he understood what Creon and Vox had. He understood why they were so protective, so possessive, so completely overwhelmed.

It is really going to suck when I tell them they were right, he thought briefly before he lost himself once again in Emma's embrace.

CHAPTER SEVENTEEN

$\mathcal{H}$a'ven watched as Emma blushed and laughed as she fingered the beautiful wrap that she wore later that evening. Sebra and Saba Monda's other wives had spirited Emma away when she and Ha'ven had finally returned to the village. They had insisted she needed to be prepared correctly for the evening celebration. When she had asked what the celebration was about, they had informed her it was for the hand-fasting for new couples. The young women would have a chance to choose an unattached male for their hut.

The men had teased Ha'ven when he had grumbled as she was being led away. While it had given him a chance to contact Adalard and Arrow, he didn't like her being out of his sight. His brothers had warned him that Kejon was not far away and to be on alert just in case Kejon found him before they arrived. Adalard said they were on their way, but it would be at least another day and a half before they arrived.

Now, Ha'ven's eyes devoured Emma as she was led past him. A possessive, self-satisfied smile curved his lips as a heated blush darkened her face when she saw the look in his eyes. He definitely liked what the women had done to her.

"You have done well in your choosing, young prince," Saba Monda said as he watched the women walking past them. His own eyes lit with pride and desire as his wives created a semi-circle around Emma. "Perhaps you will be lucky and she will choose you tonight."

Ha'ven glanced briefly at the silver-haired male beside him before his gaze turned back to his mate. "What do you mean, she will choose me? She already has," he muttered with a frown.

Saba Monda chuckled and shook his head. "Perhaps on your world," he paused a split second, leaning back before he continued. "But you are not on your world, are you?" he finished with a grin. "Tonight the women will get to choose from the new males who have returned from the Red Planet. The males will do all they can to attract the females' attention. If the looks your mate is receiving are any indication, I think you will have some competition for her affection."

"What?!" Ha'ven growled out, looking around the large circle.

Sure enough, there were several of the huge Moniker males studying Emma with interest. Rage washed over Ha'ven when one of the males stood and flexed his arms to show off the muscles in his arms and chest before he ran his hand over the soft pelt of dark brown hair covering his flat stomach.

His eyes swiveled when he heard Emma's giggle. She was studying the male as Telmay whispered something in her ear. She shook her head before turning to look at him again. A nervous smile played around the corner of her lips before she shyly looked away as the women led her past him. His eyes followed her as Sebra guided her to a small group of females who were laughing and eyeing the males.

"Yes," Saba Monda said with a quiet chuckle of delight. "I do believe you will have a bit of competition."

"Like hell," Ha'ven bit out as he shot a warning glance at the male who sat back down with a grin on his face. "I'll gut his hairy ass before I let him touch my Emma."

Laughter filtered through his consciousness as he stared possessively at Emma. Power or no power, he would fight anyone who thought to take his beautiful little mate away from him.

Emma had been stunned earlier when Telmay and Olla had shown her the colorfully woven garment that she now wore. Pollamay and Sebra had worked on her hair, threading flowers in it as they braided it around her head, leaving a few long curls to outline her face. Delicately woven sandals had been slipped onto her feet and Pollamay had shown her how to wrap the gown around her. Olla had produced a beautiful pin in the shape of birds in flight on it. She said it represented a species that mated for life and was considered to bring good luck to the wearer.

"Now, a touch of berry oil to make your lips red and shiny," Sebra had teased. "Not that it will last long if the young prince has his way."

She laughed and blushed as the small group of women she was sitting with teased her about which male she should choose. She shook her head as they kept piling food onto her plate, telling her she would need her strength tonight after the ceremony. Emma turned and looked at the young dark-brown haired female sitting next to her when the girl touched her blonde locks in wonder and sighed loudly.

"Crom wants you to choose him," Melda said, sighing again. "Did you see the way he showed off for you?"

"Crom?" Emma asked, looking in the direction that Melda was staring. Her eyes widened when she saw the huge male who had stood up as she walked by earlier staring at her. "Why is he staring at me?"

Sebra, who remained next to Emma, laughed. "He is fascinated with your hair, including the lack of it. I overheard him telling another male he wanted to see if you felt as soft as you look."

Emma flushed and looked over to where Ha'ven was sitting. She had been trying not to stare at him all evening, but it was very difficult, especially after what they had shared earlier down at the river. All she wanted was to be back in his arms again. She felt safe when he held her.

She drew in a startled breath when she saw the heated look in his eyes. She was also surprised at the touch of anger in them. Her fingers rose to play nervously with a flower at the end of one of her braids.

She jumped slightly when Sebra touched her arm. "Now, it is time for the women to make one of the men wish to belong to them. Watch," she murmured.

Emma turned in her seat to watch as Melda and two other women stood and moved to the center of the dining area. Each stood in a different area. Her lips parted in delight when she heard the faint strains of music in the background. She watched as the women began moving. Her eyes followed the moves of each dancer, hypnotized as they twisted and turned in an intricate dance. In her mind, she followed their moves while words flowed, matching the rhythm being played. Her own body responded to the music. Her heart opened like a withered sunflower kept in the dark that was suddenly touched by the sun.

She swayed in her seat, a deep yearning to join in sweeping through her as the music suddenly died down. She watched as two of the males rose and approached the three women. Melda looked them over critically before she turned her eyes to Crom who remained seated.

She looked back at the two men who stood posing for her and the other two women. She grunted out something to the women before she gave a short nod. Emma bit her lip as the women walked around each male, sizing him up. Her mouth dropped open when Melda not only felt each male's ass, but cupped the front of them as well. Her eyes flashed to Ha'ven who was watching her.

Emma forced her gaze away when she heard a low growl. A shiver raced through her when she saw Crom was watching her as well. There was no question that he was waiting for her to dance.

"Your young prince will have to work for you," Sebra said with a note of satisfaction. "Crom will challenge him."

"You don't have to sound so happy about that," Emma complained. "I don't want Crom. I only want Ha'ven."

Sebra chuckled. "A little competition will be good for your young prince. It will keep him alert and make him hornier to know that another male desires you."

Emma glared at Sebra for a moment before she tilted her head in curiosity. "How do you handle sharing Saba Monda with the other females?" she asked.

"I am very happy," Sebra responded with a grin. "He is a very horny male. I would never get anything done if I had to satisfy him alone."

"That is more information than I needed to know, Sebra," Emma grimaced. "I should have known better than to ask." She ignored Sebra when she responded by bursting out in laughter.

Emma turned as the three women led one of the men away. The young male who wasn't chosen grinned and returned to his seat. Emma watched as two other women rose and moved to the center of the dining area. Over and over for the next hour, the women around her rose and moved to dance for the men. Soon, there was only her and two other women remaining at their table.

"You will go now," Sebra murmured.

"But," Emma looked at the older female in panic. "I don't want to dance with the other women! What if they dance with me and chose a male? I don't want..." Her eyes flew to Ha'ven who was sitting perfectly still, his eyes glued to her.

"There are only two males left," Sebra said. "You will dance alone for them."

Emma's eyes moved to Crom, who sat looking at her with a burning hunger before turning to Ha'ven. The confident determination in his eyes calmed her. He promised to protect her. He would never let another male take her from him.

She rose on shaky knees. Walking over to the small group of musicians, she spoke quietly for several minutes before moving to the center of the dining area reserved for the dancers. Closing her eyes, she lifted one arm above her head while the other curved gracefully behind her.

As the music began, she let it sweep over her. The beauty of the notes poured through her blood, awakening the magic deep inside her. A soft smile curled her lips as she imagined herself back in the dance studio with her father. His arms guiding her as she took the first tentative steps.

Her arms moved in a graceful arc as she turned. She flowed around the circle, lost in the beauty of her memories and the music. Soon, her voice joined in. The clear, beautiful tones rising and falling like the waves brushing the shores of the lake. Heartfelt and pure, the sounds washed over those sitting around the circle as she danced, mesmerizing everyone with the beauty of her words and movements.

CHAPTER EIGHTEEN

*H*a'ven sat enchanted by the vision in front of him. The beauty of her voice and the grace of her body as it moved in perfect synchronization gripped him in its magic. Her aura swirled around, making her body glow in the delicate colors that were uniquely hers. The effect was pure magic at its most powerful and his own power, drained as it was, fought to answer the call of its mate.

Unable to resist when she rose up, her back arched in an elegant arc and her leg raised and bent behind her as her arms reached for the starry sky, he joined her. Moving as if in a trance, he gently gripped her tiny waist and lifted her. The moment he touched her, his power rose up to entwine with hers.

He could feel the weak threads being caught and held in the warmth of her essence. As one, they moved together to the music. Ha'ven never let her go. His hands or body touched some part of her as they danced around the circle, oblivious to anyone other than each other.

Ha'ven watched as Emma's eyes fluttered open as she slowly turned in his arms as the music faded in the background. She stood… entrapped in his arms. Her hands rested lightly on his shoulders as she gazed up at him.

Overwhelming love flooded him as he sank deeper into the blue oceans of her eyes. His lips gently caressed hers. He drank deeply when her lips parted for him. His arms drew her closer, even as her power wrapped around them, tying them together forever as one.

He reluctantly pulled back and rested his forehead against hers. "I have never seen or heard anything more beautiful, *misha petite*," he whispered huskily. "You are my love, my mate, my life. I ask that you choose me as yours."

"I already have," Emma replied as she smiled softly up at him, a tender smile curving her lips as she raised her right hand and laid it against his cheek.

A low growl sounded behind Emma. Ha'ven immediately twisted, pulling Emma behind him as Crom stepped into the circle. His face darkened in warning as the huge Moniker stepped forward.

"I challenge for the female," Crom called out in a low rumbling voice to those sitting around the circle.

"I accept the challenge," Ha'ven snarled back.

"No!" Emma said, frightened. "I don't want you to accept."

Ha'ven threw a heated glance over his shoulder. "I will not let him claim you, my Emma. You are mine!" he growled.

"Yes, and you are mine," she responded softly, resting her fingers lightly on his back. She looked over Ha'ven's shoulder at Crom, who was staring at her with dark hungry eyes. "I have already chosen Ha'ven Ha'darra."

"I am stronger. I can protect you and care for you," Crom said, standing tall and pounding his right fist into his chest. "I would be a good mate."

Emma carefully stepped around Ha'ven. She stopped beside him, running her hand down his arm, and curling her fingers around his. She looked up at Ha'ven with a tender smile before turning to look at Crom.

"I am honored by your challenge, but my heart has already been taken. You see, a very wise woman once told me there would be a man out there that would love me so much I would walk on a cloud and never touch the ground," Emma said as her throat tightened with tears at the memory of those words. "My mom was right. I found him… and I love him."

Crom stood looking at the strange but beautiful female. The tears in her eyes and the truth in her voice and eyes showed that she would not accept him. A part of him still wanted to challenge the male for her, but something told him that he could never win her. His eyes swept over her hair and the smoothness of her pale skin before he looked at Ha'ven who stood ready to strike.

"I ask for one thing before I will concede to the male," Crom finally responded.

Emma tilted her head and looked at the huge male. "What is it?"

"I wish to see if your skin feels as soft as I imagine," Crom responded with a grin. "I have never seen a female like you and it makes me curious."

Emma bit back a giggle and blushed when Ha'ven snarled a dark curse under his breath. She squeezed his fingers before she slipped her hand from his and took a step forward. A low rumble of displeasure filled the air behind her.

She glanced over her shoulder and rolled her eyes. "Behave," she admonished in a humorous tone. "He just wants to touch me."

"You are not his to touch," Ha'ven grumbled as he stepped up behind her.

Emma turned back to face Crom even as she stretched her left hand behind her to touch Ha'ven. She relaxed when his large hand wrapped around hers. She felt the familiar warmth that flooded her the moment they touched.

She bit her lip. In truth, she was a little curious herself. She reached up to timidly touch Crom's fur-coated chest at the same time as he reached out and touched her cheek. Her eyes rose to meet his. The tips of his fingers were rough, but soft as well. She tilted her head back a little further so he could run his fingers down along her jaw and throat. A low purr filled the air and the rumble of it vibrated under her fingers.

Emma couldn't hold back the giggle that escaped at the feeling of it. It reminded her of a small kitten she had when she was younger. She gasped when a thick arm suddenly wound around her waist and she was pulled back against Ha'ven's broad chest.

"You got your touch," he growled out to Crom. "We are done."

A startled squeak escaped Emma as she was suddenly swung up into a pair of strong arms. Her eyes flew to Ha'ven's blazing violet ones. The swirling of black deep inside them sent waves of heat through her blood.

"Where are we going?" she asked in confusion when he turned on his heel and began threading through the tables and down a small path into the dark forest.

"Saba Monda has given us a small hut that is used for visiting guests. I am taking you there and then I am going to let you claim me," he said in a husky, desire-laden voice. "I don't want any of those other damn males thinking that you are available again."

Emma sighed and laid her head against his chest as he carried her. She tilted her head so she could catch a glimpse of the stars through the trees. A smile curved her lips as she snuggled into his warmth.

A part of her felt guilty for not being there for her mother, but a bigger part of her felt amazement for how much her life had changed over the past few months. She had wanted a chance to find out what was out in the world. She had wanted a chance to live a little. She was finding out the world was a lot bigger than she ever imagined, and well, she had never felt so alive in her life.

~

Ha'ven strode down the long, narrow path to the hut Saba Monda had shown to him earlier. His blood boiled with jealousy. It had taken every bit of his self-control not to kill the Moniker. The thought of any other male touching her was like pouring fuel on a fire. He had wanted to rip the other male's hand off when he reached to touch Emma's cheek. His arms tightened around her slender figure as she relaxed back against him.

"It's so beautiful here," Emma sighed. "I've never seen so many stars in my life."

Ha'ven heard the ache in her voice. "What is it, *misha petite*? Something is bothering you," he asked quietly, slowing his pace so she could have more time to enjoy the stars above.

"I wonder how my mom is, and...," she answered in a small voice. "Sometimes I feel guilty that I'm not there for her... not that she would even realize it anymore," she whispered. "But other times, like now with you, I don't. I never want this to end. Do you think that makes me a selfish and uncaring daughter?"

Ha'ven's heart clenched at the hesitancy in her voice. Her uncertainty and sadness pulled at him. He knew she feared he would judge her harshly for wanting to stay with him. Did that make him any less guilty for wanting his time alone with her to never end as well?

"You said once that your mother did not remember who you were," Ha'ven replied as he stepped up to the door of the small hut. "Does she remember her life from when she was young?"

Emma reached out and lifted the latch to the door so Ha'ven could carry her over the threshold. A shiver coursed through her at the symbolic meaning. It was as if they had truly married that night.

"Yes, she remembers fragments. She especially remembers my father, though at times she doesn't remember they were married," Emma said sadly, looking up at Ha'ven's face in the dim light shining through the windows. "I don't want to ever forget you," she murmured in a hushed voice.

Ha'ven carefully lowered Emma to her feet. "I will just have to keep reminding you then," he said, brushing his fingers along her cheek. "I didn't like that male touching you," he admitted with a grimace. "You are mine, Emma. I have never felt this way before and it will take me time to understand the emotions you stir inside me."

Emma turned her head and pressed a kiss to the center of his palm. "I don't understand them either," she said. "I didn't think I would live, much less have a chance at finding someone to love. When Cuello...." her voice died and she lowered her head to hide the pain in her eyes. "I just wanted to fade away from the pain."

Ha'ven's face tightened in anger at the memory of what the human male had done to his tiny mate. He tenderly cupped her chin, lifting it so she could see the truth in his eyes. He ran his other hand up along her neck, threading his fingers through her hair. He knew he couldn't take her memories away, but he could ease them by replacing them with better, happier ones.

"Never again, Emma," he vowed passionately. "I will do everything in my power to protect you from ever having to go through anything like that again."

Emma's lips curved in a smile as she looked up at him with bright, trusting eyes. "I love you, Ha'ven."

Ha'ven lowered his head, capturing Emma's lips as his hands worked at unbraiding her hair. He wanted to run his hands through the silky strands. He deepened the kiss when her lips parted. The moment her hair was free, he moved his hands to the pin holding the colorful wrap. With nimble fingers, he slid it from the delicate fabric. Catching the wrap, he pulled it free from her body and tossed it behind him.

"Undress me, Emma," he muttered thickly as he pressed hot kisses to the corner of her mouth. "Undress me and claim me as yours."

"Forever?" she asked as her trembling fingers worked at pulling free the clasps that held his shirt closed.

"Forever," he responded.

"Oh Ha'ven," she gasped as his hands ran down to grip her hips.

Emma fought to push his shirt off his broad shoulders. Her hands roamed over his chest as she pressed tiny kisses across it. She worked her way down his flat stomach until her hands reached the top of his pants. She desperately worked at undoing the clasp at the waist and pushed them down. Ha'ven quickly toed off his boots and kicked his pants aside as Emma sank to her knees in front of him. His hands fisted in her hair and he closed his eyes briefly when he felt her hot, moist breath against his throbbing cock. Her hands ran up over his calves and clenched the back of his thighs as she pulled him forward.

"I want to taste you," she breathed.

Ha'ven drew in a heated breath, his eyes popping open to stare down at Emma's tilted face. In the dim light, her aura glowed and changed to warmer, richer colors as she opened her mouth. He swallowed several times as her lips closed around him.

"By the Goddess, Emma," he hissed out loudly. "You are mine forever, *misha petite.*"

Emma's soft moan of acknowledgement sent shivers through Ha'ven as the vibration added another layer of pleasure to the heat of her mouth. He thrust his hips forward slowly as she wrapped her lips around his shaft. He watched as she took his long length, amazed that she could take as much as she did without choking. He pulled back, shuddering at the light abrasion of her teeth against him. The sight of her loving him was the most beautiful thing he had ever seen.

Emma wrapped her hands around Ha'ven's cock, wanting to feel every inch of him. The combination of silky smooth and hard pulsing in her hands caused her own body to react. Hot moisture pooled between her legs and her breasts ached to be touched. She was desperate for relief from the building inferno inside her, but she wanted to savor this moment when she was the one in control. Deep down, she knew that Ha'ven wanted to show her that she had as much power over him as he did over her. The trembling in his tall, hard body proved that he was not immune to her touch.

She wondered vaguely what would happen if he lost that tight control. A surge of recklessness washed through her, pushing her to explore his body and push him to the breaking point. Gripping the feeling, she kept one hand wrapped around his cock while her other one explored. Her mouth became more desperate as her own body heated. She groaned around his cock, moving her mouth back and forth over it again and again. Her right hand moved with her mouth while her left stroked his stomach before sliding over his hip to grip his ass. She surprised herself when she slapped it hard.

"Goddess' blood!" Ha'ven choked out, pushing his hips forward. "I cannot take any more," he growled out.

Emma wasn't finished, but Ha'ven must have reached the limit of his control. He twisted her hair around his left fist. Pulling his cock out of her mouth with a loud pop, he reached down and pulled her up. The moment she was standing, he claimed her lips in a savage kiss.

Emma gasped as she felt his right hand reach down between them. He tangled his fingers in the golden curls and tugged. The silent demand was enough to cause her legs to part. The moment they did, his long fingers slipped between her slick folds.

"Ha'ven," she cried out as two of his fingers buried deep inside her.

"Yes, my mate. Ha'ven… your mate," he growled out as he forced her head back so he could mark her neck with his deep kiss. "I claim you, Emma. I claim you as my partner. In this life and any other the goddess gives us after, you will belong to me, Ha'ven Ha'darra, as I belong to you, my Emma."

Emma heard the words he had spoken before and felt the strands that formed between them before wrap even more firmly around her heart and soul. Her body arched into his as he pumped his fingers in and out of her as he kissed her neck. A sense of weightlessness held her as he lifted her and carried her over to the large bed in the center of the hut.

His body covered hers as he laid her down. His pulsing cock hard as it settled between her legs. The bulbous head was dark and slick with his own desire. His pre-cum mixed with her own as he started to slide into her.

"Claim me, my Emma," he begged huskily. "Claim me as your mate."

Emma stared up at him, overwhelming emotions thickening her voice as she spoke the words in her heart. "I claim you, Ha'ven Ha'darra. I claim you as my partner. In this life and any other, you will belong to me as I belong to you, my fierce warrior. Forever."

Ha'ven pushed forward as she spoke the last word, the slickness of their combined desires driving him all the way to her womb. He shuddered as her heat encased him. He groaned in pleasure when she raised her legs and wrapped them around his waist. The movement drove him impossibly deeper.

"Yes," he hissed out. "Hold tight, my Emma."

"Ahhhh!" she cried out, tilting her hips higher as he began driving into her faster and harder. "Ha'ven!"

Ha'ven ran desperate kisses along Emma's neck and shoulders as he wrapped his arms tightly around her as he rotated his hips. Each movement hit a new sensitive nerve inside her. He could feel her vaginal walls closing around the tip of his cock, trying to hold him inside her.

His mind splintered when she suddenly climaxed. The pulsing of her swollen channel around him squeezed and sucked at him. Her heels drove into his ass as she pushed him ever deeper.

With a low snarl, he pulled out of her, ignoring her cry as his cock slid across over-sensitive nerves. He rose as her legs fell away. His eyes swept over her flushed figure. Her hair was spread out wildly across the pillows, small flowers still entwined in it. Her eyes were half-closed with sultry passion as she was still locked in the orgasm that had just overwhelmed her. Her nipples were taut and rosy as her chest rose rapidly as she panted.

His eyes moved down to the tangle of moist blond curls that glistened with her orgasm. Unable to resist, he leaned over and captured her left nipple between his lips even as he pushed two fingers deep into her swollen channel. He was rewarded with her loud cry of surprise.

"Oh God!" she cried out, arching into him.

Ha'ven ravaged her taut nipple, making it swell against the onslaught of his hot mouth. He continued to work her pussy as he moved to her other nipple. He didn't stop until she shattered under him again, her hoarse cries filling the small hut. He only released her when her legs fell apart in satiation.

"Now, I will come," he growled out.

Sitting back, he gripped her left leg and rolled her over. He gripped her hips and pulled her up onto her hands and knees. The sight of her rounded ass and slick moisture of her orgasms coating the inside of her thighs drew a heated growl from him.

By the Goddess, I will never get enough of her, he thought fiercely.

Gripping his throbbing shaft in his hand, he grimaced at the sensitivity. He would not last long, but he would draw at least one more orgasm from her before he would allow himself to find relief. Aligning his swollen head with her hot channel, he watched as it disappeared into her. Just the sight was enough to cause him to almost come. Holding onto her hips, he pushed in slowly before pulling almost all the way out. Setting a rhythm that was as old as the universe, he watched as they became one. The knowledge that she was his life now flowing through him.

Emotion swelled deep inside him as her low whimpers washed through him. Her body began rocking back and forth with him. The movement pushing him deeper and deeper. He slid his left hand down over her stomach to the soft thatch of hair protecting her swollen nub.

With his other hand, he captured some of their moisture and let his fingers caress her tight rosette.

The combination was too much for Emma. Her body bucked briefly before she stiffened against him. Her soft whimpers turned to a sob as she exploded around him. His own body, tortured from him holding back, shattered. His own cries blended with hers. He could feel his release pulsing in time with hers. Her body drank his seed like a flower drank the rain. He was locked to her in a blinding orgasm. His power rose, engulfing her as it bound itself in a serenity that defied anything he had ever experienced.

"My Emma," he cried out hoarsely as they both collapsed.

CHAPTER NINETEEN

*H*a'ven opened his eyes as a loud shriek echoed through the dark forests, waking him. The shriek was followed by a second low howl. His arms wrapped protectively around Emma's sleeping form.

"Emma, *misha petite*," Ha'ven whispered urgently. "We must get dressed."

"What is it?" Emma asked sleepily as she snuggled into him. "I want to sleep. I'm so tired."

"I'm not sure, but something is wrong," Ha'ven said as he gently extricated his body from Emma and rose from the bed. "Come, we must see what is going on. I will not leave you here alone."

Emma reluctantly crawled from the bed and reached for the colorful wrap that she had worn earlier. It was flung across the back of a small stool. Pushing her hair out of her eyes, she quickly pulled the wrap around her like Telmay showed her. She glanced around for the beautiful pin to hold it on.

"Here, let me," Ha'ven murmured in a husky voice as he stepped forward with the pin in his hand and slid it through the delicate material. He touched Emma's face, lifting it so he could look her in the eye. "You must promise to do what I tell you. I am afraid that Kejon may have found us. I..." His voice faded. "He is a very dangerous male. I need to know you are safe."

Emma nodded. "I'll do what you tell me. I promise," she responded softly.

Ha'ven brushed a brief hard kiss to her lips as another low howl echoed. He turned, pushing Emma behind him when he heard a noise outside the hut they had been given. He relaxed when he saw the familiar silver fur of Saba Monda.

"What is it?" Ha'ven asked.

"You and your mate must come with me," Saba Monda said in a quiet voice filled with urgency.

Ha'ven nodded. He wrapped his hand around Emma's, squeezing it gently when he felt the slight tremble in it. He refused to dwell on the fact that he was vulnerable at the moment. While he wasn't completely defenseless against a powerful Curizan warrior with the skills that Kejon had with his power drained, it would be a difficult and dangerous battle.

One advantage he had was being able to read Kejon's aura. Not all Curizans had that ability. He had seen the dark green mixed with a dull yellow-green and the trace of black. Kejon was consumed with jealousy, greed, and the taint of evilness that created a dangerous mix. He wanted power and enjoyed hurting others.

Ha'ven's eyes jerked to Saba Monda who snarled out a command as they entered the open area of the village. Within seconds, members of the village began disappearing into the darkness.

"Ha'ven, what is it?" Emma asked in a hushed voice as she watched the older women gather the children together and disappear down the path leading to the river. "Where is everyone going?

"Intruders have entered our airspace," Sebra said quietly. "We must get you both to safety."

"No," Ha'ven growled. "They are here for me and my mate. Take Emma. Keep her safe until I return."

Sebra shook her head. "You are still weak, young prince. My people can take care of the intruders," she insisted.

"Not this one," Ha'ven said coldly. "He almost killed my brother and my mate. I will not cower when I have brought danger to you."

"You will need this if you wish to fight," Saba Monda said harshly, holding out a laser sword. "A gift from your father."

Ha'ven looked down at the intricately carved handle. "Hermon…"

"Not Hermon," Saba Monda replied as a series of low howls floated through the night air. "Melek. Come, they have landed near the lake."

"Ha'ven," Emma cried out when Sebra pulled her away from him.

Ha'ven turned and looked into Emma's frightened blue eyes. "I will keep you safe," he promised.

"But who will keep you safe?" she whispered back. "You said your powers…"

"I am the Crown Prince of the Curizan," Ha'ven interrupted, straightening his shoulders. "None will defeat a Ha'darra."

Emma watched as he turned and followed Saba Monda into the darkness. She stepped forward to follow, but Sebra stopped her. Emma started to argue, but a wave of dizziness washed over her as Sebra pressed a cloth over her nose and mouth. Emma's eyes widened before they closed as darkness descended.

"I am sorry, little one," Sebra said as she lifted Emma into her arms. "You must trust in your mate and my people to protect you both. You are too stubborn for your own good and I will not take a chance of you being harmed. The others and I have grown attached to you," Sebra said quietly as Olla, Telmay, and Pollamay gathered around to take Emma to safety.

Kejon glanced around the darkened landscape. He had beamed down the moment the advanced team located the downed transport. Now, he stood on the edge of the lake staring into the dark forest.

"The inhabitants of this moon are deadly," he said coldly. "Kill on sight."

"Do you know what type of weapons they use?" a large Marastin Dow asked as he loaded his laser rifle.

Kejon glanced at the man. The insignia on his collar showed he was an advanced tactical team leader. As far as Kejon was concerned, he and all the other men on the transport were expendable.

"They use spears and arrows," Kejon stated, looking back over the dark forest.

The Team Leader raised his eyebrow. Even in the dark Kejon would see the skeptical look on the man's face. Several other members chuckled at Kejon's statement.

"You are all dead," Kejon said dismissively.

"By a bunch of spear wielding adversaries?" one of the men joked. "We'll blow them to pieces."

Kejon gritted his teeth. "Just try not to die before we find Ha'darra," he said, walking toward the woods.

A shiver went down his spine. He could feel the eyes staring at them. The fools had alerted the Monikers to their presence. Kejon pulled on the power inside him and focused it. He pulled the shield of energy around his body. He would not be able to hold it indefinitely, but he only needed it long enough to find the Curizan Prince. Once he did, he would unleash the power he had learned to tap into thanks to the Valdier Royal, Raffvin.

Kejon wasn't a fool to believe that the Curizans were the only ones with the ability to control the energy around them. Raffvin had learned to manipulate it and used it against his own symbiot, changing it into a deadly force. Kejon had studied Raffvin and discovered a way to use what he had learned in the device he had strapped to his waist.

I will only get one chance to use it, he thought in frustration.

He stepped onto the dark path, ignoring the men coming up behind him in formation. As soon as the shadows touched him, he vanished.

CHAPTER TWENTY

*H*a'ven followed Saba Monda through the dark forest. He paused as the silver-haired Moniker gripped a long vine and began climbing up the side of one of the massive trees.

He grabbed another vine and followed. They were soon high above the forest floor. He nodded silently at Crom as the huge Moniker jumped down next to them on a large branch.

"There are thirty purple warriors," Crom said in a low voice. "Another male appeared. He is one of your people." Crom nodded toward Ha'ven. "The scouts lost track of him when he entered the forest. He has some type of shield protecting him."

"Kejon," Ha'ven growled out. "I will deal with him. Can you and your people take care of the Marastin Dow? They are cutthroat mercenaries for hire."

Crom snorted. "The others will handle them. I will go with you."

Ha'ven shook his head. "Kejon is very powerful. I will deal with him alone. I do not want to take a chance of him hurting any of your people."

Crom grinned. "I will still go with you. Do not worry, if you should die I will claim your female as my own and care for her."

Ha'ven pushed down his desire to kill the huge Moniker again. It was getting harder and harder to do so. He would be lucky to get off the damn planet before he gave into his desire to show the other male what a jealous Curizan could do even without his powers.

"I'll see your hairy ass as a rug before you touch my mate," Ha'ven growled back.

Crom grinned again, his sharp white teeth briefly gleaming to show his amusement. They all turned as another Moniker dropped down beside them. This time a tall female carrying a bow and a quiver full of arrows.

"They have entered the forest," she whispered. "They are heavily armed, but we are prepared. Once they reach the fork in the path, we will attack. This will allow us to divide them into smaller groups."

"I will oversee the attack," Saba Monda responded. "Crom, go with Ha'ven."

Ha'ven gritted his teeth in frustration. He was not used to anyone covering his back. He knew arguing would be a waste of breath as the silver-haired Moniker disappeared through the trees with the female. He turned and glared at the dark brown male who stood with his arms folded confidently across his chest.

"Kejon has powers that you cannot fight against," Ha'ven warned. "He has the ability to teleport short distances. He often comes from behind or to the left of his opponents as he is left-handed. He favors several different types of weapons, including the Marastin Dows curved blade and the Opairan's poison-tipped throwing stars. He can throw small bursts of energy that can disorient you. The best thing if you see him raise his hands is to roll to the left. It will throw him off. He will not be expecting you to know this. He can also pull an energy shield around himself to make himself invisible, but he cannot maintain it for long periods of time."

Crom listened intently. "How do you plan to kill him if you cannot see him?" he asked curiously.

Ha'ven grinned. "I may not have full use of my powers, but there are some things I am able to see even without them. His aura will give him away. You will not be able to see him, but I can."

"Let us go find your shadow-male," Crom said. "We will stay to the trees."

Ha'ven nodded. He tried to pull his power around him. He cursed when a sharp pain pierced his skull. What little that had returned he had given to Emma earlier when they came together in an explosion of need. He breathed through the pain and quickly followed Crom. It was likely he would only get one chance to kill Kejon. He refused to think about what would happen to Emma if he should fail.

Kejon slid back into the shadows of a thick tree and released the shield around him. He cursed the moment of weakness that washed over him. He had left the others back at the lake. They would draw the attention away from him. He had one goal and that was finding the Curizan prince. He didn't want to waste his energy on fighting the native inhabitants. He looked up at the branches above him. He couldn't see the movement of the creatures, but he could sense them. He waited until they were past him before he moved out from under the protection of the shadows. He remembered well where the village was from his last visit. He doubted that Ha'ven would remain behind there, but the prince now had a weakness… the whore with him. Even the brief glimpse he caught of the female on the view-screen showed she was unusual. The prince had a soft spot for females. If he could find her, he could have an added advantage and all he would have to do is wait for the prince to come to him.

Before he had stumbled upon the village, he had found a narrow cave near the river. When he had explored it, he found it contained stored items. If he wasn't mistaken, this was where the villagers who were either too young or old to fight would take refuge. If he wanted to find a weakness, that was where he needed to go.

He moved silently through the undergrowth, pausing sporadically to make sure he had not been seen. His eyes narrowed when he reached the edge of the woods near the river. He saw the dark outline of the rock wall on the other side of the river where the entrance to the cave was located.

Pausing for a moment, he focused. He stumbled when he rematerialized on the other side of the river. He sank down behind a large boulder and breathed deeply.

He wiped a hand across his brow. He pulled several small devices from a bag at his waist. The small devices would detonate, sending out a gas that would incapacitate anyone who breathed it in. Normally, he would have just killed anyone in his way, but he wanted the female alive. He wanted the Curizan Prince to watch as he killed the female. It would make his own thirst for power that much sweeter.

Rising, he stepped toward the entrance of the cave. He barely had time to raise his shield before an arrow bounced harmlessly off it. He raised the laser gun and fired.

A harsh shriek cut through the air as he hit his target. A rain of arrows burst around him. With a silent curse, he focused a burst of energy toward those high on the rocks above him. At the same time, he tossed the small balls through the entrance of the cave. A brief flash sounded at the same time as shrieks of pain echoed as those above him rocked from having their equilibrium shattered.

Several figures stumbled out of the cave. He brutally cut them down as they emerged. Tossing the last body to the side, he pulled a small breathing apparatus over his nose and mouth before entering the cave.

Bodies lay where they fell. Larger ones shielded the smaller ones. He ignored all of them. He wanted only one. His eyes fell on the golden haired female with satisfaction. She was lying on a thin cover on the ground.

Stepping over and around the others, he stared down at the still figure. She was attractive for being a different species. He decided to change his plans as he stared down at her soft features. A devious smile curved his lips as he thought of the ultimate revenge against Ha'darra.

Kejon reached down and scooped up the tiny figure. He turned on his heel. He had taken only a few steps when a hand weakly reached out and grabbed his ankle, almost tripping him. He glared down at the female holding him. Her eyes went from his to the bundle in his arms. He pulled his leg away and viciously kicked the female's rounded stomach.

He chuckled at her cry of pain. He continued through the cave and stepped out into the clear night sky. His eyes narrowed when he saw that he was not alone. A dark, satisfied smile curved his lips when he saw the outline of the male he had been seeking. It did not take as long as he expected to enjoy his triumph.

"Well, well, well. If it is not the Curizan Prince," Kejon said mockingly. "It is a shame you are too late to protect your whore, Ha'darra."

"Put her down, Kejon," Ha'ven growled back. "This is between us. We finish it here and now."

Kejon chuckled as he shifted Emma's slight weight in his arms. He palmed the device he had in his hand as he did. The sweet revenge tasted even sweeter knowing he would be able to rub in his plans before he killed Ha'darra.

"She is so sweet," Kejon said in a low menacing voice. "I wonder if she tastes as sweet as she looks. I will have to make sure I find out before I let the others sample her as well."

Ha'ven took a step forward. "Release her," he snarled.

Kejon's mouth tightened as he caught the movement of another large figure. "Tell whoever is with you to stand down or I'll snap her in half," he warned.

~

Ha'ven had frozen behind Crom when the first shrieks had echoed through the thick forests over the sound of fighting and confusion in front and to the side of them as the other Monikers engaged the Marastin Dow tactical team.

"The cave," Crom had growled out in rage. "They are being attacked!"

Ha'ven had turned even as the huge Moniker was conveying what the sounds meant. He ran along the branches, grabbing the huge vines and swinging from limb to limb. Crom followed closely beside him.

The two of them raced toward the river. They had burst out of the forest at the same time. A female Moniker lay by the shore of the river, blood seeping from her ears. She looked up, pointing with a low groan. Three bodies lay broken by the entrance of the cave where they had fallen from the rocks above. The bodies of four elderly women lay crumbled beside them, cut down as they emerged from the cave.

Ha'ven looked up as a large figure carrying another emerged from the cave. He immediately recognized Emma's golden hair. His eyes burned with rage as he pulled the laser sword out.

His blood boiled at Kejon's mocking words. "Put her down, Kejon," Ha'ven growled back. "This is between us. We finish it here and now."

He took a step forward. Fear and hatred pulsed through him at Kejon's barely veiled threat. His hand tightened until his knuckles gleamed white.

"She is so sweet," Kejon responded to his demand. "I wonder if she tastes as sweet as she looks. I will have to make sure I find out before I let the others sample her as well."

"Release her," he snarled, his eyes gauging the distance between them.

Ha'ven watched as Kejon's eyes flickered briefly to the side. The assassin's words froze him and he raised his hand to halt Crom. He could tell from the sudden darkening of Kejon's aura that he meant what he said. He would snap Emma's spine in a heartbeat.

"You want me, you've got me," Ha'ven growled out, throwing the laser sword to the side. "Just you and me. No one else will interfere. Just release the female."

"I think not," Kejon said with a triumphant grin. "Aria should have killed you when she had the chance. I will not make the same mistake. But before you die, Ha'darra, I want you to know that your female will be well used before she dies."

Ha'ven roared out in frustrated rage as Kejon shifted Emma over his shoulder as he raised his hand. Ha'ven saw the small device in the assassin's hand, even as he rushed him. A burst of black shot from the device. Long tentacles reached out toward him, wrapping around his arms and chest. The thick bands spread out over him, spreading up his neck and down his legs. The more he fought, the tighter they became until he was struggling to breathe.

"You can thank the Valdier Royal, Raffvin, for this little trick," Kejon said with a cold smile. "You see, his symbiot feeds off of dark power and you, dear prince, have the power they crave."

Ha'ven fought to remain upright, but the black bands dragged him to his knees. He struggled to gasp in a breath of air, but the black bands refused to release their hold on his throat. The dark strands stretched up over his mouth and nose until only his eyes remained free. Spots danced as he struggled with the lack of oxygen.

Crom growled out and moved to try to pull the black bands off of Ha'ven. The huge Moniker flew backwards when the black bands sent a burst of pure energy through his body. Ha'ven fought to keep from losing consciousness; his only thought was for Emma.

I am sorry, my mate, he whispered silently to her as darkness washed over him. *Forgive my failure in protecting you.*

Ha'ven? Emma's faint voice echoed softly through him.

Kejon's astonished expletive filled the air. The fury in the curse echoed as a colorful form suddenly appeared between him and Ha'ven. The figure turned to look at Kejon for a moment before it floated through the air toward Ha'ven's still figure.

The iridescent form knelt on the ground next to the shrouded body. A slender hand reached out to touch the black bands. The moment it touched the pulsing negative energy, the black bands rose up to entwine with it. The figure spoke softly to the greedy strands that slowly dissolved into it, leaving thin gold strands behind.

A shiver went through Kejon as he realized that the figure was that of the female in his arms. She was more than Ha'ven's current whore. She was a being of incredible power. As the bands dissolved, Kejon knew he needed time to explore what he held in his arms. Such power was not to be ignored or eliminated without careful consideration as to how it could be used first.

Pressing the signal for the transporter to beam him up, Kejon cast one last look at the figure that floated above Ha'darra's body. He needed to retreat to his hidden base. He needed time to plan because there was one thing he knew without a doubt... Ha'darra would be coming after the female.

CHAPTER TWENTY-ONE

"*H*a'ven," a deep voice said. "Wake up."

Ha'ven's eyes snapped open at the same time as his hand gripped the throat of the male above him. Rage glowed from his violet eyes, turning them darker. His hand tightened as his power returned. He felt a vibration and heard the sound of metal groaning ominously as he stared into a pair of matching violet eyes.

"I know he can be a royal pain in the ass, but if you kill him, mother is going to be very upset with you," Adalard said as he leaned back against the wall. "Not to mention, if you don't get a grip on your emotions, you just might kill all of us."

It took a moment for sanity to return and for Ha'ven to realize he was squeezing Arrow's throat. He released his grip and drew in a deep breath to try to calm the rage of dark power that was flowing through him.

He watched as Adalard caught Arrow who collapsed, wheezing and rubbing his throat. His eyes shot around the room that he quickly identified as being Adalard's warship. He raised a hand to his head, brushing his hair back as he sat up the rest of the way. He swung his feet over the side of the medical bay bed. Only when he felt like he was under some semblance of control did he look at his two younger brothers.

"Emma?" he asked in an emotionless voice.

"Gone," Adalard said grimly. "Kejon took her."

The walls of the medical center expanded outward before settling back into place. That was the only sign of Ha'ven's reaction to his brother's quietly spoken words. He closed his eyes as shattering pain coursed through him. The horrors Emma endured under the human male's hands would pale in comparison to what Kejon would do to her.

Ha'ven looked at his brothers. His face was pale but composed. He would do whatever was necessary to bring Emma back home to his arms.

"Do you know where he has gone?" he asked in a strained voice.

"Yes," Arrow responded. "Bahadur has an informant on the Marastin Dow ship that has been in contact with him. He is heading to Kejon's hidden base. He will be there before Kejon arrives. We should arrive shortly after. The informant says he will do what he can to keep Emma safe, but he can make no promises."

Ha'ven slid off the bed. "You expect me to trust a Marastin Dow? They would sell their own mates before they help anyone but themselves," he replied as nausea rose again. "What happened?"

"Your female saved you," another deep voice responded. "I should have gone ahead and fought you for her. If I had known how powerful she was, I would have."

Ha'ven's turned his head to look at the other side of the room. A large figure rose from the seat and stretched. His eyes narrowed on the serious look in the dark brown eyes.

"What happened?" he asked again.

Crom's mouth curved downward. "The assassin had a weapon unlike any I have ever seen." He raised his arm and showed off the golden band. "Whatever it is, it has taken a liking to me and will not come off. Kejon shot this at you only it was black, alive, and powerful. It knocked me off my feet and was determined to strangle you."

Arrow and Adalard both swore under their breaths. "That is the same thing that attacked Mandra. It is part of Raffvin's symbiot. I thought Paul and the others had defeated it," Adalard muttered. "How did Kejon get it?"

"I don't know," Ha'ven said as he thought of the power behind the small bit of symbiot. "The last thing I remember was it was draining my power from me."

"It was doing more than that," Crom said as he gently rubbed the golden band. "It was crushing you. Before my eyes, the figure of your mate, made of the colors of the sky after a shower, appeared. She touched the black bands. Whatever she said or did pulled the darkness away and into her. A living gold metal was left behind. As soon as your mate pulled the blackness away, it immediately released you. I reached down to help you and it grabbed me and has not let go since. Your brother told me it belongs to the Dragon-shifters."

"What are you doing here?" Ha'ven asked of the huge Moniker. "What of the others?"

Crom grinned. "I wish to see more than the mines of the Red Planet and the females of my world. Besides, this golden metal will not release me. I thought I should return it to its world. Not to mention, I am still hoping I get a chance to claim the little female. I cannot do that from my world," he responded. "Ten of my people perished in the battle. Pollamay gave birth early. The infant is weak, but should survive," he added somberly.

Ha'ven felt the weight of those who died on his shoulders. He looked up when he felt a hand gently touch him. The dark brown eyes looked at him for several long seconds.

"My people stand by their Prince," Crom said quietly. "We owe much to your family. Each and every one of us has taken a pledge to uphold your rule. Your father saved our world during the Great War when Ben'qumain sent in troops to kill us so he could take the resources of the Red Planet. Those that died did so with honor. Do not dishonor them by taking blame for what they have freely given."

Ha'ven nodded. "I am honored to have your support," he said quietly. Turning to look at his brothers, he drew in a deep breath. "Tell me everything you know."

Emma woke slowly. She remained still as memories crowded her. She opened her eyes and looked up at the unfamiliar ceiling. Pushing up, she sat up and brushed her long hair over her shoulder.

"You're awake," a husky voice said. "I was beginning to worry you would never wake."

Emma started and turned toward the door. A tall slender male with purple skin leaned against the wall next to the door. He was dressed in a black uniform from head to toe. An insignia and several gold stars were attached to the collar of his shirt.

"Who are you?" she asked nervously, looking around the sparsely furnished room. "Where am I?"

"My name is Captain Marus Tylis, commander of the *Traitor's Run*," the tall figure replied.

"Why...?" Emma drew in a shaky breath as she wound her hands together. "Why am I here? What is going to happen to me?"

Marus studied the tiny female. He had been surprised when Kejon had reappeared aboard the *Traitor's Run* with the female. That had been almost eighteen hours before. Kejon had handed the female over to one of the senior officers after he had told the Curizan that a fast approaching warship had entered the region.

He had immediately ordered the officer to secure the female in one of the empty cabins on the officer's level. They did not have anywhere else on board that was remotely secure. They took no prisoners and anyone who was found to violate procedures aboard was killed and their bodies disposed of in space.

It was only the fact that each member now on board the *Traitor's Run* had been specifically hand-picked for a different mission that he knew he could trust them. The former captain made the mistake of thinking that using Kejon as a cover for their true mission would be a good idea. That mistake had cost him his life and had forced Marus to change their mission. Now, he would be lucky to get his crew and himself out of the mess Kejon had made without being blown to pieces. His only hope of getting everyone out alive lay in keeping the female sitting in front of him safe.

"You were brought here by a Curizan assassin named Kejon," Marus answered in a low voice. "He is a very dangerous and powerful male. At the moment, I have been able to distract him. I don't know what he wants with you, but something tells me it isn't going to be good for either of us. Tell me who you are and what you have to do with the Ha'darra family. I need any information you can give me if I am to get us all out of this alive."

Emma bit her lip and rose off the bed on trembling legs. "My name is Emma Watson. I'm a human," she answered, looking into the cold silver eyes. "I was… taken from my world several months ago. A week or so ago, Ha'ven Ha'darra came to the world where I was taken," Emma bowed her head as fresh pain swept through her as an image of Ha'ven struggling for breath washed through her. She looked up at the male in front of her with shimmering eyes. "He kidnapped me and claimed me. I was mad at him at first," she admitted quietly. "I just wanted to… die. I had been hurt badly by a male from my world before I was taken. I didn't even know anything like this could exist." She raised her hands and swept them to encompass everything around her. "I didn't know there was such a thing as aliens. At least, not in real life."

"Who took you?" Marus asked as his gut twisted.

"A man named Creon Reykill," Emma said. "He said I was under his protection."

Marus drew in a deep breath and ran his hand down his face. This was worse than he could imagine. Forget being afraid of Kejon's powers. He had a female on board his warship that was under the protection of not one, but two of the fiercest species in the known star systems. He would be lucky if they just blew them to pieces. That would be merciful compared to what an enraged dragon-shifter and a Curizan Prince could do together.

He stared up at the ceiling and wondered how his life could have gotten so screwed up so quickly. Was this punishment for wanting to free his people from the archaic rule it was currently under? He hoped to bring freedom to his people. Instead, he and those who fought for the same thing were about to be annihilated for being in the wrong place at the wrong time with definitely the wrong female on board.

He looked back the tiny female in front of him. "You are Ha'ven Ha'darra's mate?" he asked heavily.

Emma bit her lip and nodded. "Yes," she answered.

He glanced at the door when a soft knock sounded. He opened the door a crack. A soft feminine voice said something to him and he nodded before it closed again.

"I am going to do everything in my power to keep you safe," he finally said. "It is important that Kejon not know what I am doing."

Emma nodded again. "Captain Tylis," she said as he opened the door to leave. "Thank you," she whispered.

Marus bowed his head briefly before he stepped out and closed the door behind him. Emma heard the sound of the lock engaging. She slowly sank down onto the bed and pulled her knees to her chest. Wrapping her arms around her legs, she closed her eyes and let the silent tears fall.

"Oh, Ha'ven," she whispered brokenly. "I love you."

CHAPTER TWENTY-TWO

*H*a'ven heard the softly spoken words as if from a distance. He remained frozen on the bridge as Emma's voice echoed through him. A sense of calm determination swept through him.

He bowed his head and let the powers that made up the universe open and flow through him. Since he woke, his power had returned tenfold to him. It was different than it had been before when he felt out of control and unable to harness it. Now, he felt focused and in control. He relaxed and opened himself to the power instead of fighting it.

Everything around him slowed until it was as if time itself had stopped. He moved forward, studying those around him. He could see his brother Arrow talking with the chief engineer. Adalard was reviewing information on a data tablet. Each man was at their position, ready for the battle they knew was to come.

Ha'ven turned and could see his body standing in the same position in front of the view-screen. He turned back to the front and focused on Emma. A golden strand of light flowed outward across space. He grasped the sliver of power, clinging to it. He embraced the powerful flow of energy, riding it as it swept him away from the *Rayon I.*

He focused as another warship came into view. He recognized the size and shape as being one of the Marastin Dow attack ships. His non-corporeal body flowed through the hull of the warship unencumbered. He moved along the corridors easily, unseen by those who moved about it.

He paused when he saw a tall male speaking quietly to several others. The insignia on his shirt showed that he was the captain. Rage built inside Ha'ven. The male stopped talking and looked around uneasily as the walls around him groaned. Ha'ven reined in his fury and floated closer to the male. He would not endanger Emma. He paused when the male turned back around to the other three officers standing near him.

"Whatever happens, protect the female," the male was ordering the others. "She must be returned to Ha'darra safely."

"What about the Curizan?" the female asked uneasily. "How can we possibly protect her against him? You saw what he did to Jonas. We are defenseless against him."

"We are all dead if the human female is not kept safe. She is under the protection of both the Curizan and the Valdier royal houses," the male responded harshly. "If we are to free our own people, we will need their alliance. This is more than about our lives. This is about the millions of others on our world who seek a better life. Aris, did you get the message out?"

"Yes, the Curizan general will be at Kejon's base before us and he should have notified Ha'darra," Aris replied.

"What makes you think Ha'darra will not destroy us before we have a chance to explain we had no choice but to help Kejon," one of the males asked. "As soon as they see us, they will blow us out of space."

The older male turned and looked at the three standing before him. "I have no guarantees. I will do what I can to protect those aboard the *Traitor's Run*," he replied in a low voice. "Return to your posts and make sure that Kejon's position is monitored at all times."

"Yes, sir," the three said before turning and disappearing.

Marus turned when he felt the same chill wash over him that he had felt moments ago. His eyes scanned the empty corridor. He muttered a brief oath before he straightened his shoulders.

"If you can hear me, know that we will do everything in our power to keep her safe," he muttered under his breath.

Marus didn't know if there was anyone in the corridor or not, but his gut was telling him that a power greater than any mortal had seen had been awakened. He could only hope that if Ha'darra could hear him, he would grant them mercy when this was over.

Emma raised her head when she felt a warmth caress her damp cheek. Her eyes widened when she saw the glowing image of Ha'ven kneeling in front of her. Biting her bottom lip, she raised her hand to gently touch the shimmering figure.

"Are you really here or am I dreaming?" she asked in a faint voice

Her hand brushed through the image, but the warmth that flooded her when she touched it gave her the strength to lean forward, turning until she was on her knees.

"I love you," she whispered, gazing warmly at the faint form.

As I love you, misha petite, Ha'ven replied. *I am coming for you.*

"I know," she whispered. "Captain Tylis told me he had contacted you. I saw you… I saw you lying on the ground covered in whatever it was that Kejon shot at you. I was so scared."

Emma's eyes flew to the door as heavy footsteps echoed. A moment later, she heard Kejon's voice ordering the guard outside to open the door. She turned frightened eyes to the shimmering image as the locks disengaged.

"Go," she whispered urgently. "Something tells me he mustn't realize you know where I am."

I love you, my Emma, Ha'ven said before he let go of the energy he had harnessed.

"I love you, too," she whispered as the door opened.

Emma looked up as another tall male entered. He had the same coloring as the other Curizans she had met. The biggest difference was the coldness in his eyes and the touch of insanity. She scrambled back on the bed away from him as he stood in the doorway.

"What species are you?" Kejon demanded in a frigid voice.

"Hu... human," Emma replied as she pressed back against the wall.

Kejon frowned, staring at her. Emma could tell he was assessing whether she was telling him the truth or not. He slowly walked forward, not stopping until his legs pressed against the edge of the narrow bed.

"Where do you come from?" he demanded.

"Earth," Emma said, tilting her head up in defiance.

"Earth," Kejon repeated. "Where is that and how powerful are you?"

Emma's mouth tightened. "I don't know where it is in comparison to where I am at," she stated truthfully. "And we are very powerful. Far more powerful than you," she bluffed.

Kejon stood staring down at her for several long minutes. He could see she was frightened, yet she stared back at him, refusing to look away.

A sardonic smile curved his lips. He had to give her credit for trying to hide her fear. His eyes roamed her fair hair. He reached out to touch it.

"Don't!" she said sharply, rising to stand on the bed. "You will not touch me," she hissed.

Kejon's eyes narrowed and he stepped back in alarm. Dark tentacles of black power swirled around her, lifting her golden hair until it floated around her. Her blue eyes glowed and in their depths he could see the black power in them. A shiver of warning ran down his spine. He took another cautious step back.

"What are you?" he asked as he pulled at his own power in case he needed it.

"I am the mate of Ha'ven Ha'darra," she stated, clenching her fists at her side. "I am under the protection of both Ha'ven Ha'darra and the Valdier Royal family. You will not touch me!"

Kejon fell backwards against the door when she lifted her hand up, palm outward. The force of the power behind her hand knocked the breath out of him. He pulled his own power around him like a shield. Cold anger poured through him. He needed the power inside the small female. If he could harness it and turn it against Ha'darra, he felt confident he could defeat the Curizan prince.

"Your mate is dead," Kejon lied. "I killed him. You will bow to me! I now claim you as mine."

Uncertainty flickered through Emma's eyes as her mind fought with her heart. Had she just dreamed that Ha'ven had been here with her? Had she imagined hearing his voice and feeling his warmth?

Panic and despair pierced her heart at the thought of never seeing or touching him again. Tears burned her eyes as the male in front of her took a step forward as he sensed her indecision.

"No," she whispered. "No, I will not go through this again."

She glanced around the brightly lit room. There were no shadows to hide in like before on the *Sentinel*. She closed her eyes and pictured a dark place in her mind. If her body could not find a place to slip into to hide, then her mind would. She would never let another hold her captive again.

Kejon's furious yell echoed in the room as Emma focused inward. She shut out everything but the shadows in her mind. She was safe in the darkness. She was safe since no one could find her there. She imagined the calming blackness surrounding her.

Her body tingled as she pictured herself slipping through the invisible door. Peace washed over her as she fell into the shadows. She glanced back through the doorway one last time and saw her body crumpled on the bed.

She felt a moment of triumph as Kejon turned her limp form over. He might be able to touch her physical body, but she was no longer there. She turned back, following the golden thread that guided her away.

CHAPTER TWENTY-THREE

*H*a'ven came back into his body with a shudder. He breathed in deeply as he refocused on his location. A hand on his arm drew his attention and he saw both Arrow and Adalard warily staring at him. His gaze flickered around the bridge and he noticed the other warriors were watching him with more than a trace of unease.

"What is it?" he asked, looking back at Adalard.

"You tell me," Adalard muttered.

"I think we need to take this into the conference room," Arrow suggested, giving Ha'ven a strange look.

Ha'ven nodded and strode into the conference room off the bridge. He walked over to the viewport, looking out into deep space as he waited for the door to close. He turned to look at his two brothers. They were standing with their arms folded across their chests, grim expressions on both of their faces.

"What is it?" he asked again, impatiently.

"You don't know?" Adalard inquired lightly.

"I don't know what? Will you just tell me what is going on?" he replied.

"Where were you a few minutes ago?" Arrow asked carefully as he walked over to the conference table and sat down.

Ha'ven frowned and watched as his younger brother pulled up a star chart. He frowned as he studied it. The location of the *Rayon I* was incorrect. They should be closer to the Sanapare Spaceport, not the Razzine Spaceport favored by the rougher freight pilots. It was run by the Tiliqua, a small two-headed reptile species that were skilled businessmen. It was impossible for them to have journeyed so far in a matter of minutes. Razzine was more than two days away.

"I was on the bridge," he said uneasily. "Why?"

"Yes, but where else?" Adalard insisted.

Ha'ven glanced at Adalard before he turned back to the star chart. "I was with Emma," he answered quietly.

Arrow sat back and looked at Ha'ven. A slow grin curved his mouth and excitement made his eyes glow. Adalard shot his twin a warning glance but Arrow ignored it, shrugging his shoulders.

"You were glowing, bro," Arrow said. "Hell, the entire ship was glowing with you. One minute we are almost two days behind the Marastin Dow's warship and the next we are parked next to Bahadur. I thought he was going to shit his pants when we suddenly appeared next to him. By the way, he is pissed as nothing normally shakes him. He just landed in Docking Bay 1."

"What happened? How did you do it?" Adalard asked quietly.

"I don't know. I heard Emma," he began as he studied the star chart again. "I needed to find her... go to her. I've had trouble harnessing and controlling my power since my captivity on Hell. It was to the point I feared I would have...," he paused, running his hands over his face before he sank down into one of the chairs. "I asked Melek to terminate me if it got worse. I was out of control and dangerous."

"Why didn't you tell me?" Adalard demanded, anger making the scar on his cheek stand out. "I could have helped you."

"No, you couldn't," Ha'ven replied. "We have all heard the tales of what could happen if a power is left uncontrolled."

"Children's stories!" Adalard responded, waving his hand in dismissal. "Told to keep children and young boys in line."

"No, not just stories," Ha'ven quietly explained. "Like you, I thought the same thing until… Aria awakened a darkness inside me that continued to grow. I could no longer contain or control the power inside me. I built a chamber under my home where I would go to release the excess, but even that was no longer a guarantee."

"That was why you have spent more time away," Arrow stated. "And why you wanted the *Sentinel* modified to use your energy. I couldn't understand why you would want to take a chance of draining your power when it wasn't necessary."

"You still should have told us. We could have helped you," Adalard said stubbornly.

"Emma has done that," Ha'ven admitted. "I feared the darkness that threatened to consume me would frighten her, but the moment she touched me… She is not aware of the power she holds within her body. Her touch soothes me. The magic in her soul calls to mine. She balances me."

Arrow looked thoughtfully at Ha'ven before he slowly nodded. "I've read about that."

Adalard and Ha'ven looked at their younger brother in shock. "You've read about it? Where?" Adalard demanded.

Arrow grinned. "You really should have paid better attention during our lessons. Salvin talked about it continuously for over a month. I wanted to know more so I snuck down to the archives. Took me a week to break into the forbidden section. Salvin had a ton of locks and spells on it. After I was able to get in, it took me another two years to finish reading everything in it."

Adalard rolled his eyes and sank down into the chair next to Ha'ven. "Have you ever even been laid or have you just read about it? I swear you can't have had time."

Arrow flicked his wrist at Adalard, sending a small bolt of power at his twin. Adalard barely had time to catch it before it hit him in the face. His loud curse drew a chuckle from Arrow.

Adalard growled as the shock burst through his body, making his hair stand straight up. His eyes flashed at the amusement in his twin's eyes. He hadn't been expecting the little extra 'pop' in the power-ball.

"Very funny," Adalard grunted as he sent a surge of power to relax his hair.

"I thought so," Arrow replied. "And yes, I have been laid before... more times than you can count."

"Enough," Ha'ven growled out. "What did you learn from the archives?"

Arrow opened his mouth to respond when the door to the conference room opened. Bahadur strode in without waiting for permission to enter. His eyes flashed at the three brothers.

"You startled the shit out of me!" he snapped. "Where in the hell did you come from all of a sudden?"

Ha'ven gritted his teeth and counted. The Curizan general was their best, but he also followed his own rules... which made him the best. He and Bahadur had fought side by side and he respected the other male too much to comment on his lack of respect for authority. It wouldn't do any good anyway. The other male would just agree he totally lacked the respect.

"That is just what we were about to find out," Ha'ven replied in aggravation.

"Good," Bahadur said, walking over to the replicator and ordering a stiff drink. "Then I'm just in time."

Arrow rolled his eyes at Ha'ven and Adalard behind Bahadur's back before he continued.

"I read a scroll in the archives that talked about the 'Joining'. It is said, long ago the Goddess Aikaterina gave the Curizans the ability to harness the energy around them. Each was given a different ability so none would be more powerful than the other except for one. The Goddess gave one Curizan warrior the gift to harness unlimited energy from around him but cautioned him that with that power came great responsibility. She gave him this gift because she was impressed by his courage and honor. He had been willing to sacrifice himself to protect his people. She explained that one must be more powerful than any other if balance and order was to be maintained. But, she cautioned the warrior, that if the power was not balanced within himself, it could destroy the world he had been so willing to give his life to protect. Afraid that the power would corrupt him, she told him he would need to find the one that would balance him. Only when they 'joined' as one would the power stabilize. If left unbalanced, destruction and death would follow. The Goddess, aware that such power needed to also be balanced throughout the star system so that the Curizans could not have absolute control, gave three additional species equal powers but in different forms."

"What are the other three species?" Bahadur asked, leaning forward from where he had taken a seat.

Arrow frowned. "The legend states she gave the Valdier their symbiots. The other species were the Sarafin. She gave them the gift of nine lives."

"That is only two more," Adalard said. "What of the third? Is it us?"

"No," Arrow admitted. "The scroll was torn and the description of the last species was missing."

"Great! A missing species that we have to worry about now," Bahadur muttered. "So, what has all this got to do with you suddenly appearing out of thin air?"

"If my assumption is correct," Arrow said, looking at his older brother with a raised eyebrow. "You are the one who has been gifted with unlimited power. Emma is your balance. When you claimed her, the joining was completed. You have the ability to harness and control unlimited energy. Your desire to be with her, to protect her, allowed you to bend time and space and 'transport' the *Rayon I* to the location where she is being taken."

Bahadur grimaced as he finished his drink and set the glass down on the table with a small thud. "Remind me to never piss you off," he grumbled under his breath.

Ha'ven leaned back in his chair and glared back at his brother. "Why don't I just use this energy to bring her to me?" he demanded. "Shouldn't I just be able to transport her off of the warship and into my arms if I have this unlimited power?"

"I don't know how it works," Arrow grumbled. "Hell, until you did this, I had forgotten about the legend. I would need to read back over the damn thing to figure out how it worked and that is only if they wrote down the damn directions! Gods and Goddesses don't always give specific operating directions, you know. Besides, where were you during Salvin's lessons?"

Adalard and Bahadur grinned. "Chasing the girls with us."

Ha'ven couldn't keep the grin off his face. "It was a hell of a lot more fun than what Salvin was teaching," he admitted before he sobered. "Bahadur, what information do you have?"

Bahadur touched the vidcom and changed it to a cross-section of Razz-ine. "Razzine is made from an old Antrox mining base. The Spaceport was built around it. Kejon has a hidden base located on the other side. In sight of everyone who arrives on Razzine but out of sight as it was located on the unused side of the Spaceport. This is what made it so damn hard to find. No one questioned the ships coming and going," he pointed out. "The Antrox dug tunnels on top of tunnels. I had to dig deep into their database to find the schematics for this one. Luckily, they are organized bastards. I've spent the last three days following one of Kejon's known associates. I would have lost him if not for this map."

Ha'ven leaned forward, staring at where Bahadur had tapped. The enlarged diagram showed the maze of tunnels. Bahadur highlighted the ones that lead into and out of a lower section. His eyes followed it to the remains of an old control room.

"We need to get in there before Kejon arrives," Adalard commented. "I don't think he is just going to leave it unprotected for us."

"I'll take care of his security system," Arrow said. "I can get through any lock or security. That is one of the gifts the Goddess gave me."

"What are some of the others besides being a pain in the ass and a know-it-all?" Adalard asked with a wicked grin.

"I'm a better lover than you," Arrow said, standing up.

"In your dreams," Adalard retorted back with a laugh.

"Not according to Niria, Traya, and Doray," Arrow said as he walked out of the conference room.

"What the…" Adalard said, staring at his brother.

"Aren't those your current lovers?" Bahadur asked. "Too bad, old man. Looks like Arrow sampled them recently," he added as he walked by, slapping Adalard on the shoulder in sympathy.

"Come on," Ha'ven said. "Just remember you can't kill him. Mother wouldn't like it."

"Yeah, but she didn't say anything about me not beating the shit out of him," Adalard grumbled under his breath.

CHAPTER TWENTY-FOUR

*E*mma looked around her in wonder. Her eyes moved to the ceiling, only the ceiling was a brilliant view of the universe. Nebulas in all their magnificent colors lay before her. She thought she had never seen so many stars when she was on the moon, but what she was seeing now stole her breath.

"It is beautiful," a warm, husky voice said from behind her.

Emma turned, startled. "Yes," she stuttered. "Yes, it is."

Emma studied the beautiful creature as it approached her. The figure shimmered, as if made up of gold and diamond dust. A figure became more defined until Emma was able to make out the shape of a tall, elegant woman. Her flowing gold hair matched the shimmering gown she wore. Emma tilted her head and looked up at the woman when she came to a stop in front of her.

"Where am I?" Emma asked softly. "Who are you? Am I dead?"

∾

Aikaterina studied the tiny female standing in front of her. Strength, compassion, and a gentleness radiated from her. A satisfied smile curved her lips. She had chosen well. This species continued to amaze her with their hidden attributes. She may have to revisit their world.

She had sent the touch of her own blood that would give life to the girl's planet long ago. It had taken billions of years, but time was of no consequence to her kind.

Aikaterina was considered a Goddess to those who looked at her. She did not consider herself one based on their beliefs. She simply was...

Her kind traveled through the different star systems, looking for planets with the potential for life. If a world was ready, she would leave a part of herself in the hopes it would grow and nurture life.

She moved with the universes, as much as part of them as the galaxies that made them up. At times, she was moved by a species enough to stop and to interact with it. It is what gave her the sustenance she needed to continue. The recent birth of a Valdier child had pulled her back to this solar system. But, it was the species that made up the worlds that kept her here.

Aikaterina raised her hand and ran it over the heavens. A ripple effect caused the Nebulae to change slightly and additional stars to form. She paused her hand next to a small dot and touched it. A close up image of a Spaceport built into an asteroid appeared.

"I have been called many things by many species," Aikaterina replied. "Here, I go by Aikaterina. I have brought you to a place where you would feel safe." She looked with a mischievous smile at Emma. "And no, you are not dead. That would be an incredible waste and very devastating to the one who has joined with you."

Emma looked from Aikaterina to the image of the asteroid. She stepped closer, frowning when she saw a warship docked to one of the long arms extending from it. She reached up to trace the unusual words on the side and gasped when she suddenly found herself standing inside it.

Men worked at different stations. Some called out to others while others focused on the instruments in front of them. She turned her head when a door opened to one side. Her eyes widened and she gasped as she recognized one of the men coming out of the room.

"Ha'ven," she breathed, stepping forward and reaching out.

"He cannot see or hear you here," Aikaterina replied, looking at the tall male as he talked quietly with another.

"What is happening?" Emma demanded, watching as he walked past her.

"He and the others prepare to come for you," said Aikaterina. "One of his kind has not made a good choice in the use of the gift I have given him. It is up to your male to correct that."

Emma glanced at the shimmering figure. "Why don't you take care of Kejon? If you gave him the power, couldn't you take it away from him?"

Aikaterina shook her head. "I do not interfere in the course a species has chosen. Well, not often," she added so softly Emma almost missed it.

"What do you mean? Not often," Emma asked.

Aikaterina chuckled as she moved alongside Emma. "I felt the shift in power and knew that another from the line of the one I chose long ago carried the ability to harness the powers I gave," she explained. "I was feeling very generous at the time, perhaps a little too generous. For each gift I gave, I created a need within each species for balance. It was important for the power to be shared by another who would be in harmony with their chosen mate. You are the balance to yours. I was not expecting so much power to come from such a young species."

Emma sighed in frustration. "What power? I don't have any power."

"But you do, little one," Aikaterina said, touching Emma's cheek. "Your warrior cried out for you and your heart answered his cry. You are Ha'ven's Song, the only one who can calm the darkness in him.

You do not fear that darkness, but embrace it. Only the one who can balance that darkness with light could do that."

Emma's eyes glistened with tears. She understood what Aikaterina was saying. When she was with Ha'ven she could feel the music inside. He made her want to dance on the clouds and sing to the heavens. He opened her heart and filled her life with warmth and joy, and in his arms she felt strong and safe.

"Do you think he feels any less?" Aikaterina asked tenderly. "He cannot do this alone. He needs you, little one. He needs your love and your strength."

"What should I do?" Emma asked, suddenly frightened of losing Ha'ven.

"Go back," Aikaterina whispered as she and the warship they were on started to fade. "Stand by him, hold him, balance him… love him."

Emma nodded silently. She looked one last time at the strong, determined face of the man she had come to love. She was no longer afraid. She had not traveled this far, gone through so much just to hide. She would not only stand at his side, she would fight beside him.

Emma closed her eyes. She concentrated on the Marastin Dow warship and where she had left her body. She was no longer afraid of the light.

"Praise the Goddess," a female voice whispered when she saw Emma's eyes flutter open. "I thought you were dead."

Emma blinked at the bright light. The female muttered to someone behind her and the lights dimmed. Emma gazed around the room, puzzled before everything came flooding back to her. She looked down and discovered she was covered by a thin blanket.

"Where…," she licked her dry lips. "Where am I?"

"In the medical bay," the female replied. "I am Medic Reddick. That Curizan… Kejon brought your body here almost two hours ago. He stated you just collapsed. We thought he might have..." her voice faded as she looked at the male behind her.

"We were concerned he had harmed you," Captain Tylis finished.

Emma shook her head. "I think he was going to but I... left before he could do anything," she answered, struggling to sit up. "I have to get to the asteroid."

Marus frowned. "How did you know that was where we were going?"

Emma looked up in surprise. "Aikaterina told me. My mate is there."

The female drew in a startled gasp and stared at Emma as if she had just grown another head. Marus gave her a warning glance before he stared in disbelief at Emma. Whatever she had said had shocked both of them from their expressions.

"You... spoke to Aikaterina? You... saw her?" Marus hesitantly asked.

"Yes to both questions," Emma replied.

"Captain," Reddick began, rising out of her seat.

"Not a word, Medic," Marus ordered sternly, shooting her a warning. "What did she say to you?"

"She said I was his balance," Emma said, looking up with a look of hope and excitement. "She said I was his song."

Marus wasn't sure what that meant, but he knew one thing; he would protect the tiny female with his life. She had been chosen by the Goddess herself. He had no doubt about it. He needed to get her onto the Spaceport and away from Kejon.

"If Kejon asks about her, tell him there has been no change," Marus ordered before reaching for Emma. "You will do exactly what I say."

Emma nodded. "What about you? Won't he hurt you for helping me?" she asked as he pulled her out of Medical.

"He can try," Marus muttered before turning and speaking quietly to several men standing outside the door. "How far are we from Razzine?"

"We will be ready to dock within the hour," one of the men replied.

"Kejon will be coming for the female," Marus replied. "Stall him," he ordered as he turned to another. "Get two service suits out and readied. I want clearance from the Spaceport for orbital repairs. Make sure a mobile service bike is readied as well. Ensign Marks, have our friend on the Spaceport ready for my arrival on Level 2."

"Yes, sir," the young male said, saluting.

"Let's go," Marus said grimly.

"Where are we going?" Emma asked as she hurried after him.

"Have you ever space walked before?" he asked her.

Emma stopped, her mouth hanging open at his words. Marus took that to mean 'no'. He grimly bit back the colorful expletive he wanted to say and instead focused on what needed to be done.

The last thing I need now is one very angry Curizan prince on my ass, Marus thought as he stepped into the lift and ordered it to the service level. *I'll be lucky to make it out of this alive.*

CHAPTER TWENTY-FIVE

"Sir, we are receiving an incoming message," one of the Ensigns assigned to communications called out.

"Patch it through," Ha'ven answered as he checked the laser pistol in his hand.

"This is Captain Marus Tylis of the Marastin Dow warship, *Traitor's Run*," a deep voice echoed through.

Ha'ven paused and straightened. "This is Ha'ven Ha'darra. You have my mate," he growled out.

"Yes, I do," the male responded with a heavy sigh. "A fact that will probably get me killed – more than once if that was possible," he added gruffly.

"Where are you?" Ha'ven growled out.

"Ha'ven?" Emma's soft voice suddenly echoed through the room. "Oh, Ha'ven, this is incredible! I never dreamed I would get a chance to be an astronaut! This is unbelievable."

"Where. Are. You?" Ha'ven asked again even as his stomach sank.

"We're riding around outside the Spaceport," Emma replied.

"Why do you have my mate outside the protection of your warship or the Spaceport?" Ha'ven asked with barely restrained rage.

"I'm trying to save her," Marus retorted. "We're heading for Level Two Service Bay Four B. I would appreciate it if you take your fight with that Curizan devil that has commandeered my warship somewhere else. I have my own battles to fight without getting between the two of you."

Ha'ven raised his eyebrow at the Marastin Dow's passionate statement. He looked at Adalard who shrugged his shoulders. His gaze moved to Bahadur, who folded his arms in indifference.

"I've heard rumors there is an uprising with the Marastin Dows who do not agree with the way their world is being ruled. There is talk of a revolution to overthrow the government and establish one that wants a more peaceful society."

"It is more than talk," Marus replied coldly. "We dock in fifteen minutes. I am not sure how long it will take Kejon to discover that I have taken his prize away from him. I don't expect it to be long."

"I think he may have figured it out, unless you were expecting someone else to come with us," Emma's frightened voice echoed.

Ha'ven heard Marus' curse at the same time as their connection was cut. Turning on his heel, he pushed through Adalard and Arrow. His only focus was getting to the Level Two Service Bay. He had a traitor to kill.

"Are you alright?" Marus asked Emma, who clung to his waist as tightly as the oxygen pack on his back allowed.

"Yes," she panted. "Will we make it before he catches up to us?"

"Yes," Marus tightly responded as a new plan came into his mind. "It will be close. I will do what I can to stop him. When we get close to the entrance, I am going to release the service bike. It will crash into the service bay, triggering the automatic shutdown. The doors will seal. You'll only have a few seconds to make it through the opening."

"What happens if I don't make it?" Emma asked in a trembling voice.

"You'll be trapped outside," Marus responded grimly.

"What about you? Where will you be?" she asked.

"I'm going to stop Kejon if I can," he muttered.

"Wait!" Emma started to protest, but Marus already had her arm grasped firmly in his.

She screamed as he kicked away from the service bike as they neared the entrance to the service bay. The doors were beginning to lower for their arrival. She watched as the service bike continued forward, colliding with the huge metal doors. Flashing lights on the outside of the doors flared as it detected the impact. The doors ground to a stop before they began rising again. They continued floating toward the doors.

Emma's eyes widened in terror as she noticed the rapidly shrinking space between the doors. Marus bumped against the doors. She saw him scramble to grab a service ladder.

"I'm going to push you through. When the doors close, the bay will fill with oxygen. Get out of your suit and get the hell out of the bay. My man inside will guide you to the main Level. Lose yourself in the crowd," he ordered as he pulled her closer.

"What are you going to do?" she asked as he held her.

"Try not to get myself killed," he growled as he pushed her quickly through the narrow space.

Emma floated upside down for a moment as she tumbled through the doors. She barely had time to catch a glimpse of the Marastin Dow captain before she felt herself falling to the floor below. She hit the floor hard and fell backwards. She rolled onto her knees just as another figure rushed toward her.

Hands grabbed her helmet and twisted it. A moment later a grim purple face was revealed. The male didn't speak. He quickly loosened the straps holding her suit on so he could pull it over her head.

"Come on," he ordered.

Emma stumbled over the bottom of the suit as he pulled her behind him. She bit her lip at the pain in her left ankle. She had landed hard on it and it burned.

"Captain Tylis said…" she began as she was pushed into a narrow lift.

"I know what he said," the male grunted out. "Push the top button and disappear into the crowds of the Spaceport. I hope you are worth it. He is one of our finest commanders. If he dies, thousands of others may die as well."

Emma didn't say another word. The man's eyes glowed with anger as he glared at her. He reached in and slapped his hand over the button before stepping back again. Emma leaned back as the door closed and the lift rose at a sickening speed.

Ha'ven, Emma whispered silently.

I will meet you when the lift opens, Ha'ven replied. *We need to draw Kejon out. It is time to end this.*

Emma lowered her head and squeezed her eyes shut. She refused to cry. Raising her head as the lift began to slow, she tumbled out of it as the doors opened and straight into Ha'ven's strong arms. Her arms wound instinctively around his neck and she pressed her face into his neck breathing in his familiar scent.

"I knew you would come for me," she whispered. "I love you."

Ha'ven's body trembled as he held her close. His arms were wrapped as tightly around her as he could without crushing her. He never wanted to be separated from her again.

"I swear I have come closer to losing my sanity since I met you than ever before," he grounded out harshly. He pulled back so he could stare down into her beautiful blue eyes. "You drive me crazy."

"That's a good thing, isn't it?" she teased in a trembling voice. "Captain Tylis...."

"I know," Ha'ven replied. "Arrow has gone to help him."

"Ha'ven, we need to move," Adalard said urgently. "Arrow said Kejon has broken off. He is heading for the other side of the asteroid. He won't have much oxygen or power so he will be forced to land."

"If we are going to take him, we need to do this now," Bahadur added. "Personally, I'm going to enjoy killing the bastard."

Ha'ven didn't reply. He breathed in a deep breath once more before he reluctantly stepped back. He retained his hold on Emma's hand before he turned with a nod.

The four of them moved with ease through the crowded corridors of the Spaceport. One look at the expressions on the faces of the three Curizan warriors was enough to have even the toughest inhabitant stepping aside.

CHAPTER TWENTY-SIX

*K*ejon roared out in rage as he threw the helmet of the spacesuit across the large empty room. He was going to kill the entire traitorous crew of the Marastin Dow. He had pulled the truth out of the traitorous bitch that had lied to him in the medical unit. She had fought like a Sarafin bitch in heat. His face still stung from her nails. She had resisted until the end. Only as she drew in her last breath did she finally break, spilling the truth of Tylis' deception.

He had still been too late to stop the arrogant Captain from taking the Prince's bitch. The one advantage, the one power, the one tool he needed to ensure Ha'darra's destruction, was gone. He had no other choice but to retreat for now. With his one advantage gone, and the Marastin Dow's warship no longer at his disposal, he would have to use the smaller transport he had hidden.

"I should have killed the female when I had the chance," he muttered. "None of this would have happened if Aria had done her job in the first place and killed Ha'darra instead of playing with him."

"But she didn't kill me," Ha'ven replied coldly as he stepped out of the door leading out to the Spaceport. "And soon you'll join her in death."

Kejon stopped in the middle of the open control room. Nothing remained in the room. The Antrox had dismantled and removed all the equipment when the mine was no longer profitable. He glanced at the door that led to the emergency launch bay. Bahadur stood in the doorway leading to it, a dark grin on his face and a bundle of wires in his hand.

"It would seem your transport is missing a few necessary wires from the control panel," Bahadur smirked.

Hatred burned in Kejon's eyes as he stared at the man Ben'qumain had trusted at one time. His stomach twisted at the knowledge that he had been tricked as well. He should have known never to trust anyone.

"You traitor," Kejon hissed. "You are..."

"General Razdar Bahadur at your service," Bahadur replied. "Loyal servant and protector to the Royal House of Ha'darra and Prince Ha'ven of Curizan."

A choked laugh drew Kejon's eyes to the doorway near Ha'ven. Adalard Ha'darra stood with a savage smile on his face. The muscles pulled tight over the long scar on his face.

"I'll have to remember the remark about you being a servant, Bahadur," he commented humorously before his eyes narrowed on Kejon. "You missed killing me as well, Kejon."

Kejon paled as he took a step back, his hand moving to the laser pistol at his side. His eyes darted from one male to the next before finally settling on the small pale female standing slightly behind Ha'ven. Madness flashed through his mind as he realized he was trapped.

Power had been within his grasp and now it was gone. He had held it in his arms. The pale slip of a female had escaped, leading him on a path of self-destruction. It was her fault. If she had just been another of Ha'darra's whores, it wouldn't have mattered, but she was something more. He could feel the power in her. If she had submitted to him instead of making him believe she was dying, he could have claimed that power for himself. He should have killed her when he had the chance instead of taking the chance on Ha'darra reclaiming her.

Grim determination filled him as a new plan formed. He could still destroy Ha'ven Ha'darra. He would not live to enjoy it, but he would know he had succeeded. He could kill most of the ruling family and their faithful, traitorous servant at the same time. He fingered the pistol in his hand, switching the power to full at the same time as he focused the power inside his body.

"I may have missed you once, but I won't this time," Kejon hissed out.

His eyes flashed to Bahadur who was now eyeing him with a wary caution. A nasty smile twisted his lips before his gaze rested on Ha'ven Ha'darra. Triumph flooded him when the female stepped closer to Ha'darra and threaded her fingers with the Curizan Prince.

"So sweet," he retorted savagely. "The Prince and his mate. Together in life and in death."

Wild laughter escaped Kejon as he threw the overloaded laser pistol up into the air above his head and directed the full force of his power into it. A bright flash lit up the control room before the explosion of over-charged particles sent out a shockwave as it exploded. The super-heated charge incinerated Kejon within seconds, even as the over-heated wave stretched out to engulf the room.

Ha'ven yelled out a warning as he realized what Kejon was planning. Bahadur jerked open the door behind him and fell to the floor of the outer room before slamming the heavy metal door shut with his foot. Even so, the door glowed a bright red as the overheated charge hit it.

Adalard rushed forward to protect his brother and Emma as the wave flashed toward them. At the same time, Emma and Ha'ven raised their joined hands at the on-coming wave. A shield formed around the three of them, protecting them as the wave and subsequent shock wave rolled around them.

"What the …?" Adalard murmured in a shocked voice as he watched the rock walls of the room glow a brilliant red from the superheated air. "How…?"

Adalard turned to look at his brother and Emma. Both were glowing brightly, Ha'ven with black bands with red and gold threading through it and Emma with a host of colors laced with a touch of the black. His eyes widened as Emma's colors wove in and out of the black of his brother's essence, almost as if she were dancing with him.

Ha'ven breathed deeply as the powerful explosion and super-heated air slowly pushed against the shield he and Emma had created. His power had risen immediately when he sensed his mate was in mortal danger. His only thought was to protect her. The dark mist of power inside him rose as if it was a living thing inside him. That was the second time he had felt as if another entity was inside him.

When he feared losing control, he had felt Emma's calming influence as her essence wrapped with him. He knew the moment her powers blended with his own. His mind cleared and strength flooded him as it did only when she touched him.

He turned and watched as Emma stood looking out over the room. Her face creased in concentration as her power expanded outward. The fierce determination on it drew a smile to his face.

She is absolutely beautiful, he thought in awe.

He waited as Emma's colors reached out, expanding and cooling the room until the walls once again were a dull gray. Only then did he lower his arm and calm the power burning inside him.

Emma still glowed as she continued to focus. He couldn't resist brushing his fingers through the colorful array still swirling around her. Warmth and peace flooded him.

"I love you, my Emma," he whispered as she slowly blinked. "You are truly a gift from the Goddess."

Emma started as she realized that they were no longer in danger. She blinked several times before looking up at Ha'ven in confusion. Her eyes darted around the room before she looked up again.

"What did you say?" she asked.

Ha'ven chuckled as he brushed his fingers along her cheek. "I said you are truly a gift from the Goddess. One I will be thankful for every day of our lives."

Emma's eyes widened before she giggled. "You have no idea," she murmured before she threw her arms around his neck and clung to him. "Can we go home now?"

Ha'ven lifted her in his arms and squeezed her tightly against his chest. "Anything for you, *misha petite*. Anything for you," he repeated before he pressed a kiss to her lips.

Adalard looked at his brother and Emma for a moment before he rolled his eyes. "I'll just go see if Bahadur is alive. No need to stop what you are doing. I can handle this on my own. I'm sure he is alive, so no need to worry about him," he said dryly before shaking his head in disgust. "Love! It is a good thing I'm immune to that," he muttered as he strode across the empty control room.

CHAPTER TWENTY-SEVEN

*H*a'ven ignored the stares as he carried Emma through the narrow corridors and back to where the *Rayon 1* was docked. His arms tightened protectively around her slender body as several traders looked greedily at her hair and pale complexion. Two of them collapsed in a heap on the dirty floor as he walked by. Ha'ven raised his eyebrow at Adalard and Bahadur.

"We didn't like the way they were looking at her," both men responded with a grin.

"Besides, I was really hoping to kill someone and Kejon took that pleasure away," Adalard said.

"You killed those two men?" Emma asked, shocked.

Adalard glanced down at Emma's pale face. "No, little one, we just stunned them," he assured her, shooting a warning look at Bahadur.

"Yes, just stunned them," Bahadur agreed hurriedly. "What are your plans now, Ha'ven? There are still traitors. Kejon was only one on the list we have gathered. Do you wish for me to go after the others?"

Ha'ven rounded the corner leading to the lift that would take them down to the docking bays. He stepped into it as the doors opened. Once the doors closed behind him, he turned and replied to Bahadur's question.

"Yes, I want you and Arrow to strike them hard," Ha'ven replied grimly. "I will not take a chance of them trying to kill my mate again. Arrow will need to transfer over to your transport. I will need Adalard and the *Rayon I.*"

"Are we returning to Ceran-Pax?" Adalard asked, startled.

"No, there is one place we must go before we can return home," Ha'ven replied.

He stepped out of the lift as the doors opened. Striding up the long access tunnel, he quickly gave a nod to the Ensign on duty. He nodded to Bahadur, who bowed briefly before heading off in the opposite direction to his transport.

Ha'ven continued down the long access bridge that connected the *Rayon I* to the docking station. He stepped onto the warship and continued until he came to the lift that would take him up to his quarters. Adalard scooted in behind him before the doors closed.

"Are you going to tell me where you are taking my warship?" Adalard asked in exasperation. "It helps my navigation crew if I can give them directions."

"We are going to Emma's world," Ha'ven responded. "I need you to contact Creon and ask him for the location of her planet."

"You… we…," Emma whispered, looking up, stunned at Ha'ven's hard face. "Why?"

Ha'ven didn't reply. He stepped out of the lift, leaving a stunned Adalard behind to follow through with his orders. He didn't speak again until they were enclosed in his living quarters. Only when he had her safely alone did he release the tight control he had kept on his emotions.

He gently set her down onto her feet but pulled her back into his arms. His body trembled with relief at having her safe again. He threaded his fingers through her long hair and claimed her lips in a desperate attempt to wash away the last of his fear.

"I love you, Emma," he whispered hoarsely. "I did not know fear until you came into my life. I did not understand what it was like to live in warmth until you touched me."

"Then why are you taking me to my world?" she asked in a small voice. "Are you… are you going to leave me there?"

"No!" Ha'ven swore hotly. "No, my Emma. I thought… hoped…" he breathed out in frustration as he tilted her chin up so she had to look into his eyes. "I do not want you to ever regret or have doubts about staying with me. I know you feel guilty about leaving your mother behind. I want to meet her. To let her know that you will always be cared for and loved."

Emma's eyes glittered with tears at the unselfish gift he was giving her. Unable to speak, she pressed her lips to his to let him know that he had given her a priceless gift – his unconditional love. Their lips connected with increasing passion.

"I want you," he said thickly. "I need you."

"As I need you," she whispered against his lips.

Ha'ven's lips curved and with a wave of his hand, they stood naked in the middle of his shower unit. Warm water fell around them like rain as he pressed kisses along her jaw, his hands sliding around her to lift her higher.

"I could really get used to that," she breathed out. "I love you, Ha'ven Ha'darra."

Ha'ven's heart swelled as he pressed her against the wall of the shower. "I want to touch you," he demanded in a husky voice.

Emma leaned back against the wall to give him room to explore. He was held mesmerized as he moved his hands tenderly over her sensitive skin. The feel of his calloused hands was slightly rough against the smoothness of her skin.

He leaned back so he could look down at her body. Her breasts were softly rounded, her rose-colored nipples taut with desire. His mouth watered at the thought of sucking on them.

Pouring a small amount of the cleansing liquid into his palms, he rubbed them over her shoulders and down over her breasts. He loved the way she moaned and arched into his hands. He cupped the slight weight of her breasts in his hands and ran his thumbs over the distended tips.

"Ha'ven," Emma moaned, rocking her hips back and forth to the rhythm of his touch.

"Soon, my Emma," he answered in a passion-laden voice. "Soon. I need to touch you."

Ha'ven continued his exploration across her smooth belly before kneeling before her. His hands rested for a moment as he thought of what it would be like to see her swell with his young. A sharp pain of longing swept through him.

Was this what Creon and Vox felt when they held their mates? he wondered distractedly. *Did they feel the same desire to see their mates with young the way he was feeling right now?*

For the first time, he was envious of what his friends had. Leaning forward, he pressed a kiss to Emma's stomach. His eyes closed briefly as she wound her hands in his hair and held him close.

Opening his eyes, he let his hot breath caress the soft curls covering her womanhood. His fingers massaged the cleansing liquid through them even as the warm water rinsed it away. His fingers slipped between her legs, opening her to his touch. Her hips bucked as he bent forward and nipped the soft mound.

"I want you," Emma cried out.

"And so you shall have me," Ha'ven muttered as he spread her lips.

Hot moisture touched his tongue as her essence responded to his touch. The slickness had nothing to do with the water or the cleansing liquid and everything to do with her need. He pushed his fingers deep into her vaginal channel, loving the way she clenched around him.

His tongue lapped at her swollen nub, teasing and stimulating it until she shattered in his mouth. He drank greedily from her. Her soft cries wrapping around his cock like a hard fist. With a loud curse, he rose and turned her until she was facing the wall of the shower. He pulled her hips out and aligned his aching shaft with her swollen channel. Holding her around the waist with one arm, he braced his other hand against the wall as he drove deeply into her.

A shudder coursed through him as he stretched her hot walls. She tightly gripped him, still pulsing from her orgasm. It was as if she was holding his shaft in her slender hands, squeezing and pumping him at the same time.

With a wave of his hand, they were in his bed, his body still attached to hers. She was on her hands and knees, bracing against the weight of him as he leaned over her. He pulled her hips back against him.

"I will never get enough of you," he breathed out as he drove into her over and over.

"I… Ha'ven…" Emma tried to speak, but all she could do was lean forward, spreading her legs further for him.

Ha'ven looked down between them, watching as his shaft disappeared into her. Over and over again, he watched the exotic sight as he bound them together as one. His balls drew up until he thought they might burst, but still he fought to hold back so he could enjoy the beauty of their joining. He watched as the black bands swirled from his fingers where he gripped her. His breath caught when her body shuddered as the warm bands wrapped around her.

"The joining," he whispered.

The bands slid over her shoulders to cup her breasts. More bands wrapped around her hips, circling her thighs and up along the line of her ass. Her own colors rose to dance along the bands. His breath exploded out of him as they reached out, encasing him. His head fell backwards as his hips jerked forward, his seed spilling deep inside her.

"Goddess!" he cried out.

A golden light filled the room and for a moment, Ha'ven could have sworn that he saw the universe spread open before him, the golden shimmer of the beginning of time smiling down on him and his mate before he collapsed over Emma's limp form.

"Thank you," he whispered. "Thank you for bringing her into my life," he said as he pulled Emma back against his chest and wrapped his arms protectively around her.

You're welcome, my brave Curizan warrior, Aikaterina whispered as she looked down at the sleeping couple.

CHAPTER TWENTY-EIGHT

*E*mma stood wrapped in the warmth of Ha'ven's arms. Silent tears coursed down her cheeks as she looked at the headstone in front of her. They had arrived on Earth several days before. She had been excited and nervous at the same time.

Creon, Kelan, and Trisha had talked to Ha'ven and Adalard about Paul's ranch in Wyoming. Trisha had told them that only a few humans were aware of what had truly happened. She had asked them to meet with Mason Andrews, her dad's ranch manager and Chad Morrison, his childhood friend and attorney who was managing the financial side of the ranch.

"I'd like for you to check in and make sure everything is okay," Trisha had asked. "Tell them dad is happy and that Carmen, Ariel, and I are all safe and well. Mason and Chad are aware of where dad is and will help you if you need anything."

Ha'ven had left Adalard to meet with the men while he and Emma had traveled to a place called Long Beach, California to retrieve her mother. He told Adalard that they would be a few days as Emma wanted to pick up a few personal belongings to bring back with her. They had traveled to her home first and spent two days packing and transporting the items back to the warship before she was ready to go get her mother.

"I want her to have familiar things around her when we pick her up," Emma had explained when he asked her if she wanted to see her mom first. "The doctors say it helps patients with Alzheimer's settle more quickly if they are surrounded by familiar things from when they were younger. She loves looking at the photographs of my father. I also have some of his records that were converted to CDs and some home videos. I wanted to get my Hope Chest as well. Momma was filling it for when I got married. There are some things that have been in our family for generations," she added.

It had been a shock when they arrived at the nursing home. One of the nurses who knew Emma stopped her in the corridor outside her mother's room. The woman looked at Emma in surprise.

"Miss Watson!" the nurse had exclaimed. "We were told you had been kil..." her voice faded as she suddenly realized Emma wasn't alone. "Oh!"

Emma smiled softly. "Hi Peggy, as you can see, I wasn't killed. I was kidnapped. Ha'ven, my husband, rescued me. I would like to check my mother out. We are going to be taking her home to live with us."

Peggy Mills looked at Emma in shock before a sympathetic expression filled her eyes. "Didn't anyone tell you? Your mother passed away in her sleep almost a month ago."

Emma swayed in shock. "No," she whispered as grief washed through her. "I...," she closed her eyes and leaned back against Ha'ven as he wrapped his arms around her. "Oh God!"

Emma turned in Ha'ven's arms and buried her face. Hot tears poured down her cheeks as she thought of her beautiful, gentle mother. Sorrow that she had not been there at the end for her mother tore at Emma.

Peggy timidly stepped closer and rested her hand on Emma's shoulder. "She wasn't alone," Peggy said. "I had stayed late that night. She wanted me to read a letter she had written to you. I was reading it to her when she passed away peacefully in her sleep. I have the letter." Peggy quickly walked back to the nurse's station.

Emma turned to face Peggy as she returned with a small box. Emma reached for the box with trembling hands. Her mother's life was in this small container, everything that she had become at the end of her life. Emma choked out a soft thank you as Ha'ven guided her back out the doors of the nursing home.

"I am so sorry, my Emma," Ha'ven whispered, pain at not being able to prevent the sorrow from touching her pulling at him. "I am glad that we came back. You will be able to say goodbye."

Emma nodded, biting her lip as more tears flowed down her pale cheeks. Ha'ven helped her into the small car that she had left behind before her trip to South America. She stared out the window as she quietly directed Ha'ven to the cemetery where her mother would have been laid to rest next to her father.

Ha'ven was silent during the drive. He held her hand as he drove the strange but simple transport through the tree-lined streets. They turned into the long narrow drive cutting through the manicured graveyard. Headstones stood as silent sentinels to those who had died.

"Stop here," Emma murmured thickly.

Ha'ven parked the car and turned it off. He climbed out and walked around to Emma's door, opening it for her and helping her out. She carried the small box in her arms as she walked along the narrow path between the graves.

Under a tall tree stood a simple headstone. On it were the names of Alice and Fred Watson with the dates of their births and deaths. Emma knelt in front of it and opened the small box.

On top was a small picture frame of her mom, dad, and her when she was little. She pulled it out and ran her fingers along the glass protecting it. She laid it against the headstone.

"I love you, Momma. Poppa, she's come home to dance with you again," Emma drew in a ragged breath before she continued. "I want you both to meet Ha'ven. I love him. He makes me want to sing and dance on the clouds when he holds me," she whispered. "Just like you did for Momma, Poppa. I... I... won't be back, but I want you to know I love you both very much and you were the best parents any girl could wish for." Emma put the lid back on the box and smiled weakly at Ha'ven when he bent to help her back up.

She stood wrapped in Ha'ven's warm embrace and sighed. She leaned back against him and lifted her eyes to the soft clouds that floated by for several minutes before she nodded. It was time to go home. She had nothing left here to hold her. Her home was now on a world far, far away.

"I'm ready," she murmured.

Ha'ven kept his arm wrapped around her waist as he guided her back to the car. Once she was settled in, he walked around to the driver's side. He waited until he had turned back onto the main road before he spoke.

"We will return to Paul's ranch tonight," he said. "Is there anything else you would like to do before we leave?"

Emma shook her head. "I would like to talk to Chad Morrison," she said thickly. "I want to sign whatever paperwork is necessary to sell everything here. Momma and Poppa," she stopped when emotions overcame her again. "Momma and Poppa left me very well off. I want to set up a foundation in their names to help children around the world discover art, dance, and music. Chad should be able to do that for me."

Ha'ven squeezed Emma's hand. "You are a very special person, my Emma," he said quietly. "I will always be thankful that you have chosen me as your mate."

Emma gave a strained laugh as she brushed the tears that continued to fall. "Aikaterina said that I was your balance. She told me to stand by you, hold you, balance you... and love you," she replied, laying her head back against the headrest and looking at him. "I do, you know...

love you. Not only that, you balance me. When you touch me, I feel safe. I feel like I could dance on the clouds."

Ha'ven saw the new tears spill from her eyes and pulled over to the side of the road. He put the car in park and leaned over to kiss her. He brushed the tears from her cheeks before a frown creased his brow.

"Wait a minute," he said as the name she mentioned suddenly sunk in. "Aikaterina? The Goddess Aikaterina? The ...."

"She is very sweet and beautiful," Emma said. "I liked her."

"Goddess!" Ha'ven muttered, looking at Emma in awe. "She did send you to me."

"Of course," Emma said with a tender smile. "She knew we needed each other."

"Let's go home," he muttered as the scope of the gift given to him hit home.

Emma nodded, suddenly feeling lighter. Her eyes lifted to look at the clouds above and for just a moment, she thought she saw the golden figures of her parents dancing together on one of the clouds.

Thank you, Aikaterina, Emma said silently, knowing deep down the Goddess was trying to ease her sorrow.

You are welcome, child, came the soft reply.

CHAPTER TWENTY-NINE

*H*a'ven watched as his mother embraced Emma in a fierce hug. They had arrived back on Ceran-Pax early this morning. He and Emma had spent the journey back learning more about each other.

He discovered his power, when joined with hers, was beyond anything he had ever thought possible. They had locked themselves in one of the lower storage bays and he had created a world just for the two of them. Not to be outdone, Emma had created a few illusions of her own. They had made love in tall meadows and in a crystal dome under the sea. They had flown through the air on the backs of giant birds and they had danced across the clouds on a starlit night.

Emma sang songs her father had taught her and she told him of her life. He had slowly drawn from her what happened during her captivity and held her as she cried. Afterwards, he had made slow, tender love to her on the clouds they had created together. That was the night he had given her his seed and felt it spark to life deep inside her.

It was a magical time for him. He finally understood what Creon meant when he said Carmen filled his life. Emma filled his to over-flowing.

His eyes softened as she looked over at him with a small, relieved smile. Her soft laughter filled the air as his father pulled her into his arms for a fierce hug. Her face glowed with her essence, the colors bursting out in a vivid array that warmed his heart.

Emma had been terrified when he told her his parents were looking forward to meeting her shortly before they left the *Rayon I*. He remembered how she had clung to him with her face buried in his chest.

"What if they don't like me?" she had mumbled. "What if…"

He had silenced her doubts with his lips, his love for her overflowing as he buried his fingers in her hair. He kissed her over and over until they were both breathless and trembling with need.

"They will love you as I do," he promised her.

"Do you really think so? I'm not like your species," she whispered as doubts filled her mind. "What if they…"

He kissed her again, letting her know she had no reason to doubt him. It was only when Adalard had growled at him that they needed to leave that he had pulled away. He looked at his brother's sour face and frowned.

"What is your problem? You have been in a bad mood ever since we left Emma's planet," Ha'ven growled back.

Adalard grimaced and looked away. "Nothing. I just have a lot on my mind," he said. "If you are ready, Mom and Melek are waiting."

"We're ready," Ha'ven said, sliding his arm around Emma's waist. "Adalard," he said quietly as he paused in the doorway.

"What?" Adalard said, looking defiantly back at his older brother.

"If you need assistance, I will help," Ha'ven replied quietly.

Adalard's face flushed. He glanced at Emma who was watching the exchange in silence before he shrugged. He looked back at his older brother with a crooked smile.

"I can handle this," Adalard said quietly.

Ha'ven studied his brother for a moment before he nodded.

"Ha'ven," Narissa said, looking at him with tears in her eyes. "She is absolutely beautiful."

Emma blushed as she looked at Ha'ven with bright eyes. His own darkened with desire as he saw the flush that touched her cheeks. He was remembering how she looked earlier when she was riding him.

Ha'ven! Emma's voice whispered through his mind.

"I think I deserve a kiss from my new sister-in-law," Arrow said mischievously as he swung a distracted Emma around and into his arms. "Oh yes, at least one kiss."

Emma opened her mouth to protest and found her lips covered by a set of warm firm ones. No sooner had his lips touched hers, that she found herself standing in Ha'ven's strong arms. She looked at the tall, muscular man who was lying on his back on the ground.

"Damn, you are getting the hang of those new powers of yours," Arrow said with a good-humored grin as he picked himself up off the ground.

"You'll find yourself six feet under the ground if you try to kiss my mate again," Ha'ven growled in a dark tone. "This one is off limits, Arrow."

"I know that," Arrow said as he studied his older brother. "I just wanted to see what colors your and Emma's essence changed to when you were upset. I'm working on a new theory."

"I swear, Jazar," Narissa sighed. "You and your theories. Come Emma, let me show you your new home."

"You know you are in trouble when she uses your real name," Melek muttered under his breath. "So, what did you find?"

"Emma essence definitely is needed to increase Ha'ven's power," Arrow said, rubbing his ass. "By the way, can you hit me a little softer the next time?"

"I wasn't kidding about the six feet under, Arrow," Ha'ven replied. "Keep your hands, lips, and experiments off my mate."

"Possessive characteristics," Arrow observed with a grin. "I'll have to add that as well."

"You're such a jerk sometimes, Arrow," Adalard said as he walked by.

Arrow looked at his twin's sour face before looking back at Ha'ven. "Who stuck a rod up his ass? Has he been hanging with Zoran again?"

"No." Ha'ven watched Adalard disappear down the path leading to his living quarters. "I'm not sure what happened. He has been like this ever since we met up with him on Paul Grove's ranch back on Earth. I finally had to tell him to take a break on the *Rayon I*. He was working himself and his crew into the ground."

Melek turned to look at Ha'ven. "Tell me what happened with Kejon."

"Yeah!" Arrow said. "By the way, Crom and I rescued that Marastin Dow captain. The guy didn't even give us a 'thank you' before he and his crew disappeared."

Ha'ven sighed as he realized he wasn't going to be able to escape with Emma any time soon. His eyes drifted back to his mother and his mate. His heart warmed when he saw his mother tuck a strand of Emma's hair behind her ear as she talked with her. He had definitely found his miracle.

Narissa smiled as she listened to Emma describing the gardens back on Valdier. When she had first heard that her oldest son had taken a mate from a different species, she had been concerned. She knew that some females would do whatever they could to entice or trap one of her sons. After all, they were not only royalty, but they were very powerful warriors.

"How did you and my son meet?" Narissa asked curiously.

Emma bent to pick up a fallen bud off the ground. She gently touched it with the tips of her fingers. Her eyes glowed with happiness as she thought of their first meeting.

"It was in the dining room at the palace," Emma said softly. "I was… not well. Sara, another human girl, and I were sitting at the table. Suddenly, I felt like someone had sent a huge shock through me. When I looked up, Ha'ven was standing in the doorway looking at me."

"It felt the same way when Melek and I saw each other for the first time," Narissa said with a grin. "You must have been very excited to have captured his attention. He is a very handsome and powerful man."

"Actually, I didn't want anything to do with him," Emma admitted, blushing. "He kept trying to feed me. It made me mad. I left, but he followed me, thank goodness."

Narissa stopped and looked down at Emma's bowed head. "Why? What happened?"

Emma looked up at Narissa before her eyes turned to search for Ha'ven. *I am close, my Emma.*

I just needed to know, she whispered back.

Emma glanced back up at Narissa before she continued to walk slowly along the path. "I told you I wasn't well. I had been hurt… very badly back on my world. Creon Reykill and his men saved Sara and me. I… had given up on life. If Ha'ven hadn't been there…," Emma's voice faded as she thought back to those dark days of her life.

"I will always be there to catch you, *misha petite*," Ha'ven's strong voice said as he walked up behind her and wrapped his arms around her waist. "Emma was lost in a dream of dancing with her father," he explained to his mother. "She almost slipped over the side of the cliff. I caught her and kissed her," he said huskily.

"Yeah," Arrow said with a grin. "Then she kneed him really hard according to Adalard."

Emma groaned in embarrassment and buried her face in Ha'ven's chest. She hadn't planned on telling Ha'ven's mother that part. She peeked up as Melek and Narissa chuckled.

"Narissa did the same thing to me when I kissed her the first time," Melek admitted.

"You did?" Emma breathed out in surprise as she looked at Ha'ven's mother.

"Yes, I did," Narissa chuckled. "He deserved it. He was very arrogant."

"Wow," Emma said, looking up at Ha'ven. "You are just like your dad."

Ha'ven chuckled as he swept Emma up into his arms. "You are damn right and you better never forget it," he growled out. "We will join the rest of you later this evening."

Narissa watched as Ha'ven carried his tiny mate down the path. She sighed, a smile curving her lips as Melek wrapped his arm around her. Arrow snorted and shook his head.

"I doubt we'll see them for a few days," he commented. "If my calculations are correct, the glow of their entwined auras is saying he has serious plans and it is all horizontal. Oh, and she's breeding," he added with a tilt of his head.

Narissa rolled her eyes and looked at Melek who was shaking his head. "Arrow," Melek said quietly. "One of these days your observations are going to get you into big trouble."

Arrow grinned and shrugged his shoulder. "As long as it isn't the same as what Adalard is having, I think I can handle it. Now, did someone say food?" he asked with a grin.

Melek chuckled before he and Arrow walked down the path back to the main rooms. Narissa ignored them. She knew they would be talking about the shortening list of traitors soon enough. Her eyes focused on the path that her oldest son and his mate had taken before she smiled.

"I am finally going to have a grandchild," she whispered, happily.

"Ha'ven," Emma whispered as he laid her in the middle of his bed.

"I'm going to love you, in our home, in our bed," he said quietly. With a wave of his hand, they were both undressed.

Emma raised her arms and ran her palms over his shoulders as he leaned over her. Her eyes darkened with desire as she felt the muscles bulge under her palms. It never ceased to amaze her, that strength in his lean body. Her eyes rose to meet his. Violet flames stared back at her.

"I want to dance for you," she whispered.

Ha'ven groaned and buried his hot lips along her throat. "Dance... later," he murmured.

"No, dance... now," she insisted. "There is a song I've written for you. I want to show you what you have done for me."

A shudder ran through his body as he heard the passionate desire to do something for him. Pulling back, he rolled until he was lying on his back next to her.

"I'm not sure how long I'll last," he warned her. "Your power and mine are causing havoc inside me right now."

Emma chuckled as she leaned over and brushed a kiss across his lips as her hand ran down over his chest to his stomach. She loved it when he sucked in his breath as she dipped a little lower.

"Five minutes. I promise," she said with a husky laugh.

Ha'ven watched as she slid out of the bed. He sat up. With a wave of his hand, additional pillows formed behind him as he leaned back and crossed his arms. He looked at her wickedly when her eyes widened as his cock bobbed up and down.

"You are doing that on purpose," she accused, watching as his cock grew even harder and thicker as she watched.

"Four minutes, thirty-eight seconds," he growled back.

Emma rolled her eyes before she focused inward. She was still learning how to control the powers that Ha'ven said she had. Personally, she thought the powers belonged to him, but she was willing to try. She imagined a sheer white gown flowing around her. It had thin strands of violet and was strapless.

She opened her eyes in triumph, her hands spreading the beautiful sheer material. Her head jerked up when she heard the low growl that rumbled through the room. Ha'ven's eyes were blazing with desire.

"Four minutes," he bit out hoarsely.

Emma bit her lip, wondering if she was being foolish. With a shake of her head, she focused again. Pulling on the power inside her, she let the melody in her head float in the air. As the music played softly, she looked deeply into Ha'ven's eyes and sang from her heart and soul.

Her body moved gracefully across the room to the beat. She sang of hope, discovery, and coming back to life. Ha'ven's song poured from her soul to his. The colors of her aura flowed around her, making her appear to float as she twirled and dipped.

Ha'ven's mouth went dry as the words poured over him. His heart beat with the rhythm and his own aura rose to capture hers as she floated by him. His hand rose to brush through the colors. Warmth and awe filled him as he felt the power held within it.

He reached out, capturing her hand as she stepped closer as the words faded. The music continued to play in the background as he drew her closer. He brushed his free hand over the sheer gown, making it dissolve as he brought her up against his chest.

"Time's up," he whispered.

Emma leaned forward, pressing her lips to his in an explosive kiss. Her hands cupped his face as she pressed him back against the pillows. She arched into him as his hands gripped her hips, lifting her up.

"I love you, Ha'ven," she choked out as she pressed kisses to his lips. "I love you so much."

"Emma, *misha petite*," he groaned out and pushed his legs apart, causing hers to spread as he slowly impaled her on his throbbing shaft. "Yes, my mate. Yes."

Only the music and their broken whispers filled the air as they came together. The magic of the music, still flowing from their combined powers, twisted and danced, joining in an unbreakable bond as Emma and Ha'ven came together again and again. Caught within the strands was a new glittering gold that sparkled like diamonds. Aikaterina laughed softly as she sprinkled a little of her life blood into the mix.

"A special gift for your child," she whispered before she faded away, leaving the two lovers wrapped in each other's arms.

CHAPTER THIRTY

 ive months later:

"I told you, she is staying with me of her own free will," Ha'ven snarled out. "Why do you need to speak with her? Don't you believe me?"

"No!" Four male voices said in unison.

Ha'ven glared at Creon who shrugged his shoulders and replied. "Not really. You've been known to stretch the truth a time or two."

"Stretching the truth is not a flat out lie," Ha'ven growled back. "I have never flat out lied to you."

Creon's eyebrow rose. "It is getting close to the end of your six months. Each of us has a mate who will roast our asses if we can't swear to them that the human female is safe, sound, and with you because she wants to be," he said, sitting forward. "You know what Carmen is like, Ha'ven. Give me something to prove to her that the female wants to stay with you or I'm likely to be sleeping on the couch for the next five hundred years or more."

"Cara threatened to leave the girls alone with me for a week," Trelon said. "Look at this!" he demanded, holding up a chewed leather boot in one hand. "This is the third one Jade has chewed through today! I swear her teething is going to ruin all of my boots."

"What happened to your hair?" Ha'ven asked, puzzled when he saw Trelon's closely cut hair. It looked more like the military cut that Vox and the Sarafin favored.

Zoran leaned forward with a grin. "Between Amber having a cold and burning off most of it and Jade chewing on the other half, he didn't have much choice but to get a haircut."

"Yeah, well who was in the dragonhouse yesterday?" Trelon humorously growled back. "Who lost their kid and had the whole damn army looking for him? The entire castle heard Abby ripping into you when you finally admitted you lost Zohar."

"It wouldn't have happened if Paul would quit teaching the dragonlings how to play tag," Zoran retorted. "Besides, we found him safe and sound playing with Bálint in the atrium."

Ha'ven looked over at Mandra who was sitting at an angle. He looked at Arrow who had come to support him. He drew in a deep breath and nodded his head at the huge Valdier warrior. He needed at least one of the males to support him.

"Mandra, what about you? You trust Ha'ven, don't you?" Arrow asked in exasperation.

Ha'ven bit back a surprised chuckle when Mandra turned his head to glare at Arrow before he turned his gaze on him. Ha'ven tried to resist asking the huge Valdier warrior what happened, but it was too much. He had never seen anything like the marks lining the left side of the huge warrior's face.

"I... I... What the hell happened to you?" Ha'ven finally asked. "You look like... like..."

"Like a drawing board?" Creon asked.

"Like an Antrox mining grid?" Kelan snickered.

"Like..." Trelon began before he clamped his lips tightly together when Mandra shot him a deadly look.

"Ariel thought our son would enjoy learning to draw," Mandra growled.

"Unfortunately, he found a laser pen in Mandra's pocket," Creon said.

"No, unfortunately I fell asleep on the couch after having spent the night up with that damn Pactor who ate too many Rosenberries and developed colic," Mandra growled. "Jabir decided to draw a picture on the side of my face while I was asleep on the couch."

"When he was supposed to be babysitting," Kelan added. "Cara is working on a device to remove the ink."

All the men grimaced and looked at Mandra with a sympathetic look. Ha'ven swallowed as he thought of his own pregnant mate. He was already terrified about becoming a father. What if his son or daughter disappeared or got sick or was teething?

"Ask them if they would change what they have," Paul's deep voice suggested. "I can see it in your eyes. Ask them."

Ha'ven looked back at Creon. "How did you know you would be a good father?" he asked reluctantly.

"We didn't," Creon admitted.

"But we wouldn't change it for anything in any world," Trelon replied with a grin. "I love my girls. My life has never been fuller or more exciting."

"If it wasn't for the fact that the ink makes me itch, I would proudly keep Jabir's picture," Mandra added.

"Zohar was able to elude an entire army looking for him," Zoran said proudly. "I would have found him earlier if I had remembered to call out the safe word Paul gave me, but I forgot."

Ha'ven breathed a sigh of relief. His eyes moved to Paul, who sat waiting. He turned when Emma walked into the room holding a large quilt lovingly in her arms.

"Ha'ven, I wanted to show you the quilt my mother made for my Hope Chest." Emma froze when she saw the large view-screen and all the men sitting around it. She blushed and started to step back into their living area. "I'm sorry, I didn't know you were busy."

Ha'ven reached out his hand and pulled Emma onto his lap. "I am never too busy for you, *misha petite*. I need for you to assure Creon and his family that you wish to remain with me here on Ceran-Pax."

Emma turned when Creon Reykill leaned forward and began speaking to her. "Emma, I made a promise when we brought you back from your world that I would protect you. I gave Ha'ven six months before I would come for you. I will keep my word to you. If you wish to return to the protection of the Royal House of Valdier, I can be there within a few days," he said.

Emma looked at the faces of the men staring at her. She knew that they would come for her if she asked. Her eyes lifted as more faces filled the screen. She smiled at each of them, knowing that she had been wrong not to trust them when they had reached out to her.

She smiled at Cara, who was snuggling up to Trelon. Cara winked and gave her a supportive smile. Each woman who came in was protectively held by one of the huge, unusual warriors. She turned back to look at Abby, who waited patiently for her.

"I want to stay," Emma answered softly.

"Are you sure?" Abby asked. "He isn't forcing you, is he?"

Emma blushed and covered the hands that rested on the swell of her stomach. "No, he is not forcing me. I love him. I want to stay. I've found where I belong."

"Thank goodness," Abby said with a smile. "I'm so happy for you, Emma."

"Have you… have you heard from Sara? How is she doing?" Emma asked.

"She is doing well," an older Valdier woman replied. "Jaguin is watching over her."

"When he can find her," Trisha added under her breath.

Emma was about to ask what Trisha meant when the door behind them slammed open and loud voices echoed through the room behind them.

"Who the hell are Niria, Traya, and Doray?" an angry voice asked. "If I had known you were planning on adding me to the notches on your bedpost I could have saved you the trouble! If your brother won't take me home, I'll find someone else who will."

Trisha, Carmen, and Ariel started to lean forward, but sat back when Paul let out a low snarl of rage. "Samara?" Paul called out in disbelief.

A small female hurried into the room. She wiped angrily at the tears dampening her flushed cheeks. She stopped when she saw the image of her boss on the large screen.

"Mr. Grove?" Samara Stephens whispered. "How did you get here? I was told you were on a long-term training mission."

"Samara, how did you get here?" Paul asked in a calm, steady voice.

"I…" she started to reply.

"I won her," Adalard growled out. "She is mine!"

Continue the journey with

Jaguin's Love

A Dragon Lords of the Valdier Novel

USA Today Bestseller! A human woman recovering from extreme violence and an alien male finally given hope. In this steamy story of love and comfort, what will it take to break free of the past?

Jaguin is one of the finest trackers on Valdier. To date, there is only one thing he has never been successful at finding – his true mate. That failure is eating away at him and his dragon. Even his symbiot is feeling the drain as the centuries crawl by with no end to the emptiness gnawing away at them. When the Lords of Valdier find their true mates on a distant planet, the discovery of a species compatible with their own brings hope to the warriors of Valdier where females are few and true mates almost non-existent.

Sara Wilson is a botanist whose love of plants and their potential for medicinal uses consume her life. She feels confident she is on the verge of a breakthrough when she is kidnapped by a cartel boss with only one thing on his mind – to exact revenge.

After a fruitless search for his mate, Jaguin accepts one last assignment to guard Lord Creon's mate, Carmen, during a mission to seek justice against the man who murdered her husband. Instead, he finds his true mate in the man's cruel clutches, barely clinging to life.

The scars left during her captivity run deep inside Sara as she struggles to come to terms with her new life. She is no longer on Earth, but the terror still haunts her. She needs time to discover who she is again and whether this is a life she can accept. Can Jaguin's love heal the scars on the inside or will his true mate believe she has traded one monster for another?

Find it here: *books2read.com/Jaguins-Love*

Or check out a new series!

Ella and the Beast
Book 1 of the More Than Human series

Long ago, there was a war on Earth between shifters and humans.
Humans lost, and today they know they will become extinct if
something is not done....

In this fantasy romance, the stakes have never been higher!

books2read.com/Ella-and-the-Beast

ADDITIONAL BOOKS

If you loved this story by me (S.E. Smith) please leave a review! You can discover additional books at: http://sesmithfl.com and http://sesmithya.com or find your favorite way to keep in touch here: https://sesmithfl.com/contact-me/ Be sure to sign up for my newsletter to hear about new releases!

Recommended Reading Order Lists:

http://sesmithfl.com/reading-list-by-events/

http://sesmithfl.com/reading-list-by-series/

The Series

Science Fiction / Romance

Dragon Lords of Valdier Series

It all started with a king who crashed on Earth, desperately hurt. He inadvertently discovered a species that would save his own.

Curizan Warrior Series

The Curizans have a secret, kept even from their closest allies, but even they are not immune to the draw of a little known species from an isolated planet called Earth.

Marastin Dow Warriors Series

The Marastin Dow are reviled and feared for their ruthlessness, but not all want to live a life of murder. Some wait for just the right time to escape....

Sarafin Warriors Series

A hilariously ridiculous human family who happen to be quite formidable… and a secret hidden on Earth. The origin of the Sarafin species is more than it seems. Those cat-shifting aliens won't know what hit them!

Dragonlings of Valdier Novellas

The Valdier, Sarafin, and Curizan Lords had children who just cannot stop getting into trouble! There is nothing as cute or funny as magical, shapeshifting kids, and nothing as heartwarming as family.

Cosmos' Gateway Series

Cosmos created a portal between his lab and the warriors of Prime. Discover new worlds, new species, and outrageous adventures as secrets are unravelled and bridges are crossed.

The Alliance Series

When Earth received its first visitors from space, the planet was thrown into a panicked chaos. The Trivators came to bring Earth into the Alliance of Star Systems, but now they must take control to prevent the humans from destroying themselves. No one was prepared for how the humans will affect the Trivators, though, starting with a family of three sisters....

Lords of Kassis Series

It began with a random abduction and a stowaway, and yet, somehow, the Kassisans knew the humans were coming long before now. The fate of more than one world hangs in the balance, and time is not always linear....

Zion Warriors Series

Time travel, epic heroics, and love beyond measure. Sci-fi adventures with heart and soul, laughter, and awe-inspiring discovery...

Paranormal / Fantasy / Romance

Magic, New Mexico Series

Within New Mexico is a small town named Magic, an... unusual town, to say the least. With no beginning and no end, spanning genres, authors, and universes, hilarity and drama combine to keep you on the edge of your seat!

Spirit Pass Series

There is a physical connection between two times. Follow the stories of those who travel back and forth. These westerns are as wild as they come!

Second Chance Series

Stand-alone worlds featuring a woman who remembers her own death. Fiery and mysterious, these books will steal your heart.

More Than Human Series

Long ago there was a war on Earth between shifters and humans. Humans lost, and today they know they will become extinct if something is not done....

The Fairy Tale Series

A twist on your favorite fairy tales!

A Seven Kingdoms Tale

Long ago, a strange entity came to the Seven Kingdoms to conquer and feed on their life force. It found a host, and she battled it within her body for centuries while destruction and devastation surrounded her. Our story begins when the end is near, and a portal is opened....

Epic Science Fiction / Action Adventure

Project Gliese 581G Series

An international team leave Earth to investigate a mysterious object in our solar system that was clearly made by someone, someone who isn't from Earth. Discover new worlds and conflicts in a sci-fi adventure sure to become your favorite!

New Adult / Young Adult

Breaking Free Series

A journey that will challenge everything she has ever believed about herself as danger reveals itself in sudden, heart-stopping moments.

The Dust Series

Fragments of a comet hit Earth, and Dust wakes to discover the world as he knew it is gone. It isn't the only thing that has changed, though, so has Dust...

ABOUT THE AUTHOR

S.E. Smith is an *internationally acclaimed, New York Times* and *USA TODAY Bestselling* author of science fiction, romance, fantasy, paranormal, and contemporary works for adults, young adults, and children. She enjoys writing a wide variety of genres that pull her readers into worlds that take them away.

Made in the USA
Las Vegas, NV
29 December 2023

83702571R00134